SILVER MOON

GREAT NOVELS
OF
EROTIC DOMINATION
AND
SUBMISSION

NEW TITLES EVERY MONTH

www.smbooks.co.uk

TO FIND OUT MORE ABOUT OUR READERS' CLUB
WRITE TO;

SILVER MOON READER SERVICES;
Barrington Hall Publishing
Hexgreave Hall
Farnsfield
Nottinghamshire NG22 8LS
Tel; 01157 141616

YOU WILL RECEIVE A FREE MAGAZINE OF EXTRACTS
FROM OUR EXTENSIVE RANGE OF EROTIC FICTION
ABSOLUTELY FREE. YOU WILL ALSO HAVE THE
CHANCE TO PURCHASE BOOKS WHICH ARE
EXCLUSIVE TO OUR READERS' CLUB

***

NEW AUTHORS ARE WELCOME

Please send submissions to;
Barrington Hall Publishing
Hexgreave Hall
Farnsfield N22 8LS

Silver Moon books are an imprint of Barrington Hall Publishing
which is part of Barrington Hall Ltd.

All characters and events depicted are entirely fictitious; any resemblance to anyone living or dead is entirely coincidental

Subduing Jacqueline

by

Jordan Church

CHAPTER 1

Becca thought Wendy Carter was quite a looker, especially for a woman in her mid-40s. Becca wasn't able to see Ms. Carter's face clearly at that moment due to bright light beaming through the huge bank of windows behind Carter's desk. Carter's coppery brown hair appeared nearly angelic in the slant of blazing winter sunlight while completely shadowing her eye sockets and face. For a disturbing moment the pooling of darkness on Carter's face gave Becca the optical illusion of a dirt-covered skull wearing a good wig.

"Becca, I've asked you here to discuss your prior request. You asked to be familiarized with all aspects of the Goethner-Varner Mental Health Hospital. For the most part, you have learned everything you need to be a successful Psychiatric Nurse. However, in the past I've refused to assign you to the Maximum Security ward. Now I find certain events have caused me to second guess myself. Perhaps I've been too overprotective. After all, the more you stretch your boundaries, the more your full potential is tapped."

Carter's words sounded halting and garbled. It was late afternoon. Possibly Carter was nearing the end of a particularly stressful day. Becca could hardly imagine the challenges a Director of Operations at a mental health facility must face. Still, she hoped one day she would know firsthand. That's why she tried so hard to learn everything. Becca was ambitious but in a good way, just wanting to maximize her potential and her contributions to society.

"Are you sure? I can have full access?" Up until today Carter adamantly kept her away from the Maximum Security Ward, stating Becca's natural beauty could be a source of disruption to some patients, the ones whose particular mental dysfunctions were slanted to sexual issues. Some of them were committed to the Maximum Security Ward due to mistreatment of women. Carter did not want to fan the flames by giving them any extra fuel for their smouldering fantasies.

"You'll have access but you'll find you have a lot less freedom that you could imagine. I think, oh, it would be good for you to try new challenges and interact with someone like Mr. Jones. He is truly one of a kind. I think your brightness could get his attention for the better. So, I give you my blessing. Focus only on Wayne Jones for the time being. Visit him. Try to draw him out."

"Ah, thank you, Ms. Carter."

"Becca, from now on just call me Wendy. Equals should be on a first name basis."

Becca felt puzzled but gratified and a little amazed. None of the Becca's co-workers called Ms. Carter by her first name. The name Wendy seemed too soft, an incongruous fit for the highly educated and commanding Carter.

"Sure, Ms. Car... I mean Wendy. Thanks."

"Go visit Mr. Jones. I'm sure you've already heard an earful about him from the media and the other staff members, but don't be afraid. Learn what he has to say. Study him by experiencing him. Come to understand his philosophy. Find out how we can help him be happy. Be agreeable. Do not upset him."

This all sounded pretty weird to Becca. Mr. Jones was a patient, not a valued customer. Still, she was thrilled to have access to the maximum security ward and the most intriguing patients.

"All right, I won't let you down."

"When you first meet Mr. Jones, be sure to immediately let him know I sent you. That's important."

"I will."

Becca huddled against the frigid winter air and entered the numeric code Carter issued her to gain entry through the gate to Building C. A twelve-foot fence topped with barbed wire that dripped icicles circled the maximum security area one hundred feet out from all sides of the building. As Becca started along the salt strewn path leading to the guard house, her straight black hair swept across her cheek and mouth. Her hair was long, thick, fragrant, an effective scarf to protect her from the rising winds and plummeting temperature. Becca knew there would be no snowfall tonight. It was too cold for snow.

Becca entered the warmth of the Building C lobby, surprised there was no guard at the desk. Even in the Minimum Security Wards there were usually two guards unless one was making rounds, dealing with a difficult patient, doing paperwork in the office, or using the restroom. Becca relaxed when she spotted the doors to the office and restroom behind the guard's desk, sure the guards would soon emerge.

Becca hoped Wilrey wasn't one of the guards on duty. She figured he'd fit better here as an inmate than a guard. Whenever she saw him in the cafeteria he always stared at her with a creepy intensity. She especially didn't want to knock on the office door, let alone the restroom door, to ask Wilrey for help like some scared little girl.

Becca spun the Visitor Log Book around, signed it, and entered the time and the patient she intended to visit. Everyone, even staff, had to sign in and out on the log. This was a security measure to ensure no patient could escape by pretending to be a staff member or visitor, and also to avoid forgetting a visitor and locking them in with the dangerous crazies. One of the guards was supposed to co-sign. Becca figured Wilrey or whoever could play catch up and do that later. If they bitched then she'd point out it was their fault for not being at their assigned station.

Becca skimmed the entries and noticed Ms. Carter spent the previous afternoon in the ward, reason given as visiting Wayne Jones. What would they have discussed for three hours? Becca flipped through the pages, realizing Ms. Carter had seen Jones every day including this past Sunday. How odd. Perhaps Ms. Carter took a personal interest in Jones due to all the media attention. Becca inwardly scolded herself for being cynical. Ms. Carter was a professional and wouldn't let salacious gossip influence her work habits.

Becca peeked behind the desk and realized the lock mechanism was the same as in the Minimum Security Ward. Pushing a button at the guard's desk released an electronic lock on the double doors, automatically opening them as a person approached. The guards also had controls which locked and unlocked each patient suite.

Becca figured she would run into Wilrey or another guard walking the ward hallway. Failing that, she would visit with Wayne Jones through the window in his suite door. She wanted to get started and didn't feel like waiting around.

Becca buzzed herself in, slid through the double doors, and started down the hall. Anticipation kicked up her heart rate and flushed her face pink. She found every patient interesting but these dangerous ones were especially fascinating. She'd discussed many of the most extreme cases at length with the staff assigned to the Maximum Security Ward. She'd pored over case files and studied pictures of all the resident criminally insane. However, none captivated her attention as much as the legendary media sensation Wayne Jones, also known as "The King of Rapture."

Becca wanted to make a difference and chose to work at Goethner-Varner Mental Health Hospital because of its constructive outlook. It was reflected in the name of the facility. The founders, now long dead and buried, believed mental health issues were no different than ailments of the body. If an organ was faulty, you fixed it and got the patient back on their feet and back into society. They believed the same was true of any and all mental health issues. To reflect their philosophy and encourage society to be more accepting, they named the facility a hospital.

Becca glanced at the chart hanging on the door of the first suite she passed. Radavich. His proclivity was necrophilia. They'd arrested him "getting busy" in a graveyard. Ick. She tiptoed past the room, ducking under the window. She didn't even want that guy looking at her... maybe imagining doing unspeakable things to her dead body. That would be bad luck.

Passing a cell with a chart for a Lilly Hopkins she perked up her ears. Little holes in the cell door windows of each suite allowed sound to pass into the hallway. These were closable in case the patients made too much noise. The meal slot below the window also allowed some sound through despite the metal hinged flap on it. This was for meals to slide in to the patient if they were acting too violent for dining with the other patients. Hadn't she heard some of the other PA's talking about Lilly Hopkins?

Becca heard what sounded like sex going on in the suite. She paused, frowning, about to look through the window but then remembered Lilly was a chronic masochistic masturbator. No way did she want to see that spectacle.

She thought about Lilly's case, wondering what she could learn from it. Although nearly always dishevelled, Lilly was pretty and blond. If she was normal she'd have her pick of men, but Lilly favored masturbation over normalcy. She'd heard Lilly even managed to masturbate while restrained in a straitjacket by rubbing herself all over inanimate objects. Worse, she often simultaneously harmed herself by scratching and pulling at her flesh, usually in the most tender of vulnerable areas. Poor Lilly! She probably climaxed two dozen times a day!

Obviously what Becca heard was not sex – at least not sex between adults – just another one of Lilly's lonely orgasms. Becca wondered about Lilly's limited but extreme experiences. She'd turned her back on having a role in society in return for never-ending sexual gratification. Becca shivered and felt a tightening in her lower abdomen. Her interpretation of Lilly's fate, she had to admit, really didn't sound as bad as it should. Becca maintained her decision to refrain from observing Lilly and moved to the next suite. She had no desire to view troubled Lilly in mid-act.

Becca was pleasantly surprised to pass another occupied suite. According to her colleagues who worked in Building C, usually half the suites were empty. There were many competing facilities nowadays and better treatment programs so Building C was usually slow. But business was booming at Goethner-Varner for some reason.

Becca passed another suite, observing the name on the chart was "Tillings". Becca was amused by the coincidence. It was the same last name as a psychologist who visited Jones a while back to determine if his evaluation was correct. Becca knew there were whispers that Jones was not at all insane and that some political and legal manoeuvring had committed him to Goethner-Varner.

The ward hallway turned ninety degrees up ahead leading to the longer arm of the L-shaped wing. Jones' suite was right before the turn. Becca figured a guard was just around the corner. But before she spoke with the guard, she intended to visit with Jones through his window. She could do this without disturbing other patients, as Jones was not known for loud outbursts. He was, in fact, known for his unearthly calm.

Becca was shocked to find Jones' cell door wide open with Jones alone in the suite. His back was to her while he looked out the barred window at the grounds of the Goethner-Varner Mental Health Hospital. Becca noted with alarm that Jones' arms were completely free and unrestrained. She stepped just inside the door and glanced in every corner of the room to confirm Jones was indeed alone and unguarded.

Jones spoke without turning and looking to see who had entered, "Welcome. Most welcome. You are wearing heels so you must be a woman. You have a quick soft step so I'd guess you are quite slim. Using my more special power I can tell you are most attractive and I'd guess a brunette."

Becca was startled for a moment before she realized he could see her reflection in the window. This guy wasn't going to fool her with little tricks. She may only be 20 but she wasn't born yesterday either.

Jones spun in place, his eyes zeroing in on her. Light from the fading sunset gleamed off his shaved skull. He had light hazel eyes and a deeply lined face. Becca thought he looked a lot younger than his 51 years of age.

Jones spoke, "Yes, you are very attractive. Beautiful. Ravishing. Do you know beauty is like a weapon?"

"Ah, Mr. Jones, why are you alone in here?"

"Aren't prisoners usually alone in their cells?"

"Yeah, of course, but not with their door unlocked, arms free, and no one in attendance! Besides, you're not a prisoner, you're a patient. We're here to help you."

"As far as my relative freedom at the moment, I've made known and persuaded those who needed to be persuaded I pose no risk of escape. Rather than cause any harm I plan to do most of you a great deal of good.

"As for naming me a patient instead of a prisoner you are completely mistaken. I am not a patient because I require no aid and have no mental or physical aberrations. Ironic that being a patient makes me so impatient. It is also ironic that my enemies were impatient to make me a patient. Since, despite my freedom of movement, I am not free to leave, I most logically am a prisoner.

"As for being here to help me, no, you are not. You, like others, are here to help yourself to me. Wanting to mentally poke and prod, dismantle my Id and my Ego to see what makes me tick, before putting them back together ticking in a way you find more satisfactory and less alarming. You seek to make me normal, average, to destroy what makes me special. You are not here to help me but, in the end, yes, you will be a help to me."

Jones' eyes fixed on her, calculating and anticipatory. Becca didn't know what to say. She felt like she might be in danger and that tightly wound Jones was about to make a move. But she was frozen in place, afraid any twitch on her part, any sound, would trigger him. Where were the guards when she needed them?

"Come closer, Little One. Tell me your name."

She made no move but responded verbally, "Becca."

"Why do you think you are here? What has brought you to me other than my own good fortune?"

"Ms. Carter asked me to visit you. You know; understand where you're coming from. In fact, she insisted I tell you she sent me." Becca hoped dropping Ms. Carter's name would disarm Jones and put this unsettling meeting on a more secure footing.

"Mmmm, Wendy sent you. Good work. Gooooooood work. When you see her next report back that I am satisfied and tell her the following 'Master Jones says, 'You're a good little girl, Wendy, good girl.'"

Becca was shocked by Jones' disrespect, but fear tempered her response. "I'm not comfortable telling her that. Maybe you'll have to discuss it with her yourself."

Despite her dislike and fear of the man, Jones had somehow managed to move closer to her without her noticing. His proximity made her feel like running away.

Jones spoke low and earnestly, "You think Wendy would be offended by my words? You are wrong. She will be thrilled, filled with pride. Be honest, wouldn't you like to be told the same? That you are a good girl who has succeeded in pleasing her Master, her soul's King?"

Hearing his demented words, Becca's sanity reappeared, chasing away her fear and restoring her confidence. This was just another crazy patient, and there was most definitely a guard just around the corner. It was time to take control back. "Not at all. Especially if that "Master" was you."

"Are you here to understand me?"

Becca lifted her chin. "Yes, exactly."

"To understand me you will need to understand what I can do, the effect I can create. The effect I can achieve in the emotions and sensations of a woman."

"Just what are you saying, exactly?" Becca's confidence deflated as fear raced into the empty places once occupied by enthusiasm. She desperately wanted to flee, but sensed any move would trigger his attack all the sooner. Unfortunately, doing nothing was obviously not a solution either.

"Tell me. One way or the other, do you, in fact, want to understand me?"

Becca could tell by the weight in his tone that this was a crucial moment. Could she deny her mission? Was she willing to fail in her new responsibility? Would understanding Jones be dangerous or would it be more dangerous to back down and show fear to this predator?

Becca braced herself and stood a little taller, "Yes, I want to understand you and I will."

Jones smiled broadly, triumphantly, "There it is, my pretty little new toy. The invitation was all I morally required."

With that Jones' left hand lashed out to grab her right shoulder and pin her up against the wall while his right hand plunged down just below her skirt, hooked up, and roughly slapped her pussy through her thin panties. His fingers cupped and squeezed her vulva with the base of his inverted palm, rubbing her panties harshly against the top of her slit.

Becca yelped, eyes wide. Despite bracing herself for action she was not ready for so bold a move. She had no strength to fight him, no idea how to escape the situation, and little prospect of being able to form an idea while his palm pummelled her pussy. One of her hands went to his hand on her shoulder and the other raced down to grab his right forearm. They didn't stop him. They didn't even slow him down.

She tried to close her legs but he already had one of his own between them. His hand was rubbing. Rubbing...

She thought to knee him in the crotch but he seemed to be aware of that possibility and was standing sideways. His fingers rippled pleasurable pressure back and forth across her pussy. Incredibly, Becca could feel her labia plumping with blood flow.

Becca stopped trying to kick him realizing it could escalate the situation into violence and potentially place her in greater danger. The kicks weren't working anyway. He seemed to have a strange strength while she felt weaker than usual.

Through her panties Jones' fingers gathered and pinched the flesh around her clitoris. Becca felt a spike of unexpected sexual pleasure through the discomfort.

She had to act. Pinned and immobile with Jones' hand having its way with her sex, her prospects didn't look good. The hand was getting rougher, gripping the bunched pussy flesh through her panties and jiggling up and down. As it got rougher Becca was surprised the pleasurable thrills increased, pulsing higher and higher. What he was doing was intolerable. So were her reactions to it.

Becca was feeling a sharp urgency. She had to get away. Didn't she? She gasped and shook her head. Her panties dampened with her fast flowing juices. She moaned. This bald nut was turning her on! What was wrong with her? She had to make it stop. The logical part of her brain shrieked in protest, but her body yearned for more. She bucked her hips, making his fingers pull viciously at her sweet secret flesh and then ground forward for firmer contact with his leg and fingers. Was she trying to get away by shaking his hand loose? Oh, what was wrong with her? She hadn't meant to do that, her hips had just acted.

It was all she could do to bite her lower lip and embrace the pain as an island of sanity and control in order to stop the lusty moans that wanted out. She knew she had to rein in her pussy before it just bucked and bucked and bucked right into some kind of orgasm. My God, she thought, I can't let this freak bring me off!

The self-inflicted pain in her lower lip suddenly reminded her she had another possible course of action. Her voice! She could call for help. It was her best hope for rescue, but she hesitated, embarrassed by her situation and wondering what the guards would think if they found her in a sexually compromising position with a patient. Ms. Carter had fired staff for sexual relations with patients in the past. Would Ms. Carter blame her? Jones' fingers released her bunched pussy flesh, allowing an influx of blood to rush the area and that caused an increase in unsettling pleasure and a flood of fluids. His confident fingers rolled and brushed the soaked panty to the side of her slit, divided her damp pubic hair, then slid down and up firm and complete into her vagina.

"Oh, youuu..." Instinctively she stood as high as possible on her tiptoes, trying to rise up off the invading fingers but they simply followed, stuck firmly in her saturated but still tight vagina. Some analytical part of her standing to the side of the situation noted Jones did not plunge his fingers up and down like a mini-cock but was actually twisting them to and fro in semi-circles like a washing machine. The motion kept his fingers deep and allowed him to continuously roll the ball of his thumb against her clitoral hood. The thumb pressed deeply and released pressure again and again, inducing blood to rush to the area and fatten the clitoris, bringing extreme sensitivity and extreme pleasure.

Instead of helping her escape his clutches, rising onto her tiptoes made her more helpless and now her voice, her potential avenue of escape, worked against her to egg him on, "Oh, ohhhh, oh, ohh. God. Fuck!"

Jones was calm, his eyes warmly analytical, his mouth twisted into a patronizing half-smile, "God of Fuck? I like that. If you'd like to worship me I will allow you."

His fingers twisted in her pussy with extra harshness.

"Oh, you! No! Quit it. Quit it. Stop. Please!"

You're obviously hysterical, Pretty Toy. Why would you want to stop receiving all this divine pleasure? You should embrace your new destiny. It makes no sense. Since Pretty Toy is hysterical, no, wait, hysterical is not the correct term. Malfunctioning! Since Pretty Toy is malfunctioning I'll make the decisions from now on. I'll make all the decisions!"

Jones' pressuring thumb and penetrating fingertips dug deeper into her delicate folds and pinched towards each other, apparently trying to do the impossible and make contact through her flesh. It was uncomfortable, disturbing and a bit painful to Becca. It was also wonderful. It was too wonderful.

"No, no, no, no. Ohhhhhhhhh, no, ohhhhhhhh," Becca's distress needed verbal release. What the hell, she thought, why were her hips bucking up against his hand as if... she wanted this? It seemed like her pussy wanted more contact, more of everything, even more pain. Her pussy was rebelling and making its own decision. A bad one!

Jones continued talking. He seemed to enjoy the sound of his own voice. "With all decisions handled for you by me you will be able to focus your programming on your central missions, Pretty Toy. One, feel physical, mental, and emotional pleasure at every sensation I give you and every act I command you to complete. Two, focus on your main task which is to please me. Give yourself over to your destiny and never look back."

This Jones guy was a certifiable lunatic, saying crazy things. On the other hand, the pleasure flowed steady and strong, commanding all her attention. It was making it hard for her to think, hard to resist. Jones' crazy words, spoken so matter-of-fact, made them sound… almost sensible. She shook her head, trying to dislodge the ideas seeded in her brain. She knew she had to stop them from sprouting, growing into foul ideas, overgrowing her will and sense of self-determination. Could she actually just give in to him and start doing anything and everything he dictated? To Becca it was a nightmarish but tempting prospect. No! She must resist this insanity!

"Noooo. Mr. Jones, just stop. Ummm, uh, just please. Please, oh, please!"

"If you want me to stop why are you grunting and moaning and pushing your pussy on my hand?"

The words actually made her buck her hips harder. Her pubic mound smashed against his pinching thumb and fingers, "Because, ahhh. Ahhhhhhh!"

"Is it because it feels so good?"

"Yes, dammit, it feels soooo good. God!"

"Is it also because you love it? You love what I'm doing to you?"

"Yes, yes, that's why. It just feels so good!"

"Pretty Toy, you must pay attention. I said 'love'." His left hand released her pinned shoulder and he mauled her breasts roughly, quickly locating one hard nipple on her right breast and pinching viciously.

"Aahgh. No!"

He added pressure to his grip through her top and bra and twisted the nipple through her clothing, thanks to how erect it had become from the hand fucking. Becca knew Jones would find it significant that, despite the pain and her cries of protest, she still pushed her pussy hard onto his fingers and made no effort to escape. She didn't care what he thought. All that was important was the pleasure and the pain, the pain and the pleasure, the pleasure-pain.

"What was it I said, Pretty Toy?"

"You… aaaah, you said I love it."

"Good. Good girl. Now, how does Pretty Toy feel? What emotion do you feel?"

On some level, despite her aroused passions, she still noted that Jones seemed to hold his breath, waiting for her answer as if this was something crucial. Becca could feel it, too. Her eyes rose to his and cleared a little despite the potent mingling of pleasure and pain. She blinked, knowing her response was important. Not as important as continuing and increasing that pleasure, somehow getting those fingers deeper in her pussy, swallowing them with her pussy lips. Not as important as twisting her torso to and fro, not to escape, but to increase the stretch and pain on her nipples as his vice grip switched between them. Fuck it. Whatever he wanted she would just give him. He'd made it clear what he wanted to hear and it didn't feel like a lie when she said it.

"I feel love! I love it!"

The hand at her pussy applied so much pressure she slid a few inches up the wall. She squealed like a wounded rabbit. Her hands were on his shoulders. They were not trying to push him away but her fingers were gripping him tightly. They were in this together now.

Becca realized she was getting more pleasure than pain. Jones seemed to think that wasn't fair. She thought Jones must definitely have a sense of fair play because he sought to increase her pain to a level that would come to match her pleasure. She knew he couldn't squeeze the nipple any harder than he already was, at least not through her shirt and bra. His right hand, soaked in her juices, was having fun wreaking havoc in her pussy. So he leaned in and down and bit her on the side of the neck.

"Ah! Ahh! Stop! No!"

Her cries seemed to delight him. His teeth clamped harder on her delicate neck skin and he even ground his teeth back and forth a little. She felt her neck muscles stiffen instinctively but she dared not pull away or the teeth could rip her skin. She knew he must be leaving a nasty bruised imprint of his front teeth on the side of her neck. She wondered how she would explain that mark to people who saw it. Was Jones trying to mark her as his territory? Was she now an added territory in King Jones' kingdom?

"No, oooh! It hurts! Stop!"

He must have thought he was overdoing the pain because he relaxed the finger pincers on her abused nipple which allowed blood to rush back into the bud, then sawed the fingers of his right hand faster and possibly even deeper into her pussy. He was still biting her throat, though. Becca wondered for a fearful moment if Jones was some kind of vampire but knew he wasn't breaking the skin.

"Oh, please. Please!"

Jones pulled his teeth off her neck to speak into her ear. "You are a polite and pretty toy. Since you asked so sweetly I grant your request. You may orgasm."

His hand at her pussy gripped a handful of slick sensitized flesh and he jerked her back and forth. He pulled her groin towards him, her toes tapping at the floor and then banged her back against the wall, smashing her ass. He did this again and again. Even through the pain, her thin arms around his neck cradled the ruthless predator, her soft cheek grazing the gray fuzz on his shaved head.

His pushing and pulling hand was vicious. The harshness was painful to both her pussy and her ass. The pain was nothing compared to the sheer pleasure which was made somehow all the greater by the pain experienced. It made no sense but it was exactly what she wanted. No, what she needed and had not known she needed. It was the right combination to unlock her orgasm even in this bizarre situation. It was by far the greatest orgasm she'd ever known in her young life.

"Ooooohh, yes, yes, yes, I'm doing it. I'm coming!"

Her arms gripped him with all her power, her slim hips thrusting back rapid-fire, her verbalizations becoming animalistic. Jones kept her going, kept the orgasm growing hotter and more intense, like blowing on coals.

She rode his hand and had orgasm after orgasm, four powerful ones and numerous smaller ones. It was Becca's first ever multiple orgasm. She was sweaty and exhausted. Her passion still flared bright but her body could no longer sustain. She wound down, writhing much less vigorously, eyelids drooping in ecstatic exhaustion.

Jones pulled his slippery digits out of her and his hand off her twitching pussy and then lifted her entirely in both arms. The chewed area of her neck was bright red and swollen. It was going to darken and bruise dramatically and would sport clear tooth marks. He'd marked her body to reflect the mark he'd left on her soul. Jones carried her to the narrow cell bed and laid her down.

A little rest before the next step in the delicate toy manufacturing process...

CHAPTER 2

Jones watched her while she rested. He admired his bite mark on her neck. Jones enjoyed biting. He knew that lovers left hickeys on their partners supposedly as a psychological sign of possessiveness. Jones knew he was possessive. He was possessive of all his lovers. Lover was the wrong word. They were slaves, not lovers. He supposed his bites were a sadist's version of possessiveness.

When Jones bit a woman it made him feel like a vampire. He felt like he was a vampire, though not of the sort depicted in the movies. Vampires sucked life force out of people to sustain their own life force. Many victims fell in order to sustain a single vampire. Jones felt he was a bit like that. He took away their current way of life in order to improve his own quality of life.

He also felt like a sexual saint for not having taken his own satisfaction despite his total control and ability to have done so. He had no intention of keeping that halo. Her pleasure had literally come first and repeatedly. Of course, that had nothing to do with chivalry. Even strong-willed women had a hard time denying him anything he set his sights on. A young girl like Becca, given so much overwhelming pleasure, would soon find it almost impossible to deny him anything. Exactly as it should be.

When Becca woke nude in an unfamiliar location, her blue eyes darted around the room in alarm. The walls and ceiling were sterile white and she realized she was still in Jones' suite at the Mental Health Center. She wished she wasn't there. She wished she had never been there.

Waking up inside a suite designed to contain mentally deranged persons made her feel highly vulnerable. She wished she was wearing clothes. The site of her own nudity made her feel ten times more vulnerable. Looking up to see Jones studying her made her feel a hundred times more vulnerable.

Oh my God, thought Becca, that sick skinhead old freak shoved his fingers up her pussy. She had come. Actually, she hadn't just come, she had had multiple orgasms. That was a first! It had been wonderful but how horrible that she had done it!

At that moment Jones started tugging gently but insistently at her pubic hair. The sensation made her look down there. With shame she noted her dark little bush was plastered to her pubic mound and gleaming from her pussy juices.

Jones' cold eyes noted her alarm, "Wakey wakey, Pretty Toy. Time for you to perform the function you were built for."

Becca was groggy and off balance. "What?"

"Fucking. Why else are you equipped with a pussy? That added feature clearly has a purpose. Fucking."

"Get your shitty hand off me, you sick creep!"

"The staff members here seem to be insensitive to the needs of the patients. No wonder why the recovery rate is so low. I'm thankful I don't have any mental issues to recover from or I'd begin to despair."

"Get away from me, Mr. Jones!"

"You are slightly more respectful in use of title but not in tone. When I first met you I told you beauty is like a weapon. I'll explain. You are beautiful. To utilize your beauty weapon you must exercise it in sex. Remember, a weapon unused is a useless weapon. No one wants to feel useless. I'm here to help you."

Becca thought Jones's voice and word pattern both had a singsong hypnotic quality. It was doing something to her. She shook her head, not in denial, but just to try to clear it of the webs he was spinning.

"Go to hell."

"That's too bad. Pretty Toy is malfunctioning. I'll need to hit the reset button."

Jones, less than average size himself but still far bigger than delicate Becca, grabbed her left bicep which was nearest to him and flipped her over onto her belly. The fact she was attempting to rise at the time actually assisted him. On her belly she levered her knees underneath to attempt to rise again but his left hand pinned her face to the pillow by pressing on the back of her thin neck. His right hand, covered with her dried secretions from their previous interlude, returned to work at her displayed pussy.

Becca discovered she was helpless, blinded and partially muffled by the pillow he pressed against her face. She wanted to resist but it seemed so hopeless. Oddly, she was also worried that in violently struggling she might hurt him. It was a crazy thought but he was a patient after all. That made her the responsible party. She actually felt guilty for all they had done and even felt herself make a down payment of guilt for what was about to happen.

She stopped struggling but he kept her face pressed into the pillow and continued working about her pussy, spreading the outer and inner lips, fingers pinning them aside and making her pussy gape, cool air rushing in.

Where the hell was the damn guard? She managed to twist her eyes towards the door to the room and saw it was still open. The fool hadn't closed the door! If she could yell out a guard anywhere up or down the ward hallway would hear and come to her assistance.

His index and middle fingers pushed in and out of her vagina while the pad of his thumb palpitated her clitoris, "Ahhh, here is that reset button."

"Ahhhh." Her "ahhhh" was of a far different tone and nature than his.

She couldn't let this happen again. Since she didn't have the physical strength, she was going to need help. Jones was distracted trying to overwhelm her pussy with sensation and the grip on her neck had loosened. Becca mustered her strength and reared up with all her weak might. It was enough to raise her face several inches off the pillow just long enough for her to yell, "Guard!"

He muffled further cries by pushing her face back into the pillow.

He continued working at her defenseless glistening pussy. When he spoke he did not sound angry at all, "Pretty Toy, when I hit your reset button apparently I put you on the wrong setting. I'd meant to switch you to "Monogamous Service" so you would give me all your attention. However, it seems I have accidentally set you on "Multiple Sexual Partners". Why else would you want the guard to join us?"

Becca was angry now. This guy was molesting her, mistreating her, disrespecting her, and now he was mocking her attempt to get help. Like Wilrey, or whoever the guard was, would actually join them in some perverted three-way.

Although Becca was furious with Jones, she was even angrier at her own body. Her pussy streamed with juice, her knees trembled, and the extreme pleasure Jones induced made it hard for her to think coherently. Humiliating recollections flashed through her mind. Jones, mocking her. Her body, selling out. Jones, suggesting pasty fat-faced Wilrey could join in and have at her. Recalling the exquisite humiliation spurred new waves of pleasure in her body. She grunted and issued a long reluctant moan, her body stiffening and pushing her hot pussy into the palm of Jones' hand. She was so angry and hot, troubled and aroused.

She pictured Wilrey shoving his pale thick cock into her wet defenseless pussy. Mentally, she clung to the picture like she was drowning as a way to tame her arousal. Instead, it had the opposite effect. The more she pictured Wilrey's cock shafting into her little pussy the hotter she became.

Jones flipped her onto her back, grabbed both her ankles in his hands and lifted her legs up and back until her feet spread wide and even with her face. This raised her ass off the mattress and it quivered just inches from his arched hard on. Dimly, she realized he was about to screw her. She knew she should struggle to stop him but stopping him didn't seem as important to her as the pleasure she stood to gain if he fucked her.

If he did fuck her that would just be completely unprofessional of her. Besides, who knew where an accomplished pervert like Jones had stuck his cock in the past? So many women! This was horrible, unthinkable. Becca was embarrassed by the lewd acts of copulation her mind conjured. But her pussy wasn't embarrassed. It was all for getting fucked, absolutely insistent.

Desperately, Becca cried out again for help, contradicting the longings of her pussy. "Guard! Guard!" Becca knew guards anywhere on the wing would hear her passionate pleas for help. Any second now, someone would arrive at the room to rescue her.

Jones seemed unconcerned by Becca's loud cries echoing in the small room. Even though Jones had no actual history of violence, with a small chill, Becca considered the possibility Jones had done something terrible to the guards.

"Pay attention, Pretty Toy," Jones said. "I am going to inaugurate you off the assembly line with the gift of my cock. No champagne bottle so my cock has to do the job. Plus, I need to quality test your pussy. After all, I wouldn't want to put my brand name on an inferior product."

With a delighted smile Jones shoved his cock deep into her wetly grasping pussy. Becca gave a grunting, agonized but delighted cry in response. His cock speared her, thick and full and all the way in. Horror and disbelief filled half of her mind while the other half savored the thrill of the dubious accomplishment. Her mental battle of pleasure versus self-preservation was at an impasse, neither side in control of her body. Her body was on its own, surrendering to pure sensation. Her hips immediately slammed her pussy up onto his cock, craving the depraved contact.

Jones smiled with knowing satisfaction, pleased by her reaction. She could actually hear him humming. He must view her response as a definite sign of success on his sexual assembly line. She thought he was sick in the head but, then again, she also felt pride in pleasing him. With this irrational feeling of satisfaction Becca realized if Jones was sick in the head, he was no longer the only one.

Jones halted his thrusting and leaned back to examine her analytically. Becca was desperate for more contact. She slid her ass up his folded thighs and crammed her wetness on his cock. She closed her eyes tightly, unable to bear watching him observe her, not wanting to imagine what he was seeing and the judgments he was making about her. Becca's face twisted and frowned in pleasure concentration, her mouth open and gasping passionate "ohhhhs" and delirious "ummms".

"Pretty good, Pretty Toy. You are doing most of the work as is appropriate. Now, open your eyes and keep them open and focused on me or whoever is fucking you in the future. While you're at it, make sure to fill those eyes with gratitude and worshipfulness, too. As your owner and re-creator I know you're into me but you wouldn't want anyone I gave you to for sex to think you were picturing someone else fucking you instead of them. That would be inconsiderate of you. Remember, it is not about you anymore, it is all about how you can please and serve your owner. That is a Pretty Toy's purpose."

To Becca, Jones' words were a bothersome distraction to her ongoing all-important effort to mash her pussy flesh onto Jones' dick. Jones disgusted and scared her but she needed his cock. She tried her best to ignore his words, but they insidiously wormed through the red clouds of confusion in her mind. They were persuasive, compelling. Without conscious permission Becca opened her eyes wide and tried her best to fill them with the desire she felt and the gratitude he demanded.

He pressed her legs down, feet over her head, her calves knocking her face while he thrust hard and steady into her sensitive sex. Becca felt appallingly vulnerable, not only because of the awkward helpless position she was shaped into but even more because Jones' predatory gaze made her feel feeble in her own mind, pinned and perfectly vulnerable. She felt as mentally penetrated as she was physically penetrated. The start of a physical and emotional orgasm built higher.

Jones spoke. "I'm giving you what you need when you didn't even know you needed it. The least you can do is thank me. A Pretty Toy like you should always be polite to its owner and users. Go ahead now."

Becca felt shocked and dismayed by his order to thank him for his invasion. It was humiliating and unjust!

"Pretty Toy, is your voice box malfunctioning? Give your thanks. Speak now."

He seemed intent on this, as intense as her own arousal. She should tell him no. She should tell him to go to hell. However, a part of her, a part growing louder and taking more control, was appreciative of what he was doing to her.

She opened her mouth wider, panting but about to speak. She had no idea what she was about to say. Suddenly Becca's view of Jones' intense face framed by white-painted sterile ceiling was joined in the frame by the fat face of Wilrey, the security guard.

Becca was relieved to see Wilrey knowing he would quickly stop the ordeal. Although she'd never admit it, truthfully, she was a little disappointed she would never know how huge that orgasm would have been.

Wilrey's eyes opened wide with surprised delight. She couldn't blame him, given her exposed position, but her cheeks burned red with embarrassment. What must he think of her seeing her naked, exposed pussy fucked by a patient? Surely he wouldn't think this situation was consensual?

"Wilrey, help me!"

Jones twisted his face around and spotted Wilrey, "Yes, help her out, Wilrey. Shove your dick in Pretty Toy's mouth. That's the kind of help she wants."

"Wow, Mr. Jones, that Becca is a real prize. Good score."

"Go ahead and shove your dick in her face. I believe in sharing the wealth."

It's a good idea and all but I just got done with the Hopkins doll. I'm not sure my dick is up to the job."

Jones sighed and continued mechanically thrusting into Becca's tight pussy like a cook stirring a pot of stew, keeping it on an even boil, "Only one way to know for sure, Wilrey. Give it a try. Even if she can't get it up for you, she'll clean Doll's juices off you."

Wilrey paused, a big leering grin breaking out on his fat round face.

Becca froze, outraged out of her passionate daze. Was Wilrey admitting he'd had sex with Lilly Hopkins, the chronic masochistic masturbatory patient? When she passed Lilly Hopkin's room, is that what she'd heard, Wilrey giving it to Hopkins? It was one thing for a patient like Jones to assault a staff member like her, but something else for a guard to take advantage of a female patient. It might be sexist but the expectations were different. Becca was a "victim" of a patient, not a victimizer of a patient. Sexually using poor Lilly Hopkins was a horrendous moral violation.

"Wilrey, you monster, how could you do that to poor Lilly? She's a patient, you sick freak! I'm going to report you to Ms. Carter. You'll be fired and prosecuted!"

Jones still thrust his cock into her pussy but she shut out the pleasure now. It was a matter of principle, of protecting a vulnerable patient.

Wilrey looked scared for a moment and his eyes darted to Jones. Unconcerned and relaxed, Jones continued to thrust, but addressed both of their concerns.

"Pretty Toy, the one we call Doll and who you know as Lilly Hopkins, is not an actual patient here. She is a fraud. She is one of my people. She is one of my many subjects. She didn't want me to get too lonely while incarcerated. Why do you think business at Goethner-Varner is booming? She isn't the only one "committed" to serve me. They help me pass the time and amuse my new friends such as Wilrey here. When I am freed, they will be "cured" and freed as well. Despite what you may think I am a principled man. You may not agree with or fully comprehend many of my beliefs, but one area we surely agree on is the humane treatment of the disadvantaged. Wilrey, tell her if I lie."

Wilrey spoke earnestly, his eyes wide like a child's. "It's true, Pretty Toy. I was lonely before Mr. Jones allowed me to join his kingdom. I used to do bad things and sometimes hurt patients. Not anymore. I don't need to. Now I just hurt the women who enjoy being hurt."

Jones thrust particularly hard as if to punctuate Wilrey's statement and drive the point home, "I've actually improved the lot of the patients here. They are off limits to my people and have no idea his Majesty King Jones runs the show. I do believe in humane treatment. The first Friday of every month I dispatch many of my female subjects to find vagrants on the streets to orally pleasure them. This King is magnanimous. Now, Pretty Toy, back to your purpose, which is fucking my dick and licking Doll's juices off Wilrey's."

Becca felt the urgent need to remove Wilrey from Jones' plan of action at war with her urgent need to come. Once Jones banished her concern for Lilly, all of her erotically pleasurable sensations returned to swamp her. She wanted to stop thinking and get to coming all over Jones' cock, but wished the prospect of sex with Wilrey was out of the picture.

Becca panted, "Wilrey, just leave us alone."

Wilrey grinned, "Listen to that, Mr. Jones. You must have pulled the Pretty Toy's string. Now she just wants to be with you. She doesn't want to be saved now."

Becca triple flushed from her shameful embarrassment, her racing blood, and her rising need to orgasm. Her number one priority was keeping her pussy in colliding contact with Jones' cock. All her physical energy was going towards fulfilling goal number one. That Jones was nibbling her nipples while holding her ankles above her head did not distract Becca from goal number one. Goal number two, a distant second, was to keep Wilrey away from her.

Wilrey dropped his pants, eagerly stepping out of them but keeping his dirty white socks and heavy black shoes on. Instinctively Becca found herself taking note of his penis. It was big and getting bigger despite its recent use. She could see areas of it still glistened with Lilly's juices. He wasn't really going to shove that slimy penis into her mouth, was he?

"Wilrey, get the fuck out of here," she said. "Leave me alone!"

Jones spoke up, "Wilrey, ignore Pretty Toy's malfunction. She'll soon be repaired. You have my permission, help yourself. Perhaps if I adjust these dials a little…"

Jones released her ankles to pinch her nipples, twisting so hard she thought they might tear off.

Becca groaned in pain and frustration, "You fucker!"

"Yes, very accurate, Pretty Toy," said Jones as he twisted her nipples in time with a series of faster harder thrusts.

Becca's body shoved her pussy back at him eagerly and she thrilled in the harsh wonderful contact. Her mind lingered over the exquisite sensations of pain rippling from her savaged nipples. She became distracted again when Wilrey rubbed his damp hard cock lengthwise across her full lips, practically humping her lower face.

Wilrey urged her, "Come on, Pretty Toy, open those soft lips you're equipped with and suck me. Get my dick all clean. Do it real good. I'll give you a taste of my ball milk to swallow down."

Becca opened her eyes and kept her mouth shut, feeling disgusted, helpless, and aroused. What could she do? Dimly, she realized she had to choose between continuing to resist or giving in to them and being what they wanted. Pleasure surged through her body as she realized she could relinquish all control to Jones and become a human fuck toy obeying commands. She wouldn't be responsible for the pleasure she felt.

Her sharp arousal now surpassed her combined disgust, horror, and angry helplessness. The arousal wasn't just from the physical actions of Jones cock skimming in and out of her sex or the compelling mix of pain and pleasure stemming from Jones twisting her inexperienced nipples.

No, the true source of her arousal was degradation. Their humiliating words, their utter lack of respect for her, all the wrongful mistreatments, her lewd and helpless nakedness, and even the grossness of Wilrey's slimy penis sliding crosswise against her lips all pumped accelerant on her internal fires, driving her flames higher and spurring her arousal to billow to uncontrollable heights.

What if she just opened her mouth as wide as she could? It was an alien and insidious thought but the moment she conceived it she acted on it.

Wilrey groaned and slid his slimy cock into her widely gaping mouth, moving back and forth between the soft folds of her lips. She was doing it! She was actually doing it! She kept her wet little tongue working the sensitive underside of his cock, following the rhythm of Jones' thrusts into her pussy. In a moment of unity she could sense all three of them taking pride and pleasure in the submission of her mouth to their will.

Becca pictured herself sucking in gross Wilrey's dick and the repulsive image stoked her fires. She imagined Wilrey's gratitude to Jones. Obviously, there was no way she'd be doing this for him if Jones hadn't softened her will. Before today, she wouldn't have given a creep like Wilrey the time of day and now she sucked him deep and wriggled her tongue on his cock with all her might.

Becca first mentally recoiled as she tasted the juices of Lilly Hopkins on Wilrey's cock, but she quickly recovered, her tongue pushing harder. She eagerly swallowed a mouthful of her saliva, Wilrey's pre-come, and the faint remnants of Lilly's pussy juice. It was an unholy cocktail which made her thirsty for more.

Wilrey used undue force to jam his groin against Becca's mouth, bouncing Becca's head against the mattress. Apparently, he was not satisfied to let her service him, because he was actively face-fucking her.

A newly subjugated part of Becca's rational mind rebelled, insisting she should be angered by the treatment, appalled by her own cooperation, sickened that she had slurped up another woman's juices, and worried about the men and their depraved plans for her. Becca's new persona, Pretty Toy, quickly quelled the rebellion, assuring her none of those things were important. Only pleasing the men and obtaining the greatest orgasm had any relevance now.

When Jones suddenly pulled out of her pussy, Becca whimpered, feeling a profound sense of loss and emptiness. Her skyrocketing pleasure halted and began to plummet back to Earth. Becca's legs were still held in place due to Wilrey's wide thighs pinning them while he dipped his cock down into her mouth.

Still servicing Wiley's cock, Becca was completely unprepared when Jones wound up and delivered a full swing spank to her stretched taut ass cheeks. Five more followed while she choked around Wilrey's cock.

Wilrey's cock choked off Becca's outraged screams of pain. All she managed was an inadequate muffled wail. Although upset by the spanking pain, she felt more cheated by the loss of Jones' cock.

Jones spoke, "Wilrey, pull out. Before you interrupted us I was performing an important quality test on this toy."

Wilrey pulled out with great reluctance, disentangled his legs from her and staggered several steps backward from Becca. Becca started to put her legs down.

Jones addressed her, "Pretty Toy, stay as you are. Recall our conversation just before Wilrey joined us. You are to thank me, your Creator. As well, you should kindly thank Wilrey for honoring you by putting his dick in your facial orifice. You should also give further words of appreciation and express what you want now. Do well, and you will be rewarded with the return of our cocks."

Becca's mental fog lifted for a moment, allowing her to think clearly. She had to have those cocks back in her mouth and pussy. The only way to get them was to thank their owners and then to beg for what she wanted. So she clearly had no choice and would have to do exactly as Jones commanded.

A wiser part, far back in her consciousness, Protested that thanking them and begging them would change her forever, but her newly dominant sexually submissive side didn't give a damn.

Her voice sounded foreign, more husky and sexy, "I thank you, Mr. Jones, for everything. Please, please put your dick back in me. I love it."

Jones seemed to consider, even halting Wilrey who had begun to step back into position, "Good, Pretty Toy. However, you are programmed to do even better. You should be more specific, more sexually graphic in your request. If you want your mouth and your pussy fucked you need to make the offer a tempting one to us."

Becca didn't hesitate. It seemed like a part of herself had secretly hoped he would demand more of her, "Please, Sir, Mr. Jones, I beg you to shove your dick back in my pussy. Please fuck me hard. I need it so bad, Sir, and I think I'd go crazy without it. I will be so grateful if you will fuck me. My little pussy is dripping for you. I want to suck Wilrey off too. It would be an honor. Anything you want, Mr. Jones. I'm all yours! I'll do anything in return for the return of your dick!"

Becca held her ankles up by her ears and bared her pussy, her wide eyes pleading and begging Jones for his cock, waiting for any signal he found her complete capitulation acceptable.

Jones delivered a vicious spank to her ass, sending a shockwave of pain and disappointment through her. She must not have thanked and begged good enough to satisfy him. His next words greatly reassured her.

"Wilrey, I do believe this one now has my stamp of approval. The red hand print will temporarily do for the time being under these conditions. I'll mark her permanently later."

Jones resumed his position and thrust back into Becca's soaked pussy. Becca found herself eagerly grabbing Wilrey's cock in both hands and guiding it into her mouth. She angled her neck to push her mouth up and forward so her mouth could engulf the maximum amount of cock. It was awkward and her neck hurt but the sensation of being completely stuffed seemed worth it at the moment.

The three of them worked rhythmically like precision parts in a well oiled machine. In less than a minute Becca was coming while whining, her mouth still wrapped around Wilrey's cock. It was the best orgasm of her life. A record, the orgasm held for about three minutes until she came again as Jones blasted come into her wildly flexing pussy.

Through both tremendous orgasms Becca focused as much of her will as she could muster to continue to suck and lick at Wilrey's cock. She was determined to make him come. As the second orgasm began to pass she grabbed his testicles and gave them a light squeeze. That seemed to drive him over the edge and he came deep in her throat while he yelped and groaned. She swallowed and moaned, sharing his excitement.

Becca amazed herself by eagerly swallowing down all his sperm and licking his cock clean. It was like her submission turned her into an expert whore. She was a sexual automaton, a flesh machine whose purpose was to satisfy others. Somehow, it was wonderful to feel that way and tempting to imagine transforming permanently into a sex toy.

As Wilrey pulled his dick away from her mouth, a few droplets of sweat fell from his face, splashing her nose and cheek. Even this comparatively light sensation was enough to bring her back to reality. What had she been thinking? Why had she let them do this to her? She had to get away from these freaks before she lost herself. Before they did even more to her.

Becca relaxed her legs and pulled her pussy off Jones' still throbbing cock, which tried to pump sperm into her but had nothing left to deliver. Becca slowly stood on shaky sore legs, aware Jones stared at her with a clinical, detached gaze.

"Do you think what we just did was crazy?" he asked.

Becca hesitated. The use of the word "crazy" was, of course, frowned upon in a psychiatric ward. "It was not right," she said. "It was not smart. It was not sane."

Jones smiled with smug satisfaction, as if she had performed exactly as he expected. "Since you say it was not sane it must be the opposite. In your view, it must have been insane. People must be judged by their acts within the framework of their own viewpoint. For instance, to a true cannibal eating a human being is not insane or bad because he believes it to be a correct act. What Mr. Wilrey and I did was perfectly sane within our moral framework which tells us you are here to serve us in any way we see fit. So, Wilrey and I are totally sane. You, however, as defined by your own logic framework, are insane. So, as an insane person, you need to be committed to this facility until you can be declared sane. That will only be when you view the various sexual acts we engage in as completely sane, logical, appropriate, and desirable. Believe in me, and we'll soon have you cured. It won't be long before you can re-enter society as a much more useful Pretty Toy."

Becca stared at him while fumbling to put her clothes back on. What was this madman talking about?

Jones leaned back on the mattress, his cock gleaming with her pussy oils.

"Wilrey, for her own good, go ahead and place Pretty Toy into her toy box."

Wilrey looked confused, "Toy box, Mr. Jones? What toy box?"

"Wilrey, what does one store in a toy box? Pretty Toys, Dolls…."

"Ohhh! I get it!"

"Give Pretty Toy an official ward outfit too so she'll fit in, just in case. Do have her cleaned up by Doll in the usual way."

Wilrey leered with renewed eagerness, grabbing one of Becca's thin biceps in a powerful grip that was beyond her ability to escape. He jerked her arm and she staggered along behind him. Feeling hopeless and exhausted, she didn't even try to resist. If she had known what was in store for her, she would have fought, clawed and kicked all the way to her new toy box.

After unlocking the door with his code, Wilrey shoved Becca into Lilly Hopkins' room. Becca did not resist as he pushed her onto a narrow bed and used leather straps to secure her delicate wrists to the top of the bed frame. Lilly Hopkins observed from a second bed through hunks of blond hair pulled over her face. Absently, Becca studied Lilly's features and found her pretty, especially for a woman nearly as old as her own Mother. Oh, if Mother could see her now! How awful!

Wilrey finished pulling the straps secure and turned to Lilly, "Doll, Mr. Jones says to clean her out. His spunk is up her cunt. Lick her out good so she'll be ready for more of the same."

"You gross jerk!" Becca yelled yanking and struggling vainly against the straps, which cut and stung her pale flesh. She turned frantic pleading eyes on Lilly Hopkins. Surely, the lady wouldn't do what he was asking? Hope turned to dread when Lilly walked straight to her without hesitation or expression.

Lilly knelt on the bed between Becca's feet, slid her hands between Becca's inner thighs, and began pulling them apart to expose Becca's hairy little pussy. Becca struggled wildly in an absolute panic, although deep down she recognized she couldn't stop it.

She held Lilly off by wind-milling her legs, her feet churning and kicking and bruising Lilly's arms. As she realized she was lucky Wilrey failed to tie her legs down, her eyes caught Wilrey chuckling and leaning against the sterile white wall. The jerk had left her legs free on purpose, hoping to see a one-sided catfight. This realization made her recognize Lilly Hopkins was as much a victim as herself.

Becca refused to continue to hurt Lilly for Wilrey's entertainment and gave up the struggle. It was inevitable anyway.

Workmanlike, Lilly returned her dislodged hands to Becca's soft inner thighs and spread her unresisting legs wide. Becca watched in horrified fascination as Lilly's full red lips descended on her helpless pussy.

Lilly Hopkins clamped her mouth onto the pussy, lips to lips, and mechanically began to suck, suck, dart tongue in, suck, suck. Repeat. Repeat. Becca started feeling a potent mixture of awful wondrous sensations. Lilly's eyes held a wicked delight in their depths as she watched Becca's expression while she sucked and licked at the swollen folds of Becca's pussy. As Lilly's eyes darkened with arousal, they suddenly struck Becca as very similar to the black button eyes of an actual doll.

Trying to hold still despite the ungodly good sensations Lilly stirred in her sex, Becca laid passive and just tried to get through it. Becca stared as Lilly dropped her hand to her own pussy and started masturbating. Lilly's pointer and middle fingers applied slow circular pressure to her clitoris. As Lilly pleasured herself, she moaned with pleasure against Becca's pussy, causing delightful vibrations and tingles in the tender pink flesh.

Shocked by the twisted passion on Lilly's face, Becca averted her eyes and tried to distract herself by watching the giggling Wilrey. But somehow thinking about Wilrey enjoying her predicament just boosted her horniness. Her pussy became even more sensitized, even more attuned to Lilly's agile tongue. There was nothing she could do, she was at their mercy, and, God help her, she was starting to relish her helplessness. It felt like along with Jones' come, Lilly was sucking her soul out through her pussy.

As she felt herself start up the pleasurable ascent towards climax, she bit her lip and shook her head. This was crazy. Maybe she was crazy. She tensed her leg muscles and pushed her butt down into the mattress to escape, but Lilly's darting tongue and vacuuming mouth simply followed her the couple inches she gained. When she surrendered and relaxed, raising her ass back up, the tongue delved particularly deep until Lilly's nose ground against her clitoris, causing the clitoris to harden and swell painfully.

Wilrey chimed in then with mocking, haunting words, "Becca, Becca. Your pussy looks so wet. Hopkins must have sucked out all the come by now. Not all that wetness can be her spit. Hell, I can smell you. You're a real lesbian slut. Who knew? I bet you didn't even know you're an-all-the-time-with-anyone slut. Now we all know, including you, and now that you know it you can't unlearn it."

As Wilrey mocked her, Lilly worked diligently at her pussy. She drilled it with her tongue and every few seconds pulled it out to lick hard and quick up and down both sides of her labial lips, first the outer, then the inner, then a swipe across the clitoris, then back to tunnelling her tongue deep up Becca's pussy. Becca felt like she was going crazy. She could hardly think. She wanted Lilly to continue tonguing her pussy, from then into infinity. Nothing else mattered. If Wilrey had offered her immediate freedom without first allowing Lilly to bring her to orgasm Becca would have turned him down. All her priorities had flipped upside down. More accurately, she only had one priority now. Orgasm.

Without permission her trim hips shoved her pussy deeper onto Lilly's tongue, grinding her pussy hair hard against Lilly's face. Pussy and mouth mashed together again and again in violent kisses. Sometimes Lilly's nose would mash Becca's clitoris, causing a powerful good/bad pain/pleasure and sometimes Lilly's teeth would scrape her most vulnerable skin, causing her to gasp in pain before returning to groans of fuller pleasure. The wild bouncing smeared pussy juice all over Lilly's face. Lilly didn't seem to mind, she seemed to revel in it.

"Ah, ahhhhh!," Becca howled as all of her muscles tensed. This madness was going to drive her mad. "So good - I'm going to - I'm going to come again!"

Moments later she did come again. Her orgasms continued to grow successively stronger despite her repeated mistaken beliefs no higher peaks could be achieved.

Lilly pulled her wet mouth off Becca's pulsing pussy and fondled her own pussy quite harshly until she, too, came a minute after Becca's orgasm. Becca watched the process with lewd fascination, wondering why watching the pretty older lady diddle herself was so arousing.

After Lilly came Becca glanced at Wilrey, feeling slightly repulsed by his self-satisfied smirk. She found her eyes automatically checked his groin for a tell-tale bulge. It was there! Was he going to fuck her? Surprisingly, she did not dread the thought. If Wilrey decided to fuck her she guessed he could help himself and she wouldn't mind as long as he made her come again.

Wilrey noticed her look, "Not yet, little slut. You need to learn some manners. Doll here sucked your pussy. Only fair you return the favor."

"Go fuck yourself!" Becca yelled.

Wilrey ground his hips in slow circles, accentuating the bulge in his pants. "Now why would I do that when I've got you?"

Becca eyed Lilly's blond furred pussy, dreading crossing that lesbian line. Getting licked by a woman against her will was one thing but sucking another woman's pussy would be a mental stigma that would brand her psyche forever.

Lilly Hopkins eyes sparkled with delight as she rose up, straddled Becca, and mashed her thick blond bush into Becca's face. Becca kept her mouth closed, lips pressed so tightly together they were turning white. Lilly lightly bumped her mound against Becca's closed lips, leaving a dewy covering of pussy juice all over her jaw.

Sudden pain flashed in Becca. Her pussy! Aargh! Wilrey was pinching her clit viciously. Not only pinching, but twisting and pulling.

"I'll just keep doing this until you lick Doll's cunt and suck in her juices, Pretty Toy. We both know you'll give in sooner or later so go ahead and put that tongue to work."

Becca couldn't think through the pain. She parted her lips to scream, to release some small portion of the pain. As she screamed against Lilly's pussy, Lilly cooed with delight, the first vocal sound she'd made during the encounter.

Wilrey relaxed his clit pinch a little. Becca was grateful and she flicked her tongue through Lilly's swampy bush and tentatively licked at her sloppy pussy lips. Wilrey continued to squeeze Becca's clitoris gently, sometimes just rubbing the super sensitized node of flesh. Becca was going wild from the pain, the tremendous pleasure radiating from her little clitty, these bizarre people, and these humiliating acts she was compelled to carry out.

She knew she should hate the degradation. On a moral level perhaps she did, but on the physical and sensual planes she loved it and felt grateful. She was irrevocably changed, like the old Becca no longer existed.

Suddenly her resistance broke and she abandoned reason for passion, craning her skinny neck forward and plunging her narrow tongue as far up and deep as it would go into Lilly. She liked tasting her! Not the taste exactly, but the sensation of being forced to taste her. She liked everything now. They could do anything to her or make her do anything and she knew she would enjoy it.

She wished her hands were free not to escape, but to cup Lilly's luscious ass. The passionate thought drove her arousal even higher. She imagined Wilrey's hard cock sliding up her pussy. It was bigger than Jones' cock. Would it feel better? Could Wilrey get it up a third time in less than an hour? Her imagination fired, picturing her and Lilly teaming up their mouths on Wilrey's cock. The nasty thought of her and Lilly's tongues simultaneously licking Wilrey's cock while he leered down at them made her shudder with passionate revulsion.

Although unable or unwilling to service Becca's pussy, Wilrey rewarded Becca's efforts by using his fat fingers to roughly fondle her pussy. He alternated thrusting his fingers in her pussy and then pulling them out to pinch and sometimes pull at her labial lips. He mixed pain and pleasure in equal measures, making Becca's pussy quiver.

Becca avidly tongued Lilly's vagina while Lilly ground her wet bush against Becca's face. Wilrey wickedly flicked Becca's clitoris with a thumbnail and Becca felt her ass alternately grinding downwards and thrusting up into the sensations. She had no control over her own ass. She loved her complete and utter loss of control.

When Lilly grunted and howled ferociously in orgasm she smashed her groin hard to Becca's face, almost suffocating her. Excited by Lilly's grunts, Wilrey thrust three fat fingers in Becca's soaked little pussy and used the thumb and index finger of his left hand to pinch and rub her swollen clitoris. The combinations easily drove Becca over the top into yet another orgasm.

After Lilly and Wilrey got off the bed, Becca didn't move, closing her eyes and savoring the aftershocks of pleasure. Her legs remained spread wide and she didn't bother wiping Lilly's musky, glistening come off her face.

Through tired, slitted eyes, Becca studied Wilrey as he drank in her condition of disarray. He mumbled, "Mr. Jones is a fucking genius."

Becca's eyes fluttered closed. She still made no attempt to speak, close her legs, or to pull her strapped hands free. She felt completely exhausted and no longer cared what happened.

CHAPTER 3

Jacqueline Thorpe pushed wide the door leading to Dr. Arlington's waiting room and strode inside. She stepped over to the receptionist's desk taking long firm strides. Her apparent confidence directly contrasted the lack of confidence she felt. Jacqueline knew her body movements lied but she did not feel guilty. After all, perception was reality and everyone has an equal chance to make their own reality. It was also why, professionally, people knew her as Jacqueline while in her personal life to friends and family she was known as Jackie.

"I'm here to meet Dr. Arlington. I have an appointment. Dr. Jacqueline Thorpe."

The receptionist was new or at least different from the one Jackie met on her first visit when she interviewed for a job as Psychoanalyst and junior partner in Dr. Arlington's practice. The older woman she'd met then, Ruthie, had been kindly and affectionate. This younger woman seemed cold to Jackie. She was quite attractive, even gorgeous, but her face remained as expressionless as a field of snow.

"You're early. Go sit in the waiting room and I'll call you when he's ready."

Jackie noted that rather than looking her in the eyes, the receptionist appraised Jackie's tight coils of pinned up bronzed hair and her apparel. The long look seemed to focus especially on Jackie's ample breasts that she always tried – but with only partial success – to conceal with thick shapeless tops. From the receptionist's nasty I'm-Laughing-At-You-Not-With-You smirk it was apparent she found Jackie's fashion sense lacking.

Jackie felt a flash of anger. People were so superficial. Men and women too often seemed to judge others by appearance, physique, and fashion. It was the demeanour, the personality, the actions of a person that really counted. Jackie knew she was beautiful but actively worked to downplay her appearance. She didn't want to make her way through life by depending on her beauty.

If she'd been willing to succeed in life by leveraging her beauty and her body she would have given in to the boss's sexual advances at her previous job at Thurgood Joiner instead of quitting in outrage before she even had another job lined up.

Jackie found a seat in the empty waiting room and waited, examining the pastel paintings of landscapes adorning the walls. They were clearly meant to relax antsy patients. Of course, they were all just prints. Dr. Arlington's patients all had mental or emotional troubles and no one would be unwise enough to risk leaving original paintings in a room with them.

Jackie grew more and more nervous about her meeting with Dr. Arlington. She had met him once already and admired the successful elderly man. Of course, since he was a Psychoanalyst, she had no idea what he thought of her. All Psychoanalysts were masters at reading the emotions of others while concealing their own. Although Jackie had only earned her PhD in Psychoanalysis two years ago, she hoped she was not the exception to the rule.

Jackie heard a sharp intake of breath and a low moan and swivelled her head to look at the receptionist. The receptionist, about twenty feet away, held up her right index finger. Two bright beads of blood spotted her index finger pad.

"A fucking staple stabbed me. It really hurts."

The receptionist watched Jackie with a hint of predatory anticipation, waiting for Jackie's reaction. She placed the injured finger into her mouth and sucked languidly, her ruby painted lips pulsing around her finger.

Jackie looked away, disconcerted. What was that girl's deal anyway? Was she Dr. Arlington's receptionist, or his patient? Jackie heard her sucking on the finger for long minutes before removing it from her mouth with an audible pop. Why did she have to suck that finger so long?

A moment later she heard the sound of a stapler in action and another intake of breath followed by a throaty and extended moan from the receptionist. The moan sounded like one of pain, frustration, and... arousal? Jackie pretended not to notice.

"Hey, look!"

Jackie glanced at the receptionist, hoping it was time for her meeting. But the weird receptionist held up her hand and spread her fingers wide. The previously sucked index finger gleamed with saliva. The middle finger had two droplets of blood beading on the tip.

"I think it wants my blood. That stapler has two little fangs just like a vampire."

The receptionist waggled the stapler with her uninjured hand, her grin like sunlight reflecting off the field of snow, her teeth bright and perfect, "No, Little Vampire, my blood belongs to me."

Eyes full of poisonous humour, the receptionist stared into Jackie's shocked eyes, leaned towards her hand, and used her flicking tongue to scoop up the beads of blood.

Just then Dr. Arlington came out of his office and seemed surprised to see Jackie, "Oh, you're here, Dr. Thorpe. Good. Good to see you. Please, come right in."

He motioned for her to come in to his office and then looked pointedly at the receptionist. "I hope you haven't been waiting long."

"Just a few minutes, but I was early."

A small surge of satisfaction flooded Jackie when Dr. Arlington shot a frown of fatherly reprimand towards the receptionist. Despite Dr. Arlington's authority the girl seemed nonchalant as she went back to stapling.

Dr. Arlington ushered Jackie into his office. It seemed more like a home library than an actual office. There were three beautiful antique lamps and a huge cherry wood desk. Thousands of leather-bound books lined the fourteen-foot tall floor to ceiling bookshelves. Jackie sat in one of two high backed chairs lined in front of Dr. Arlington's desk as Dr. Arlington sat in his executive leather swivel chair.

Dr. Arlington noted her awed perusal of their surroundings, "You know, Dr. Thorpe, the empty room next to this one possesses the same dimensions and features. It is just waiting for an occupant to fill it with décor suiting their own personality."

"Yes, you showed me last time and it's been on my mind. Please, call me Jacqueline."

"You also, of course, should call me Robert. We're both doctors and titles between doctors are tedious. Especially given that I'd like to work in partnership with you for as many years as I have left before I retire."

Jackie felt a surge of glorious happiness. Dr. Arlington, Robert, had chosen her! After all the candidates he must have interviewed he selected her to become a junior partner in his psychotherapy practice.

"Thank you, Dr. Ar... ah, Robert, I'm looking forward to..."

Robert raised a hand to intercept her words. "I want to make you a partner in my practice, and I anticipate doing so. However, we're not quite there yet."

Jackie's elation turned to dismay. "Robert, I promise to be the perfect partner. I'll work hard and represent you and your therapeutic philosophy in every way."

"You must realize though that every applicant either has said or would say much the same. Some are truthful and would do as they say. Others are truthful but are unable to actually do as they say. Still others just plain lie. This is a crucial decision that will impact my practice and my legacy. I must be absolutely certain of making the correct choice."

"Robert, how can I reassure you?"

"You embody the right attitude, Jacqueline. I want to hire you on a temporary capacity as a consultant. I will pay you generously to perform one challenging but rewarding task. Successfully complete the task as professionally and competently as I envision, and I will make you a long term junior partner in my practice and assure your professional reputation in the field."

"I am intrigued, Robert."

"Are you familiar with the Wayne Jones case?"

"Wayne Jones, "The King of Rapture?""

"So you are familiar with him, at least enough to know his media nickname. "King of Rapture" indeed! It is ridiculous to treat a serious mental condition with such flamboyance and disrespect. In the future, please be professional and refrain from using the media's moniker for him. Just Wayne Jones or Mr. Jones will be fine."

Color stained Jackie's her cheeks and she wished she could take back her unprofessional words.

Robert perceptively noticed her discomfort, "Don't worry, no harm there, Jacqueline. Please speak freely in private with me. Don't let my irritation with the media disconcert you. Not your fault at all. It pains me how insensitive the media, and the public in general, are to mental illness. When a criminal suffers from mental illness they should be pitied as much as their own victims."

Although Jackie doubted the victims would agree, she concurred with the point of view that the mentally ill victimizer was also a victim.

"The nickname "King of Rapture" is inaccurate and unfair. Firstly, the word rapture is normally used to refer to the penultimate religious experiences. To compare the effects of anything Jones did to a religious experience is offensive. For that matter, calling Jones a King is offensive to royalty of all nationalities. The focus should be on the criminal act and on the man's mental condition."

Jackie recalled the origin of the nickname. When a neighbour reported hearing screaming from inside his residence, police discovered Jones in the middle of a sexual act with a beautiful 22-year-old woman named Cassandra Zane. The woman claimed to be a victim of rape, contradicting Jones' assertion that the sex was consensual. The fact that the police found the woman bound and covered with painful welts lent believability to the woman's story. Complicating matters for Jones, the young woman was the daughter of an old money tycoon. The tycoon's money and celebrity, combined with the sexual factors, ensured the case became a media magnet.

As the media investigated, they found Jones had a number of female followers or fans. One fan interviewed on video stated that sex with Jones was like experiencing the rapture and that Jones was "the King of Rapture." Quickly all the newscasts saturated the airwaves with the quote, creating both a nickname and a media star. The youth, beauty, and high social standing of the young woman should have sealed the deal in convincing everyone Jones raped her, especially since Jones wasn't much of a looker. But Jackie had always sensed there was far more to the story than what the media uncovered.

Robert continued, "Justice in the Jones case took a path that avoided the courtroom. The young woman's family abhorred the media circus, plus a trial would have exposed the young woman's every act and every previous entanglement. There were questions about her honesty after reports surfaced indicating she'd flirted with Jones and was seen willingly accompanying him around town. The prosecution tried to bargain with Jones for a lesser conviction but he refused. At one point, they almost dismissed the case, but then Mayor Harrell became involved. Few know this but the girl's father, Wilford Zane, is George Harrell's number one campaign contributor. Harrell, motivated by his interest in pleasing Zane, is the reason Jones was committed."

"That's incredible! If you know this, why doesn't everyone? Why isn't that in the media?"

"News people around here are told what to care about. Harrell wanted them to ruin Jones' reputation. He didn't realize the media frenzy would turn Jones into a celebrity. With the quote "he's the King of Rapture" Jones became a hit, earning a multitude of weak-minded females desperate to experience the sexual rapture of "King Jones".

"Harrell's break came when police searched Jones' residence. They found homemade pornography, instruments of sexual torture, and Jones' diary detailing his exploits and twisted thoughts. The diary outlined beliefs such as women being objects to be used, pain as equal to pleasure, and Jones considering himself "King" of all persons he selected as subjects. Turns out the King title was not something the follower conjured on her own. The search revealed Jones was both a deviant and insane."

Jackie questioned the validity of Robert's last statement and had to interject, wondering whether he was testing her, "Not necessarily. Egomania and narcissism are dysfunctions but not insanity. A truly insane person, the type who would need to be indefinitely committed, cannot function in society and is a threat to themselves or others."

Robert paused and studied her. She could see his tongue working inside his mouth as if trying to taste an expensive wine. He almost said one thing, but decided on a different direction, "Yes, you're right. The thought process is only dangerous if acted on through violence. Jones had no history of that at all. But in Jones case he did qualify as a danger to society. It wasn't the arrogance expressed in his journal, his philosophy that all others existed to serve his curious sense of pleasure, or even his belief he was King in a world populated by peasant women ripe for the harvesting. No, Jones became a threat to society after his population mushroomed and he attracted so many like-minded followers. Did you know his followers sold thousands of T-shirts that read "I bow down to the King of Rapture"?

"No, I hadn't heard that."

"If free, a notorious man like Jones could exert enormous influence over a community, particularly young impressionable men and women. Harrell convinced the psychiatric board of review assigned to Jones' case to diagnose him as mentally deranged and a threat to society. That led to his indefinite committal to the maximum security ward at the Goethner-Varner Mental Health Hospital. Jones' committal neatly avoided an actual trial. He'll likely be confined longer this way, perhaps his entire life.

"Now, six months after Jones' committal, there is a small problem for which I require your assistance. A few of Jones' deluded followers are lawyers. They appealed Jones' diagnosis through state channels where Harrell's influence doesn't stretch. As a state consultant I've been tasked to assess Jones' mental condition and formulate an opinion on whether he should be released into society. I would like to handle the case, as the fee involved is most attractive, but I have strong social connections with Harrell and Zane. This obviously raises questions about my objectivity, so I'm turning the task to you. This way Jones is treated fairly in the eyes of the public and my practice gains the fee."

Jackie had a sudden realization, "You're leaving something out! Whoever declares Wayne Jones sane will be seen as a laughingstock. Their career, my career, would be publicly ruined. I'd never be able to overcome the reputation as "The woman who freed the maniac Jones"!"

Robert sported a sly smile. "Smart girl, you're right about that. If you approve his release I would most certainly decline to take you on as my partner due to the media embarrassment."

"I refuse to flush my career down the toilet!"

"That is not my intention. Look, Jones is insane, at the very least a threat to the community. Simply interview him a few times, review his records and case file, and make an assessment that agrees with the original determination. Spend a couple weeks, be thorough, and make it look good. Document all of the hours you spend with him in the visitor log so no one questions your judgment. I can't make this next point strongly enough. To be freed, Jones requires three state assessments that recommend overturning the state board's findings. He has already acquired two. Whoever those doctors were, they must have been fans or otherwise off kilter to submit such preposterous findings. Luckily, your third and final recommendation will ultimately decide Jones' fate."

"I don't believe in deciding an outcome before completing an assessment. It isn't professional."

"Powerful people will be indebted to you. You'll have a junior partnership with yours truly. I'm in my sixties, how much longer can I last? You'll inherit this practice in just a few short years. Besides, Jones is a fascinating case doctors would kill for. His mentality is fascinating. You'll be able to publish articles in the best mental health journals."

"Objectivity and fairness don't matter?"

"The odds of you finding this patient sane are astronomical. Make your own judgments, but you are right that your reputation is at stake."

Jackie sensed a trick, but she couldn't put her finger on it.

"Do you accept, Jacqueline, or shall I call one of my many other eager applicants to offer them this life-changing opportunity?"

Hearing footsteps out in the hall, Becca glanced at the locked exit to the suite she now shared with Jones devotee Lilly Hopkins. "Jail cell" was more appropriate than "suite", although the food was pretty good and the suite was much larger than the prison cells she saw in movies. Still, if given the option she would immediately trade her suite for an actual prison cell, or at least she hoped she would. With a bitter, hopeless laugh she realized this experience might actually make her a better Psychiatric Assistant. She finally understood the powerlessness and frustration her patients felt with incarceration.

Sharing a cell with the sexually hyperactive and insistent Hopkins woman – Doll – had drained her physically and emotionally. She glanced nervously over at Lilly in the other bed, relieved she seemed to be sleeping.

Four days of imprisonment had been hell so far. All of the degrading sex... All the orgasms she hated herself for enjoying... It was just a living hell! At first she thought obsessively about escape, then about being rescued, but now she just wondered what would happen next.

Like right now. Becca got up and pressed her ear to the meal slot in the door, listening to the echoing footsteps grow louder and louder. Who was it? Would they stop at her suite? What would they do to her and what would they make her do?

She straightened, stared through the square window in her cell door, and waited to catch sight of the owner of the footsteps. Again for the millionth time she cursed that the window was Plexiglas, not real glass. She knew because Day Two she'd spent an hour bouncing a chair off it trying to break it.

The footsteps stopped and the head of a black guard appeared in the window. He leered at her, his lascivious expression a jarring contrast to the distinguished band of white hair at his temples. Even though she'd never met this guard, Becca didn't bother pleading for help. They never helped her. Instead they helped themselves to her.

Damn her curiosity! Why did she look through the window? Why hadn't she thrown the covers over herself and pretended to sleep? It was her best and only defence. Sometimes they didn't want sex from a groggy girl with morning breath.

"Power up, Pretty Toy, time to play."

He stared at her and waited for acknowledgment of his command. What was she supposed to say? The word "no" was useless. When she acted "against the manufacturer's specifications" they "fixed her" using pain.

"I don't have time to come in there unless you malfunction. If it isn't broke I won't need to fix it."

"How may I please you from in here, Sir?" She'd found showing obedience was a sure-fire way of acting in accordance with Jones' specification. She had to admit being their little actress and assuming the submissive role turned her on, especially when they forced her to vocalize her subservience

"Simple. I don't have to enter the room to get serviced by you. I'll push my cock through this here little opening for food trays, and Pretty Toy will suck it. Don't worry; my dick belongs there because it is food for you. I won't touch you any, but you'll make me happy. Playing with Pretty Toys is meant to make people happy. But first show me your working parts, Pretty Toy. Make my cock stiff."

She knew what he wanted. She moved back five feet from the door and spread her legs wide, hands under each breast, plumping and displaying them to advantage. She was, of course, completely naked.

The guard's eyes centred on her pubic mound, her black pubic hair untrimmed but not thick enough to conceal and protect the modesty of her pussy. She shivered, feeling his eyes, hot and wet, invade her most tender place.

"Pretty Toy has a nice little pussy. If Pretty Toy sucks me real good, I'll give her permission to pet her pussy."

These people made her so angry! Talking to her like she was some kind of inanimate object. She'd heard of the objectification of women but this was ridiculous. Suggesting she would want to finger her pussy while she sucked him off. Like he was kindly giving her a present!

"Pretty Toy, switch into blow job mode."

She tried to keep the outrage and resentment off her face and failed miserably. She glanced up at the camera mounted in one corner of the room. He'd probably made a bet with another guard who would be watching her performance on the cameras. But, she had already donned her Pretty Toy role and that meant following instructions, whatever they were. He just wanted an unusual blow job, nothing worse than what she had already done.

Becca's poor abused body protested as she squatted until her mouth was level with the metal shelf that stuck out from under the tray opening in the door. Squatting caused her little ass to clench and spread under the window for his viewing pleasure.

The guard pushed his stiff black cock through the opening until it rested on the cool stainless steel shelf. She looked at it with a hollow feeling in her stomach, then opened her lips and made contact with his dick.

First she kept her lips together and used the tandem to skim from tip to base and back, again and again across the top of the cock. She heard him groan in delight and felt pleased with producing such pleasure in him.

"I give you permission to pet your pussy as a gift for gobbling my cock so good. Compromise, Pretty Toy, that's what life is all about."

She pressed her left cheek against the cool stainless steel shelf and slid it forward toward his cockhead. As she tried to guide it between her lips, a streak of pre-come created a snail trail across her chin. She popped his cock into her mouth and tasted the salty, slimy pre-come, an unexpected amount of saliva pooled in her mouth, almost as if she was starving for cock.

"Oh yes, Pretty Toy, you are definitely so compromised."

Starving for cock? How ridiculous, she asserted inwardly as her lips, mouth, and tongue teamed up to synchronize the best possible blow job. At least, her mouth wasn't starving for cock. She admitted her pussy was hungry for... something.

Maybe it wouldn't be so bad if he did come in the cell. Maybe she should stop pleasuring him to incite him to come and get her.

Although her pussy longed to be fucked, she hated the idea of disappointing the guard, whoever he was. Disappointing him was not part of her programming. Part of her instructions, she corrected herself. Maybe getting fucked wasn't in her current instruction set, but he had given her permission to "pet her pussy".

Becca's left hand gripped the metal shelf for balance, and her right hand darted to her pussy. Before she could get a grip on herself and reconsider, her fingers got a grip on her dripping, hungry pussy. All of her fingers strained to thrust into the heat of her tight slit, competing deliciously to gain entry.

While fingering herself, she licked all over the guard's cockhead. Wanting the entire length of his cock inside her mouth, she slid her whole head forward and back on the shelf through a large pool of her own drool, trying to take the dick as deep as possible.

She felt slimy, awkward, and passionate. She was such a slut. Her pussy squished hard down on her fingers. What a whore she was. Her arousal spiked dangerously. The worse she thought of herself the closer she came to coming.

The guard's cock jerked and pulsed. "Ahhh, I'm coming! All over your face, Pretty Toy, make it go all over your face!"

Becca quickly and unquestioningly obeyed instructions. She was desperate to come and was so close, her fingers frantically working in her pussy folds, but it was even more important to do as she was told.

She pulled her face off his cock and moved back about half a foot. She waited for the spray of whiteness, her eyes blinking defensively. She kept her face sideways and her previously drooled saliva dripped off her lower cheek onto the metal shelf. He blasted his climax into her face and hair, and she obediently held still for it. As the hot come dripped down her face, she quivered with lust and degradation, hoping the act and smell would take her over the edge into her own orgasm. It wasn't quite enough. The fingers in her pussy slowed their ministrations. She could still finger herself to completion, but it wasn't the same.

Thick white come coated her face. Some was stuck in her hair, but most of it slid off her face to pool below on the stainless steel shelf.

"Don't you be wasting food, Pretty Toy. Eat it all up, yum yum."

Becca went to work licking up the mixture of his warm spend and her cooled saliva. It was a twisted, shameful turn on, and her fingers picked up speed again, working to satiate her needful pussy. She was getting desperate for release.

It only took a long minute for her to polish the entire shaft, all of his sperm soon digesting in her belly.

The guard pulled his cock back, and she heard the zip of his pants going back up. Without a word he left her with only the sound of his receding footsteps and an unfulfilled pussy.

She stood up, aching, dizzy, and lusty, only bothering to clean her soiled face with a single swipe of her hand across one cheek. She would have been shocked at the heavy white dapples all over her face and hair if she looked in a mirror, but mirrors were banned from suites, as patients could break them into shards and cut themselves or others.

Seeking a solution to her desperate need, her eyes scanned the cell and found a brave volunteer. Lilly Hopkins sat in bed watching her with a wide voracious smile. She tossed the thin blanket off her nude form and patted the bed next to her.

Becca really disliked Lilly, and it made her angry to Lilly had clearly enjoyed watching her debasement, but Becca's desperate need for completion made her grateful. Plus, Becca's distaste for Lilly combined with the delicious idea of reprehensible lesbian acts poured gasoline on Becca's little crotch campfire.

Becca ran to Lilly's bed, jumped on it, and surprised Lilly by straddling her and cramming her pussy onto her mouth. Lilly's tongue snaked in and within moments Pretty Toy finally climaxed with a yell, her come-stained face turned straight up to the ceiling.

CHAPTER 4

Jackie had a job, three weeks to complete a mission, and a signed Permission to Conduct Case Review to present to Ms. Wendy Carter, Director of the Goethner-Varner Mental Health Hospital, in order to gain full evaluative access to Jones. Full evaluative access included unlimited interviews and a complete copy of his case file.

On the drive to the Hospital, anxious thoughts darted through her mind and she clenched the steering wheel. She was still uncomfortable with the idea that her diagnosis was already made, before meeting the subject or reviewing his history. But the thought of tarnishing her professional reputation and giving up the chance for her own practice for a sexual sadist was unpalatable. She shook her head and tried to reassure herself. It wouldn't be an issue. Jones was insane. He had to be.

Although Jackie the woman dreaded meeting a freak like Jones, Jacqueline the professional looked forward to it with excited anticipation. It was wrong to categorize a mentally unfit person as a freak, but the descriptions of the sadistic tools and bondage gear he used on women made Jones far more alien and freakish than any Martian marching out of a flying saucer.

Jackie slowed as she approached the discrete sign bearing the Goethner-Varner name and turned up a long drive that wound into a hilly, wooded area. Like most mental health facilities for the criminally insane, tall pine trees hid the Goethner-Varner complex from sight of the main road. Although the facility was only a mile outside of a small town, Jackie guessed most the town's residents had no idea that Goethner-Varner existed though Jones arrival may have changed that.

As Jackie approached the complex, she noted the jammed visitor parking lot. A group of people swarmed in front of the main gate, some holding signs that sported slogans such as "Free Sex Prophet Jones" or "Just Listen to Jones" or "Jones = Joy". Other people milled in the parking lot, even grilling food like tailgaters at a sporting event. The cold air didn't seem to bother them perhaps because of the heat from the grills. Were all these people here because of Jones?

A redheaded woman about forty stepped in front of her car, holding out both hands and smiling widely. Jackie braked her car sharply and frowned at the woman. She wore a long lined trench coat but it was open despite the cold. Jackie was surprised to see that under it she wore a tight halter-top and tight cut-off jeans that exposed shapely pale legs. Big boots made her look especially slim. Jackie thought this woman must have been waiting in one of the running cars in order to stay warm enough in that outfit. Her front bumper stopped ten feet from the woman and her blinding smile. Jackie waved her hand, signalling at the woman to move, but the woman maintained both her position and her huge smile.

A rap on Jackie's driver's side window caused her to flinch. A pretty teenage girl with eager brown eyes motioned for Jackie to roll her window down. Jackie eyed the girl through her window, assessing her age between 18 and 20. She wore a bulging blue ski jacket and her long coppery hair cascaded down to brush the top of her butt. Jackie saw a tattoo on the left side of her neck. It was Chinese symbols in fiery form coloured red and gold. The girl's beauty was startling. She seemed friendly and harmless, so Jackie rolled her window down, but slowly, cautiously, and only part way. Who were these two and what did they want?

"Are you here to see King Jones?"

"Why are you asking?"

The girl and her joyous smile ignored Jackie's question and her tone of suspicion. "Tell him Kira is here. I'm here every day. Tell him Kira and Monica are both here rooting for him. Tell him we'll do anything he wants. Anything!"

How could Jackie respond to that?

"Ahh, great, Kira. I've got to go. Bye."

Jackie started rolling her window up but stopped when she saw the girl's delicate fingers gripping the top of the window. There was a blazing flame tattooed on the back of her hand.

"Oh! One more thing! When you go to King Jones will you do me one little favuor? Please! It's easy and you'll like it I promise."

"Well, I'll be busy and probably won't even see him."

"Oh, you will. He'll see you, see how pretty you are, he'll want you to see him. You will see him, yes you will lucky lady."

At this point Jackie would pretend to agree to anything if it would get these odd women out of her way. "Fine, what's the favuor?"

"Like I said, tell King Jones Kira and Monica say hi but, first, give him a nice long blow job."

Jackie stared in disbelief at the innocent-looking girl, whose happy and enthusiastic expression remained unchanged as she made her shocking statement. At least she released the car window.

Jackie made a noncommittal noise and watched as the red-headed older woman stepped out from the front of the car and joined Kira.

As Jackie drove past the pair, just before her window fully closed, she heard Kira say, "I told her Mom. I told her."

As she waited for Director Carter, Jackie reflected on her surreal entry into Goethner-Varner. All of those happy people holding up signs calling for Jones' release.

People" wasn't quite accurate. The term "females" better fit the bill. The phrase "female groupies" was even more precise. Jackie had to admit Jones had a fine taste in "supporters". They ranged from good-looking to beautiful.

Feeling slightly disgusted with herself, she wondered if Jones would find her attractive. She supposed he would. She knew he would. Number one, if she started enhancing her natural assets rather than obscuring them, she'd be at least as desirable as the beautiful woman in the parking lot. Number two, if he was a sexual deviant he was probably attracted to any and every female regardless.

The receptionist actually got up and walked over to Jackie. "Wendy will see you now."

Jackie wondered at the woman's use of Carter's first name. The receptionist had a pierced nostril and a four-leaf clover tattoo on her right ankle. Things seemed pretty informal around here. The pink streaks dyed into her brown hair made her look more like a groupie ready for her band to take stage than an office professional.

Jackie self-reprimanded inwardly for judging the woman by her outer appearance. Just because the woman had a tattoo and a facial piercing did not mean she was bad at her job.

She'd didn't have to wonder for long why the receptionist walked over just to tell her to go on in. She found out when the girl walked before her and opened the double doors for her. The gesture was reminiscent of a man on a first date. It felt odd and wrong to Jackie to be treated that way by a woman.

As Jackie passed the receptionist and entered Carter's office, Jackie could have sworn the woman checked out her ass. She wondered if the woman was a lesbian.

Oh well, thought Jackie, other people's lifestyle choices were none of her concern.

Carter tilted back in her leather armchair, her eyes assessing Jackie.

Jackie donned a competent smile and her professional demeanour. "Hello, Ms. Carter, I'm Dr. Jacqueline Wilson. I assume Dr. Arlington called ahead to inform you of my visit?"

Carter stared at her for two seconds before answering, "Please Jackie, call me Wendy. Robbie did call and I did expect you. But you aren't here to see me, are you?"

"Well, it is professional courtesy to meet with you. It is your facility."

"I just work here. It is no more my facility than it is the janitor's. If this place belongs to anyone, it's the patients."

Jackie considered those words and found them quite strange. Although Carter seemed sincere, her words sounded overly diplomatic, too rehearsed, like someone trained Ms. Carter to say it that way. "That's an interesting perspective Ms. Carter."

"Please, don't call me Ms. Carter. I certainly won't be calling you Dr. Wilson. Just call me Wendy. I consider you and I to be equal, Jackie."

It grated on Jackie that Wendy wasn't calling her Dr. Wilson, or at least Jacqueline. In all of her work relationships she insisted on being called Jacqueline. The more formal name provided an intangible barrier, allowing her to keep co-workers at a professional distance. Jacqueline sounded more cultured, less familiar, more sophisticated, and less accessible. But as this was a temporary assignment, it wasn't worth correcting Wendy.

"Wendy, I appreciate your hospitality. I plan to study Wayne Jones' psychology in detail over the next few weeks. Any insight you provide will be greatly appreciated. His is a fascinating case."

"My recommendation is to take your time and to conduct an in-depth study on Jones' philosophy. Jones is not insane. He has much to teach you."

Jackie's mouth nearly fell open. What was Wendy talking about?

Wendy chuckled, "Did you believe me, Jackie? I see you did. You are dangerously gullible. Untested. If you're not careful Jones is going to eat you up. Manipulate you. You're here to take measure of his state of mind. He will take your measure. He will understand your weak points better than you. He'll find weak points you did not know existed. I went through the same thing with him. It's a process. I was professionally fascinated. He put me through the wringer."

Wendy's dark brown eyes held a distant misty look while her hand fiddled with the blouse button positioned between her breasts. Her delicate fingers plucked it outward and then released it, repeating the process again and again. The motions caused Wendy's inner wrist and forearm rhythmically pushed on her right breast, plumping it up and outward.

Although Jackie found Wendy's actions odd, she found her advice sound. She determined to be calm, reserved, and rational with Jones. Maintaining purely professional conduct could influence him to mirror her behaviour. If she kept him calm and rational she'd be able to draw him out more, assess him more completely.

"Under what conditions will I meet with Mr. Jones? Will I need a guard?"

"No, you won't need a guard. Although he possesses a philosophy found unacceptable by society, he is not violent. In his own way he is really quite willing to please, and he won't do anything you don't want him to do. We don't even need to keep him confined. We do, but we wouldn't have to. The only potential problem I foresee is you. Since he won't do anything you don't want him to your only possible danger would be yourself. The things you want. I don't know. Do you find that reassuring or concerning?"

Jackie couldn't understand Wendy's point. "If you say he wouldn't harm anyone, I'm sure I'll be safe."

"Good for you, Jackie, though that is not exactly what I said. Your confidence is an asset. Very appealing. I'm sure Mr. Jones will agree."

"Have his followers been any sort of a problem?"

"Not at all. Quite peaceable. They tend to be passive by nature. They are just big fans of Mr. Jones. Good people."

"Good people? Good people don't idolize a rapist who thinks the world and the people in it exist for his own use and enjoyment. These "fans" worship a mentally deranged man. The police found torture devices in his basement, in his attic, and in his garage!"

"Come now, Jackie, people's desires take many forms. There is a wide spectrum. They may not be your particular shade but surely you don't think every person unlike you is a bad person? Another point, are you certain you are different from them? You have yet to meet Mr. Jones. Maybe you'll be a big fan too!"

"That's..." Jackie nearly said 'crazy' but knew better than to use than word, "a bizarre comment to make. I'm here to analyze Mr. Jones, not idolize him. I don't mean to be rude but I find your words patronizing and demeaning. I'd like to get on with my task. Can you assist with that?"

Wendy spent a moment considering Jackie, "Your outer shell is pretty but also, I think, thick and tough. Tough to crack. You'll have an interesting time with Mr. Jones and vice versa."

"There you go saying odd things again. Why would you say something like that?"

Wendy looked amused and chose not to answer. "When Robert called me I had my Administrative Assistant prepare a portfolio for you. It's on her desk. In the box are all of the Wayne Jones case materials, so you'll have as much background on him as possible. On top are a map of our facility and a permit badge that will give you free access. Of course, guards still need to unlock doors for you and such."

Wendy's calm professional response made Jackie regret her outburst. She shouldn't have let a stranger ruffle her like that.

Jackie got verbal directions from Wendy to the maximum security ward, thanked her with whatever grace she could muster, and left her office. The tattooed and pierced secretary had a frown on her face very different from her earlier smile.

Jackie retrieved the portfolio. The large cardboard box contained heavy objects that shifted and scraped when she lifted it. Jackie made a point to make introductions and shake the secretary's hand. So many people treated each other unequally just because of status or lack of status in the workplace. So superficial! Jackie felt that everyone should be treated as equals who fulfil different functions in life. She'd found this attitude won her a lot of friends among "the little people".

The young woman resumed her sunshine of a smile, "Oh, thank you, I'm Anni spelled A-N-N-I. If you get lost or have any questions just pick up the nearest wall phone and dial *-3-6. That's for this."

As Anni pointed at her desk phone, the fluorescent light gleamed off her nose ring, the tiny diamond in it acting as a prism for the light. Jackie wondered why people pierced themselves in non-traditional, publicly visible locations, branding themselves as freaks and depending on piercings to differentiate themselves from others.

Anni's sweet smile twisted into a lascivious smirk as she continued, "I tried to get *-6-9 but they wouldn't give it to me. But you can call me anytime for anything. Any number of things."

"Ah, sure, Anni, thanks for your helpfulness. Have a nice day."

As Jackie struggled to tote the box out of the office as quickly as possible to escape Anni's lusty little eyes, Anni still spoke in a rush, "Call me anytime. I'll do whatever I can to help you. Any way you want. I might not know the answer because I've only been here about five months but I'm willing to do anything."

Upon Jackie's departure, Wendy leaned her fine leather chair back and closed her eyes, daydreaming the meeting between Jackie and Mr. Jones. She hoped Jackie would captivate Mr. Jones. She'd attempted to make Jackie particularly intriguing to him by firing her up and triggering her defences. Mr. Jones always enjoyed challenges.

Wendy cared for all the patients at Goethner-Varner like she was a big sister to them. But Jones was different. His happiness now determined Wendy's happiness. It didn't make any sense and it was wrong but it was also true. She knew the exact day of her transformation, August 18th, four weeks after Wayne Jones' incarceration. It was the day Jones sprayed his come on her face, baptizing her into a new path of addictive sin, abuse, and capitulation.

Wendy glanced at her desk planner, still open to the week of August 18. Up until that day, she maintained the planner in precise organized detail. But since August 18, there were no additional entries, not a single pen stroke. Wendy perpetually lived in the current moment, forming no plans for the future.

If she'd been sick and stayed home August 18th, she might still be "old Wendy" instead of "new Wendy". New Wendy would do anything to please Jones. New Wendy sent trusting young ladies like Becca into his clutches. Wendy hated the new Wendy. New Wendy disgusted and shamed her. But the things new Wendy did, felt, and had done to her enthralled her in forbidden delights. In the end Wendy knew that how she felt and what she wanted didn't matter. Jones morphed her into his creation, and she would exist to be whom and what he wanted for as long as he wanted.

The ball of Wendy's palm pushed at the tight skirt material stretched over her crotch, massaging her needy pussy in order to quench its thirst for sensation. Instead of quenching her pussy thirst, the indirect contact only watered the growth of lust. She closed her eyes and imagined Jackie's showdown with Jones, picturing Jones spraying his come all over Jackie's face. She felt disgusted with herself because she envied Jackie and longed to be baptized in Jones' come once again.

"You stupid slut!" The air-tearing sound of a whip in rapid motion accompanied the woman's harsh voice. The stroke ripped through her blouse and bra and made vicious, stinging contact with the upper slopes of Wendy's breasts.

Wendy sucked in a trembling breath and tightened her closed eyes further. She had no need to open them, she already knew what they would see. She made no change in her position even allowing the ball of the palm of her hand to continue in its hopeless venture to satisfy her pussy. She felt the chair and her body pulled away from the desk and spun so she faced the whip wielder. The whip screamed through the air again this time slashing the masturbating hand and catching her forearm and one skirt-covered thigh. Her burning hand froze its movement but, contradictorily, the flames in her pussy rose higher.

"You dumbass piece of shit!"

The owner of the voice grabbed the wrist of her burning hand and jerked her out of the chair to sprawl awkwardly on the carpeted floor. The whip sang again, laying a line of fire across her back. The angry whip wielder stepped two feet to the right and the whip scored another burning line, combining with the first to form an X on Wendy's back. Wendy sobbed with pain and unexplainable depraved emotions. The whip wielder took three more steps, seconds later three consecutive whip slashes paralleled across Wendy's buttocks.

Wendy emitted a long and tortured groan, her face sinking to the floor. Her arms collapsed under her and her chest pressed into the plush carpet. This movement made her rear rise higher, stretching her tender ass flesh tauter. As the whip lashed her three more times, she couldn't decide if this position made it better or worse.

Although her back and ass were raging infernos of pain, her pussy was hotter now, much hotter, and her rock hard nipples poked into the plush carpet.

"What the hell is wrong with you, Dummy?"

Four more steps and the abuser was behind Wendy. Wendy knew what was about to happen but did nothing to stop it. It was fate and, more importantly, it was Jones' will working through the body of another. It was meant to be.

The nose of a high-heeled ladies shoe blasted unerringly and perfectly into the centre of Wendy's pussy, causing her to rise up several inches. The stretched skirt protected Wendy from some of the kick's force, but it still triggered contradictory blasts of intolerable pain and addictive pleasure. Wendy had grown to hate-love the intense formula of pleasure and pain, dreading and treasuring it simultaneously. Wendy had long since given up trying to understand it. She'd also given up trying to avoid it.

"Answer me, Dummy! Why'd you get that sexy bitch all on guard? What the fuck?"

"I did it for Mr. Jones."

"Bull. He told you to be sweet and welcoming, to lull her into relaxing her guard. You did the fucking opposite. I heard every word over the intercom, Dummy."

Wendy peered up and behind at Anni through her tears from the pain and insidious pleasure, "Mr. Jones, I know he likes a challenge. I just want to make him happy. I thought if I…"

Anni planted the V-shaped tip of her pink high-heeled shoe into Wendy's pussy and pushed it as deep as her slim short leg could drive it into Wendy's groin. That effectively cut off Wendy's words as she groaned and wailed like a lost soul.

"Dummy, the reason you're called Dummy is because you think you're so smart you do what you think is smart and that's dumb because sometimes your smart ideas don't agree with what's on Mr. Jones' mind. That makes them dumb ideas and that makes you Dummy."

Wendy doubted that was the real reason Jones called her Dummy. She believed Jones gave her the nickname to keep her in her place, to remind her of how little significance her intelligence had to him. She waited, face in the carpet, for the next strike of the whip. She had not followed Jones' instructions regarding Ms. Jacqueline Thorpe. She deserved to be whipped even longer and harder than a dumb slut like her normally warranted.

Anni withdrew her pink shoe tip from Dummy's pussy, "Lift your dress up around your waist, Dummy, and pull your panties down to your knees."

Dummy did as ordered. Anni used her shoe tip to lightly trace the lips of the wounded vulva through her damaged panties.

"Now put your hands on each side and hold your dress in place clear of your ass."

Dummy followed the orders quickly without question, knowing she deserved Anni's punishment.

"Now I'm going to whip you, but instead of being lazy you have to knee march in a circle around this room until you pass out or I tell you to stop."

Dummy 'walked' on her knees while Anni whip-slashed her exposed ass. While Dummy struggled to keep her balance and continue moving, she suffered the double agony of new whip lines stinging across her ass and third degree carpet burns on her poor knees.

Blinded by luscious pain Dummy never saw Anni stare at her glistening pussy mound, never saw Anni's eyes devour the image of translucent fluid dripping down the insides of her trembling thighs. Deafened and hypnotized by the song of the lash, Dummy never heard Anni murmuring throatily behind her.

"Or until you come…."

CHAPTER 5

Jackie placed Jones' portfolio on the floor and consulted her map of Goethner-Varner before exiting the administration building. The facility consisted of the outer parking lot, the main gate and security, several hundred feet of grounds leading to the inner parking lot and administration building, and several smaller buildings for staff and equipment. Behind and to the right of the administration building stood Building A and Building B, which contained troubled but typically harmless resident patients. Tucked far back and to the left, a thick wall of planted trees, labelled as 'wind breaks' on the map, surrounded Building C. Jackie tucked the map into her jacket pocket, grabbed the portfolio, stepped outside, and headed for her car in the parking lot.

After placing Jones' portfolio in her vehicle, Jackie's nerves gathered force as she walked the paved pathway toward the 'wind breaks' obscuring Building C. She cynically noted she didn't see any crops that needed protection from the wind. Clearly, the true intent was to conceal any view of Building C and the towering barbed wire fence surrounding it. The structural strategy seemed to be "out of sight, out of mind".

Jackie punched her temporary code into the console at the gate outside Building C, noting the small camera mounted at the top of the barbed wire fence and pointed at the gate. A disembodied electronic voiced demanded her name. As Jackie complied, her voice trembled with nervousness. Surprised at her sudden lack of confidence, she reminded herself that studying dangerous psychosis in college was far different from studying a real psychotic in person. Potential psychotic, she corrected, striving for fairness despite her own self interest in the final outcome.

As she approached the building, dread assaulted Jackie and she fought the urge to flee. Picturing the crazy women holding vigil in the parking lot, she emitted a bitter laugh. She imagined dozens of Jones' fans would regard her as lucky, who would give their right leg to be in her position. Maybe literally.

Jackie entered the building and spotted two men sitting behind a wide metal desk, a middle-aged heavyset black guard whose name tag proclaimed him to be Hotchkiss and a younger overweight white man named Wilrey. Jackie pasted on her best smile as she gave her name. A cold professional demeanour would be ineffective with gentlemen of this ilk. It would cause them to brand her a bitch. She'd be seeing a lot of these guards in the next few weeks and her safety might depend on them.

Hotchkiss handled her check-in with a friendly grin, "Welcome to Building C, Dr.Thorpe. Ms. Carter called ahead and told us to expect you, though when she described you she didn't mention how beautiful you are. Did she, Wilrey?"

Wilrey didn't look at Hotchkiss, his eyes fixated on Jackie's high breasts and long legs. "No, Hotchkisser, no idea at all. You're welcome here Dr. Thorpe any time day or night. Especially night. Welcome with wide open arms."

Jackie struggled to keep a friendly smile on her face, especially after she noted an odd smell wafting from their twin desk. Sweaty but also bleach-like. She thought her sense of smell was tricking her until she saw little beads of sweat on Hotchkiss' forehead. Same thing with Wilrey's temples. It didn't seem hot in the room to Jackie. Maybe they had just walked rounds? Maybe they had passed the time with an arm-wrestling contest. Guards were famous for finding unconventional ways to combat the boredom. Jackie congratulated herself on the keen observation.

Hotchkiss shook his head at Wilrey's comments. "Never mind Wilrey, ma'am. Us guards get a little lonely. In Wilrey's case it's made him dysfunctional. Few more years likely he'll go from guard straight to patient."

Wilrey tore his avid gaze from Jackie's well-concealed breasts and shot Hotchkiss a look brimming with hatred. For the first time Jackie's smile faltered. Quick as a lockdown, Wilrey's face reverted to simple lust and his greedy gaze returned to Jackie's body, scanning her trim waist, skirt, and the small amount of leg that showed.

Hotchkiss failed to notice Wilrey's hatred. "Head on inside. If you're not comfortable talking to Jones on your own, one of us can go with you. Otherwise, we'll watch on the monitor. We'll be in there in an instant if you need us. He's in suite eight, on the right, just before the hallway turns. I'll buzz you into his room."

"I'll be fine on my own. I understand Mr. Jones is cooperative and incident free since his incarceration. But I appreciate your offer. Thanks guys."

Wilrey grinned, "Mr. Jones is very cooperative. Hell, he's downright helpful. He's a real Godsend."

Hotchkiss scowled, "Shut up, Wilrey! Miss, we'll be right here watching. You need anything, let us know. If you think you're in some kind of trouble we can't see – like, theoretically, Jones issues some kind of verbal threat – just put a hand on top of your head and we'll know to come running."

Wilrey failed to shut up, perhaps just to spite Hotchkiss, "Yeah, we'll be watching. Hotchkiss can watch whatever he wants. I'll keep my eyes glued on you Dr.Thorpe. I'll study every move, every little twitch, just looking for any sign of trouble I can help out with."

"Good God, shut up already, Wilrey. Miss, don't mind him. He's ugly as a barn spider but just as harmless too."

"No bother, Mr. Hotchkiss. I have a good sense of humour."

Jackie didn't feel Wilrey's comments were at all humorous, but she would tolerate it to make her task as smooth and efficient as possible.

She moved toward the entrance to the ward, feeling highly attuned to the crawl of Wilrey's wet eyeballs up and down her legs. As the door buzzed unlocked, she made a note to wear slacks on her future visits.

As the Thorpe woman moved through the ward Wilrey's eyes stalked her, flicking instantly from camera view to camera view. He didn't like how she dressed, like an uppity bitch who thought she was better than him. Her prissy dress suit left far too much to the imagination. Her skirt covered her legs to her knees and she made no attempt to show any cleavage.

"That bitch should dress a lot sexier." Wilrey scowled when Hotchkiss was too engrossed to respond. "Hey, my turn, give me some!"

Licking his lips, Hotchkiss closed his eyes tight and swiped at the sweat beading by the white hair streaks above his ears. "Fuck off, Wilrey. You just keep watching Miss Thorpe. That should be enough entertainment for you."

Wilrey pursed his lips in frustration but turned back to the monitors. Thorpe stood outside Jones' door, waiting for the guards to buzz her in. On another monitor view Jones reclined on his bed, lost in thought, meditating or just plain zoning. He did that a lot. Wilrey hadn't figured out the reason though he didn't much care.

ilrey purposely waited extra seconds until he saw telltale signs of Thorpe's impatience. He enjoyed watching her check her watch, glance at the camera, and shift her feet restlessly. Oh yeah, watching Jones break the Thorpe bitch was going to be fun. As Thorpe entered Suite Eight, Wilrey turned back to Hotchkiss. As much as he liked keeping a pretty woman waiting he himself did not like to wait.

"Now, Hotchkiss. My fucking turn!"

"Fine. Four minutes then we switch again." Hotchkiss leaned back and pushed his chair back, widening his legs as well as he could with his pants down to his knees. His penis stood fully erect and gleaming with spittle from the woman under the desk. The woman wordlessly crawled on her hands and knees over to Wilrey and immediately swallowed his shaft into her tireless mouth.

The woman, Wilrey thought her name was Kianna, was one of Mr. Jones' fans. Life was good for those who helped Mr. Jones. Wilrey grabbed handfuls of Kianna's short blond hair and slammed her face harshly against his groin. Wilrey had no worry the woman would bite him or allow her teeth to scrape him. All she cared about was pleasing others at the direction of Jones. Like all of his fans, that was her whole life now.

No one watched the monitors any longer. Wilrey concentrated on the oral though he fantasised it was Thorpe sliding her soft wet tongue all over the underside of his engulfed cock. Hotchkiss watched the action while one hand stroked up and down his cock to maintain his erection. They were unworried about Jacqueline Thorpe. She was in Jones' hands, and he alone would now determine her fate.

After the door electronically buzzed unlocked, Jackie knocked politely and waited for recognition. She had butterflies in her stomach. She couldn't help it.

Jones in person was less threatening than the images she'd seen on television and in newspapers. She suspected news organizations doctored his photos to make him appear more malevolent, as evil villains made for compelling news and larger profits. Nowadays the inflammatory news programs outperformed the fair and objective ones.

Jones sat on the side of the bed watching her with interested eyes. He was very pale, albino-looking, with gray stubble speckling his shaved head. He was surprisingly slight and short, perhaps 5'8" standing. At first, Jackie felt disappointed. Jones seemed entirely average, nothing special. Then their eyes locked and she gasped as fear zipped through her body. Strange lines shot through his hazel eyes making them look like cracked glass marbles. Something dominating, predatory, and completely unpredictable lurked in their depths. Jones truly looked insane. Jackie steadied herself, slid her professional smile like armuor over her face, and prepared for battle.

"Hello, Mr. Jones, my name is Dr. Thorpe. I'm a Psychoanalyst, and I'll work with you over the next few weeks. I wish to better understand your unique needs in order to best help you."

"Welcome to my humble abode, Jackie. I know who you are and exactly the nature of why you are truly here. I look forward to my complete exoneration. While you are "working with me" in order to "best help me" I will also be working with you in order to best help you."

Jackie froze for a moment in shock. Jones called her Jackie. How did he know her first name? She hadn't told him yet, so who had? Who informed him of her visit and its purpose? She gathered her wits, knowing she couldn't retreat. She had to forge ahead and figure it out as she went along.

"Mr. Jones, I want us to form a working relationship based on respect. Please address me as Dr. Thorpe. I'll continue to call you Mr. Jones. Mutual respect is one of my rules, another is complete honesty. As such, I'll tell you I am here on behalf of the state to determine whether you belong at this facility. In return, I'd like to know who told you I was coming."

"Establishing ground rules. Very nice!" Jones' cracked glass hazel eyes lit with a lantern glow and he leaned forward on the bed. Heart thrumming with fear and eyes darting to the camera overhead, Jackie shrank back, certain Jones was about to launch off the bed and attack her. A flash of smug satisfaction flashed through Jones' eyes as he remained composed on the bed, "I like ground rules. They provide a framework to accentuate and propagate the game. It is a two-way street, though. Since you want to base the relationship on respect there must be allowance for my own ground rules. Yours have nice potential, like an egg in a womb. I'll fertilize your egg and we'll see what grows. Each rule is like a gene. If rules are in disagreement the dominant gene will supersede the recessive one. What is a recessive gene if not a submissive one? Domination and submission exist in every level of creation from the atomic to the galactic. By the way, both my genes and my rules are, of course, dominant to your own. I'm sure you won't mind given your nature."

"Mr. Jones, as I said, I'll treat you with respect but we are not equals, we have different roles."

"I could not agree more, Jackie Rose."

Jackie felt herself go pale with shock. How did he know her middle name? She struggled to maintain a calm pleasant expression. "I thought we agreed on titles and surnames, Mr. Jones. Please refer to me as Dr. Thorpe."

"We agreed to nothing, other than that rules should exist. You suggested using titles and surnames as one of your ground rules. I have yet to present mine. Your other rule was that we would be completely honest at all times. I approve of that one. As for names, my rule is we call each other whatever we want. My name for you will likely change over the course of time as I get to know you better. I know my rule and yours are at odds but the solution is simple, my rules are dominant to your recessive, submissive ones."

Wayne Jones watched her, his eyes as bright and alert as an owl's on the hunt. She still felt bewilderment and panic that he knew her middle name. What other tidbits did he know about her? Though she tried to be stone-faced, she could tell the extremely perceptive Jones saw through her facade.

He had used her middle name as a drill to bore through her defences. This realization added anger and frustration to her unexpected cauldron of emotions. Blessed with a superior intellect and education, she typically possessed more knowledge than other people. Knowledge was power. When others had knowledge she didn't, they held some degree of power over her. She hated that feeling.

"Mr. Jones, how do you know my middle name?"

"I'm psychic."

Jones had an amused crinkle at the corners of his eyes. Jackie didn't reply and stared at him with a calm, slightly bored expression, trying to wait the truth out of him.

"I am psychic," Jones said. "My power, besides allowing me to know your middle name, also lets me see your innermost self. Your truest desires, ones you hide even from yourself. Should I tell you what they are?"

"Mr. Jones, I'm here to help you, to understand you. Let's focus on that."

"Of course, Jackie Rose, I do understand. It would be inappropriate, embarrassing even, for a psychoanalyst to get counselling from a patient. Sometimes the nature of the messenger is more important that the message. At least that's how you feel now. As you learn you will change. Would you like me to come over there and teach you?"

Jackie sat at the small table a good distance from Jones' bed. "You look comfortable, Mr. Jones. You can stay over there."

Jones smiled tolerantly examining her body as thoroughly as she planned on examining his mind.

"Now, you were placed in this facility by judge's order nearly six months ago. That was based on the recommendation of state appointed psychologists. They found you a risk to others and ill-equipped to fit in with society. For safety reasons they recommended admission until such time professionals deemed your mental state no longer a threat. I'm here to re-examine your mental state, assess progress, and to make recommendations."

"I know, Jackie Rose."

"Please don't use that form of address, Mr. Jones."

"Apparently you did not pay attention to the ground rules. I'll name you as I see fit. You can always leave. Unlike me, you are free to go. I'm not. This room, and, to a lesser degree, this entire facility and everyone in it is part of my environment. You are now part of my environment. For the time being, I'll call you Jackie Rose. Why do you find Jackie Rose so unwelcome?"

"It ignores my title and status."

"Your title and status are still in question. Tell me, who last called you Jackie Rose?"

Jackie studied Jones for few moments. Obviously, she would have to tolerate his mannerisms to accomplish her mission. So who had called her Jackie Rose last? It had been years.

"My mother did, just before she died."

"Tell me, did your mother treat you with respect?"

"Of course."

"Then it is settled. I'll call you Jackie Rose. It seems appropriate. If the woman from whose womb you slid out called you Jackie Rose it seems right the man who will slide his cock into your own womb should address you the same way. Of course you must first prove yourself to earn my cock."

Jones' words shocked Jackie into silence. His passive aggressive but eloquent conversation had almost lulled her into thinking him sane. Now she knew the man was truly mad and understood why he'd been committed. The only question now was whether Jones was actually dangerous. Unfortunately, this was now more than an academic or legal question. At this point, Jackie felt vulnerable to the man. He seemed guided purely by his own will without regard to social norms. For the first time in her professional capacity, she feared she was in danger!

Even as the thought developed, Jones levered himself off the bed and moved fluidly towards her. Jackie immediately put one hand on top of her head, palm flat against her tightly wound blond locks. Hotchkiss and Wilrey would be in the room in a few seconds, maybe ten, maybe fifteen.

When Jones reached her side, Jackie remained sitting in the chair, perfectly still to avoid provoking an attack. She estimated they were around the same height and weight, but as a man, he would be far stronger. She wouldn't have a chance if she fought him on her own. Thank God for the guards!

"Look, don't do anything foolish. You won't help your situation. I'm here to see if you're dangerous. You attack me and you won't be free again for a very long time, possibly never." Jackie didn't know how long she could stall Jones with talking. Where were those goddamn guards?

"Jackie Rose, fearing me is like fearing your destiny, your calling in life. Instead of fear, you should feel eagerness. I will teach you. You have no need for the protection you so desperately pray for, your false idols will not answer your prayers anyway. You could say I've used my powers to block their view of us. But I won't touch you until you want it, until you beg me to. Politely, might I add. All in good time. You are indeed here to help me, more than you know, and in ways that are foreign to you now but will soon become the fabric of your existence."

Jones stood over her another moment. "Jackie Rose, I will be free again and it will be thanks to your recommendation. I won't be attacking you. I'm not an attacker. I never even did what I was accused of. They knew it. Fabricating a story was the only way for them to lock me up. I just give people what they need though they often don't yet consciously acknowledge what they want at a deeper level, a level I can always see. I will not touch you until you've made me a free man. You see, that is another one of my ground rules. That one is personalized just for you. It does not apply to any other females I met or will meet here."

Jones pulled out the chair opposite her and sat down, putting them at equal eye level and defusing her trepidation.

"Oh, well, thanks, Mr. Jones, for your special allowance to me." Jackie struggled a moment to extinguish her sarcasm. "I wanted to meet you today, but I still need to review your file in detail. Ms. Carter gave it to me and it is quite thick. I'll be back in a couple days."

"You do that, Jackie Rose. You'll find lots of thought-provoking photos in the file and even some of my favourite personal tools. Look at every photo carefully. They should be quite enlightening. You want to know me? I understand my journals of personal thoughts are also in there. Remember what curiosity did to the cat? Curiosity can also enslave a pussy and make a mind slave to the pussy. Your pussy, your mind."

Jackie realized the conversation was over. She wasn't about to argue with him. There was no point. Jackie backed out of Jones' room as he smiled at her, his eyes full of mad energies.

Still no guards Jackie thought in numb dismay. When she pulled her hand off the top of her head it left a damp patch.

Jackie was furious but kept her anger drowning below the surface as she stood on the other side of the guard desk. Jackie breathed through her mouth, wondering what the guards had been up to during her visit with Jones. The room smelled worse and Wilrey and Hotchkiss were even sweatier than before.

"Did you watch my meeting with Wayne Jones?"

"Wilrey did. Those are his monitors."

Wilrey leaned forward. Both of them had their bellies pressed firmly up against the desk. "I watched you every second, Miss Thorpe. Your visit almost makes me wish I was a patient here."

Jackie ignored his leer. Obviously, Wilrey hadn't seen the hand on top of her head, the signal of possible danger. Probably too occupied with trying to see down her blouse. Thank God she dressed conservatively. There was also a chance he had seen the signal and chose to ignore it. Maybe he'd wanted Jones to attack her to take her down a notch. A man like him had no respect for women. Jackie knew a woman like herself – confident and well-educated – would threaten Wilrey's perception of women's role in society. He was a caveman without the hairiness and with a lot of extra fat.

"Why do you ask, Miss Thorpe?" Hotchkiss asked deferentially.

"No reason, just checking. Thanks, guys."

Jackie realized it would do no good to make an issue of it. Nothing bad happened and she didn't want to show any weakness to confirm Wilrey's view of women. She planned to ask Hotchkiss to watch over her next time.

She walked to the exit a few feet away, highly aware of Wilrey's creepy crawly eyes scurrying up and down her body. She heard sucking slurps like a fat lollipop pulled from a mouth and then sucked back in. She turned at the door to give a falsely friendly wave goodbye expecting to see Wilrey had been popping his finger out of the corner of his mouth just to harass her. But both guards sat quietly with their hands below the desk, their sweaty faces placid.

CHAPTER 6

After five days of imprisonment, Becca was piecing together how the world worked under Jones' rule in the maximum security ward. The information gathering process was slow going, as she was still stuck in Lilly's locked suite Becca's only information was from random comments and glimpses through the door's window of people walking by in the ward hallway and from Lilly. Lilly's information could hardly be trusted. She was one of "them" as Becca had come to think of Jones' followers.

Becca learned though "they" gave Jones the respect usually reserved for a revered prophet, they weren't a cult, but more than a club. It was all more like a powerful lifestyle choice – like Amish refusing to use electricity – with Jones as the guru. They were united by a commonly held addiction.

Becca learned that once Jones arrived at the centre, combinations of bribes, seductions, and Jones own mind-clouding words led to the enlistment of the male staff as his henchmen and to submission of the female staff. Jones himself declared all actual patients completely off limits. To them everything continued as normal.

Jones tasked the staff to provide false papers and room accommodations for an unknown number of Jones' female groupies and male followers. The guards and male followers enforced Jones' will. The females served the men sexually and in simple manual tasks like cleaning. There were two dominant-type ugly women who heaped lesbian abuse on the subjugated women. The attractive nurses were all enslaved to Jones, and, by extension, to the guards and the two dominatrix's who used to be their friends and co-workers. Becca marvelled that they had somehow managed to enslave all the attractive ones.

The nurses that were not considered attractive and had no dominant nature to tap into were forced out. Early retirements were offered. Systematic unfair treatment caused some to resign. Arranged transfers to other buildings were the main method. The transfers out were often replaced with transfers in of unsuspecting attractive nurses from other wards.

Others were replaced by new hires who were Wayne Jones converts from the outset. All of them pretty to beautiful and willing to do anything for Jones. Willing to suffer or allow anything in his name no matter how contrary to their best interests.

Becca had previously been kept out of this area due to her inexperience and great beauty. She hadn't had the opportunity then to pick up on the unusual staff turnover or high ratio of beautiful women in the suites and servicing the suites. They could take this group of women and match up evenly with the contestants in a beauty pageant.

Becca didn't know how this worked yet. She was stuck in the locked suite and she had been there for five days. Her only information was from random comments and glimpses through the door window towards people walking by in the ward hallway and from Lilly/Doll. Lilly could hardly be trusted. She was one of "them" as Becca had come to think of... them. Jones' followers.

Becca spent her time trapped in the suite trying to analyze "them", trying to analyze her own reactions, and trying to get away. She also often wondered why no one had come to save her yet.

Life in this room was 90% boredom and 10%... things she'd rather avoid remembering. In a lot of ways the boredom was worse than the other 10%. Sometimes she caught herself looking forward to the other 10% just to relieve the boredom, she was certain.

Every few minutes, Becca glanced out the little window in the suite door. It was late afternoon and soon another night of hard sex would begin. Earlier in the day she spotted a beautiful bronze-haired woman who strode down the hallway with far too much confidence for a subjugated woman. Was she a dominatrix? She considered banging on the door, but was too afraid of more punishment and abuse. Only after it was too late did she realize the woman's conservative suit precluded her from being one of them. If only she'd realized it in time!

"What are you thinking about, Pretty Toy?"

Becca hadn't noticed Lilly creeping up on her. Not only because she was lost in contemplation but also because Lilly had literally crawled on her hands and knees over to the side of Becca's bed and was peering over the mattress like a shelf troll.

"Nothing. Stay away from me."

Lilly leaped onto the bed, straddled Becca's waist, and ripped off Becca's gown. Becca didn't bother struggling though she gave a convincing flinch. Lilly always got her way sexually with Becca, and Becca was tired of fighting for a lost cause.

"Pretty Toy, I'll give you a choice. Would you rather bare your private thoughts or lick this bared private part?" Lilly vigorously rubbed her bare pussy against Becca's breast, as if she hoped the nipple would penetrate her pussy.

Becca knew she would end up licking pussy one way or another but figured chatting Lilly up could garner useful information. "I'm curious about the dominants and the submissives. That relationship."

"What input does Pretty Toy require?"

"I can understand why the dominants do what they do. But I don't understand the submissives."

"You don't understand yourself? How pathetic." Lilly humped her hot pussy against Becca's nipple and giggled.

Becca glared her answer and stiffened. However, the giggles were a delightful sound and the bouncing heat was sending blood rushing to fill her mashed nipple.

"Silly Pretty Toy, I'll tell you. The dominants and submissives are like Ying and Yang. Submissives are opposites of the dominants. Together, they exist in perfect balance. As for the nature of submissives, once we accept an authority, most of us follow orders from that authority without question, even sick and disturbing ones. We show no compunction, no self-respect other than pride in obedience, suffered punishment, or being chosen to be used."

"Most?"

Lilly slid her body down Becca's, leaned down, and swiped her muscular tongue warmly into Becca's left ear before she whispered, "There are two more kinds of women here not counting the dominatrixes. The second kind resist to various degrees and then give in as a sport to amuse and entertain themselves and the dominants they serve. They aren't rebels, they're entertainers."

Lilly scooted back up Becca's body, grabbed both of Becca's ears, and moved Becca's face liberally all over her breasts. As Becca spoke, saliva smeared slick and gleaming all over Lilly's rubbing breasts. "What umph, about the, umph, third type?"

"Oh, them! The third group is comprised of women who are fully resistant, immune to this sort of activity, intent on escape and resistance, and focused entirely on winning their freedom." Lilly pressed Becca's face hard and deep into her right breast and laughed so hard it hurt Becca's nose, "So far the third group is purely theoretical."

Lilly reached down between their legs, and her fingers tweezed Becca's loosely wet labial lips. Lilly wiggled her own pussy until it split along her wrist. Lilly's body undulated, fucking her arm her weight adding force to the fingers pulling at Becca's pussy, while her eyes held steady on Becca's. Lilly's manipulations caused alarming pleasure in Becca's pussy, while Lilly's words spawned worrisome thoughts and ideas in Becca's head.

Becca was no longer sure if she would fit in with the elusive third group. In a sudden revelation, she admitted she probably belonged to the first group. After all, when Wilrey fucked her, or the black guard Hotchkiss ordered her to suck his cock, or when Lilly made yet another lesbian assault on her, Becca enjoyed giving them pleasure as well as taking her own pleasure.

Lilly ground down on her wrist and started twisting Becca's pussy folds tighter.

Becca gasped, but continued thinking about her repeated submissions. Over the past few days she tried to reason with her dominants, to persuade, to beg for release at times. But why? She knew all along they wouldn't listen.

Lilly's mouth fell open releasing a gasp and a small dollop of drool that landed on Becca's smaller breasts.

Sometimes Becca ran or climbed furniture in the room to escape her dominants. But why? There was no escape, and she always waited until the door latched securely shut behind her visiting dominator. She waited until it was too late to escape before she tried to escape.

Becca's own gasps were filling the gaps between Lilly's. Mostly Becca did as instructed. She put up with the humiliating things the dominators did to her. Putting up with it wasn't quite the right description. Not unless 'putting up with' meant the same as 'enjoyed', or 'had lots of mind-blowing orgasms'. Just as there was no escaping the cell / suite, there was no escaping the fact in less than week she'd had far more and infinitely better sex than all the rest of her sexual experiences combined. After her experiences here, those encounters seemed unimaginative and dull.

Becca's hands grabbed Lilly's slick ass cheeks and jammed her down on the arm and hand, increasing both of their pleasures and discomforts.

Becca could no longer think of herself as a fully resistant victim when every day she desperately begged the dominants humping cock into her to shove harder and come deep inside her. If she wasn't yelling encouragements she was either gasping in pleasure or her tongue was deep-probing Lilly's pussy or anus. At those times providing as much pleasure as possible to her dominator consumed her, drove her. There were no thoughts of resistance, of rescue, or escape.

"You're going to come, Pretty Toy, like a bitch in heat." Lilly's tone swelled with victorious self-satisfaction.

Becca wanted her freedom. But she also didn't want the twisted adventure to end. Her dominators made her do perverted, unimaginable things and made her love it, even need it. If she was free, how would she get what she now needed? No one man or woman could meet her new needs.

Lilly made a show of working her mouth full of saliva and then spit straight into Becca's face. Becca moaned and panted, enjoying the debasing wetness running from the bridge of her nose onto her cheeks and lips.

If Becca won her freedom she would lose her triumphant orgasms and hard earned depths of submission. She could only retain these by giving up her independence. It disturbed her that the trade was worth considering.

Lilly violently bounced up and down and began coming with wolfish growls while Becca's own cries sounded more like a bird in distress.

It also disturbed Becca that no one discovered her captivity or came to save her. Although now she wasn't entirely sure she still wanted a rescuer, she'd probably go if one showed up. Still, she was hurt no one cared enough to notice her absence.

It was partly her fault since the dominators made her name her family and friends. They also forced her to send text and e-mail messages and voice mails at late times when no one would answer their phones. She'd told them all she was unexpectedly going to Africa on a psychiatric mission and would be incommunicado for four weeks. Apparently they thought four weeks would be enough to convert her. As it had only been a week and she was almost converted, Becca knew they were right.

Lilly's gripping hand shuddered with her orgasm, driving Becca into another perspective-altering climax.

Becca left the messages but still believed someone would come for her. Where was Wendy Carter? She wondered if Wendy was involved in this but the thought of intelligent, successful Wendy subjugated was ridiculous. What about Anni, Wendy's secretary? She was always so sweet and helpful. Wouldn't she have informed Wendy that no one had seen Becca in days? Well, not 'no one'. Jones' followers had seen entirely too much of Becca, up close and personal.

Lilly dug into Becca's wet slot and swirled her fingers. She pulled out a wad of come and shoved her hand into Becca's mouth, smearing her tongue with tangy juices before withdrawing and finger painting her face with a mixture of come and saliva.

Becca figured Jones wasn't in control of the entire centre, perhaps just the maximum security ward. After all, if Jones controlled things, why wouldn't he free himself?

A light knock sounded at the door before it clicked unlocked and opened. Usually dominators walked right in and helped themselves to Becca's charms. She wondered if it was a guard, a fake patient, or one of the dominant nurses. She was sort of in the mood for one of the older rougher guards.

"Becca, how are you?" asked a smiling Wendy Carter, peering past Lilly's naked hip.

"Oh my God! Ms. Carter!" Becca pushed Lilly off her, rushed to Wendy, and flung her arms around her slim body. Lilly hissed but took no action other than watching her with hostile, snake eyes.

She was saved! Ms. Carter would set things right. Ms. Carter would save her from them and from herself.

Ms. Carter's left hand grabbed Becca's right shoulder and shoved her to arm's length. Her open-palmed right hand shot up to slap Becca's face.

"Stupid slut, I told you to call me Wendy!"

Wendy forced a dazed Becca down to her knees. Anni stepped into the room wearing a sly, anticipatory smirk. She planted one thigh-high black leather boot between Becca's bare breasts and kicked her onto the floor.

Lilly hopped off the bed and passionately kissed first Anni and then Wendy. Becca curled into a ball and watched from the floor, her chest smarting and her mind processing this new turn of events.

Anni placed the pointed toe of her boot between Becca's breasts and studied Becca with dark intent, "I heard about your new name, Pretty Toy. You got lucky. You should hear some of the new names. Do you know what the best thing is about toys?"

Becca didn't know the answer, and feared Anni would punish her for her ignorance. She was smart to be scared.

Anni raised a double-headed shocking pink dildo and a black strap-on. "The best thing about toys, idiot, is attachable parts."

Anni and Wendy stripped completely nude. Even though Anni removed her boot from her chest, Becca made no move to resist the current twist of fate. She saw what direction this was going in.

Curiosity penetrated Becca's resignation. How would a scenario with four women, a double-headed dildo, and a strap-on dildo play out? Would they pair up? The idea of doing anything sexual in nature with Wendy was shocking and intimidating.

As Becca watched from the floor, the three bizarre sexual allies gracefully assembled themselves and the "attachable parts" like a synchronized swimming team.

Lilly and Wendy slobbered each head and shaft of the double dildo, crouched on their hands and knees with legs interlaced, and pressed butts against each other. Anni fitted the enormous pink double-headed dildo between them and levered each end into each of their ends. Becca was shocked as she realized Anni had crammed the plastic cockheads into their assholes, not their pussies. Several harsh spanks urged the women to vigorously grind their asses, Anni effectively forcing them to ass-fuck each other and themselves.

Anni slapped Becca's thigh to get her attention and ordered her to stay on her back and crab crawl until her head and shoulders rested on Lilly's and Wendy's calves. Becca maneuvered until her face was directly under their wet pussies, which pumped back and forth making wet kissing contact whenever they rammed the double-headed dildo completely up their poop chutes.

Anni gave her a simple command, "Lick."

There was no room for misinterpretation so Becca craned her neck to clumsily deliver sweeping licks to the two gyrating pussies above her.

Moments later Anni laced the strap-on around her hips and thrust the huge black plastic head into Becca's pussy. Becca's lubricated pussy offered no resistance as it plunged into her liquid depths. She shamefully admitted to herself it wasn't still wet from her interlude with Lilly. This sick scenario inflamed her beyond measure.

As Anni crammed the huge dildo into Becca's dripping pussy, she lashed her open hand against Lilly's and Wendy's ass cheeks, adding significant pain to contrast the strange pleasures invading Lilly's and Wendy's assholes.

After long minutes building the other three to the edge of climax, Anni stopped and jerked on Becca's dark pussy locks. Becca stopped licking to peer at her from between Lilly and Wendy's conjoined legs.

"Call Ms. Carter Wendy. I don't care what you call this other bitch. However if you don't give me the respect I deserve, I will punish you." She twisted the tender flesh just above Becca's clitoris to make her point.

Becca quickly devised a title Anni would find pleasing. She answered meekly and far more sincerely than she intended, "Yes, Mistress.

Anni smiled with cold satisfaction. "Perhaps Pretty Toy is finally defect-free." She thrust the dildo so hard into Becca's pussy, tears of pain filled Becca's eyes. Immediately the synchronized swimming restarted into motion with Anni thrusting, Becca slurping wet bushes and bumping her pussy up to meet false cock, and Lilly and Wendy sodomizing each other and themselves. At short intervals the smacks of blistering spanks delivered by Anni punctuated the gasps, pants, and moans emanating from the women.

In less than a minute all of them were coming. Becca knew this was only the first of many orgasms her new Mistress would give her. Becca found, for the moment, she no longer dreaded anything they might do to her. She looked forward to it.

As she lay gasping from her orgasm, the dildo still buried deep in her sex and ready to bring her back to orgasm, the anxious feeling of having forgotten something important consumed Becca. What was it?

A tiny droplet fell on her face from the trembling buttocks and pussies above her. She didn't know if it was a droplet of sweat or sex juice. It did help her remember what she had forgotten.

Becca cleared her throat, "Mistress Anni, thank you for fucking me."

That wasn't it though.

"Um, Wendy? I have a message for you from Master Jones. He said to tell you you're a good girl."

CHAPTER 7

The mother and daughter team smiled at her as she left the facility. She just wanted to be alone. She felt watched. Feeling paranoid, she switched lanes and made unnecessary turns to determine whether she had a tail. She concluded the feeling was just her nerves.

Jackie entered her large ground floor apartment and exhaled with relief. She wanted a full retreat from the day. Between Jones, Wilrey, and all those Jones fans it felt wonderful to finally be free from scrutiny.

As she carted the heavy Jones portfolio through her front hall, items rolled and slid around in the box, inciting her curiosity. Jackie entered her home office and placed the heavy box on her small desk. Although she longed to look inside the box, she made herself wait. She required food and rest and wanted to be in peak mental condition during her analysis.

Jackie made a microwave veggie dinner, watched the news, and took a dreamless nap. Feeling recharged, she opened the file box.

After she examined each item, she laid them across the desk. Stack of folders, stack of three journals, stack of photos, stack of pornographic magazines, and a pile of... things.

The strange objects sparked her imagination, but it took several moments for her mind to define what they were and their probable uses.

The main attraction was a huge dildo with a switch on the side. The idea that any human female could fit that thing into her vagina was preposterous.

A dozen large silver rings with sharply pointed connectors gleamed up at her. As she laid them on the desk she realized with disgust these weren't just large rings to wear in pierced nipples, they were rings that could actually pierce nipples. Or other places her imagination refused to consider.

Next, she removed a smaller, oddly shaped dildo. A butt plug she decided.

She peered into the box, spotting a heavy, oiled leather whip curled like a snake at the bottom. Maybe that, not the dildo, was the real main attraction! What kind of monster whipped another human being? Or wanted to be whipped? Deriving enjoyment from pain was madness.

She removed a stiffened leather collar, wide, banded with metal. She noted the brass nametag: Good Girl. How patronizing! Who in their right mind would want to be Wayne Jones' "Good Girl"? Jackie personally found both his looks and alien perspectives on life unattractive. Still, she guessed his crazy fans would probably line up and fight for the right to wear it.

A ball-gag, a leather hood, lengths of Teflon cords, handcuffs, and a wooden paddle rounded out the collection.

A complete sadist's fun kit, she thought, attempting humour to calm her feeling of dread. Or it was a complete masochist's fun kit? The breathless, guilty little roller coaster thrill she felt while handling each of these forbidden items surprised Jackie. The thrill she felt when she realized Jones had used these on women sickened her.

Why would someone place these unhygienic items in the portfolio? None of them proved Jones was insane. Jackie wished they had taken photos and thrown the nasty paraphernalia away.

Even in the privacy of her own apartment, Jackie battled shame before picking up the oversize dildo by the handle and examining it. It had a hand grip and hilt like a sword and was unexpectedly heavy. Batteries slid into the handle. The shaft, incredibly, was translucent and several inches in diameter at the base, expanding even wider until the top where it mushroomed out in simulation of a real penis. Of course, a real penis wouldn't be anywhere near this colossal. A candy cane twirl of copper coils stretched from the base of the shaft up to the head. Mystified, Jackie couldn't imagine how poking a monstrous, metallic sword at the most tender of areas would turn women on.

Jackie's free hand massaged the shaft, digesting its tactile capabilities. How on earth did it work? Had it ever been used? Did some women, either forced by Jones or overwhelmed with masochistic arousal, actually stick part of that thing into their vagina?

Jackie studied the hilt, noting a thick flange curving up and out about four inches. Jackie gasped as she realized that part was meant to simultaneously penetrate a woman's anus! Disgusting! Why would any woman desire anal penetration with the vagina available?

Why would any male enjoy placing part of this object in a woman's exit hole?

She reminded herself not to judge others based on her perceptions of normal. It did not matter if Jones deviated from society's norms. What mattered was determining whether he was a threat to himself or others. Consensual sadomasochistic sex did not make him a threat. He was never even brought to trial for the alleged rape, false imprisonment, and torture of Cassandra Zane, probably because the charges were false. To keep him contained, she had to show an intent or willingness to harm others or self and an inability to control that urge.

She caressed the wide leather collar. It was nearly square, its width almost equalling its height. A woman wearing it would be unable to bend her neck to see her own body. Several thick metal rings decorated the leather. Two smaller rings, perhaps for a padlock, stuck out from each end of the collar. She dug in the bottom of the file box. There it was, a small silver padlock! She felt proud of herself for figuring it out. With a grin she imagined Jones applying the nameplate moniker "Good Girl" to herself. She blushed, still smiling, but shaking her head.

Suddenly she felt watched, and the blood drained from her face as she imagined his smug, knowing eyes dissecting her blushing smile. Weren't some psychics also clairvoyant? As a scientist she found the idea of psychic powers highly suspect, but as a woman, alone and vulnerable in her home, she just felt nervous. Jones' professed belief in his powers showed disconnection with reality. A disconnection that went a long ways toward sealing his fate. She still wondered how he knew her middle name. Someone must have told. That had disturbing implications, as disturbing as the idea of Jones clairvoyantly viewing her.

She took a break from the unsettling portfolio and checked her e-mail. There was a message from Robert. She read it quickly:

"Jacqueline, I hope your task is proceeding smoothly. Wendy Carter may be a good resource. She is likely to have useful insight into Wayne Jones. Whatever the finding of your appraisal, there is an excellent opportunity for you to write a journal article on Jones. Once you make a diagnosis, the case is quite compelling and a good sell. I'd be happy to help you write the article, which could lead to a book deal and talk show appearances. One thing, I think it crucial you develop a complete understanding of Jones' perspective and that of his followers. Take your time, be thorough. If you need an assistance let me know, and I'll do my best to help."

So many of her ambitions could come true so quickly! To think she had second-guessed herself for leaving Thurgood Joiner. Obviously, sticking with her principles paid off big time. Although discouraged by Jones' initial lack of cooperation, Jackie vowed to arm herself with knowledge, giving herself the upper hand for her next visit.

Her first step was to learn more about Jones' philosophy and thought process. Consulting his handwritten journals could provide compelling and undeniable information. No one could accuse her of fabricating the information or of biased judgment.

She sifted through the stack of dated journals, grabbing the most recent. His recent state of mind would be the most applicable, the most damning. Jackie still wanted to conduct a fair appraisal, but had to admit Jones hadn't been a sympathetic figure in their meeting. She possessed no mixed feelings or qualms about ultimately finding in favour of his continued incarceration.

She liked to be comfortable and focused while working at home, so she changed into a T-shirt and plaid pyjama bottoms, then took the journal to the living room. She lay lengthwise on the sofa, flipped the television off, and cracked open the journal.

Recorded in small, neat handwriting, the brown leather journal captured Jones' laundry list of sexual conquests and sexual acts. Jones wrote in a matter-of-fact tone showing utter disregard for the women. A typical entry:

"Next one, black hair, white, medium build, 28 years old. Newly divorced, no children, just moved in to neighbourhood. Helped her move in. This one turned down offer of help but gave in to insistence. Later, she claimed not interested, too tired for sexual activity. Again, gave in to insistence. Very responsive, adapted quickly to pain. This one's knowledge of true self close to surface. Easy acquisition. Made do with bungee cords from boxes. Required her to sleep in one of largest cardboard boxes that night. Perfectly obedient so soon. As instructed, still in box noon following day even though I was three hours late. Fed her after she earned privilege. Will be useful for certain tasks. Have named this one Bungee Bitch."

Jones' perspective appalled but fascinated Jackie. His crazy journal musings suggested he was an alien separate from the human race. Or he considered himself a herder and his women like cattle. However, she now understood why prosecutors found his journal worthless. Jones failed to date or record real names in any of the entries. The journal contained no descriptions of illegal acts. If true, the journal suggested Jones had no need to falsely imprison or rape women to get them to submit. If false, the journal held no relevance. Jackie realized after reading a few entries the journal was pure fiction, just Jones transcribing fantasies. That many women willing to be mistreated simply didn't exist in reality!

Still, considering the journal was pure fantasy, she expected to find more detail, more flamboyance, and more delusions of grandeur. Jones wrote the entries in a matter of fact manner, as if ticking off actual events. Although to him they probably felt like actual events. Perhaps she could use the journal to support a diagnosis of psychosis, the inability to distinguish between reality and fantasy.

As she continued paging through the journal, a folded piece of parchment covered in Jones' handwriting fell to the floor. She opened it and read it:

"A hierarchy, a system of superior to inferior, dominant to submissive, appears in all groups, all organizations, and all systems. This is true in civilization and in nature. Some systems are obvious, such as in the workplace world of bosses and underlings, while others are nearly imperceptible. One practical example of a stealth system, arguably the most important of all, is the world of sexual preferences and practices. Sexual behaviour is the doorway to evolutionary success, passing on one's genes. Myself, while unsuccessful in business and unassuming in appearance, in the sexual realm I wear the crown of King. The sexual realm of each person is secret to most but obvious as a sunrise to me. My realm is all around me. I immediately know who is a sexual serf, how much and what kind of sex they have had. I can see it in their eyes. I read it in their aura. I lack respect for and may not even speak to someone who has had no sex, not even masturbation, for more than a week. This is because they have spurned my sexual realm. The women who achieve the most orgasms, the most powerful orgasms, and the deepest levels of submission, masochism, and humiliation successively rank higher in my realm. It is the only realm that counts. Of course, no matter how high they rank they can never be more than slaves."

Heart racing, Jackie clutched the paper. This "document" provided a window into Jones' deranged thought process. Its bizarrely titillating nature made it perfect for inclusion in a paper or book on the Jones case. She pictured a photo of the parchment filling an entire medical journal page. This letter was a big gold nugget!

However, a complete, professional appraisal required far more than journals or a piece of parchment. Jones' cooperation was absolutely crucial to her future success. During her next meeting with Jones, she planned to use his words and the king/serf analogy to draw him into conversation, to encourage him to reveal more of his dysfunctional philosophy.

As Jackie reread the parchment, her face flushed with embarrassment. If Jones actually saw the nature and degree of Jackie's sexual experiences in her eyes or "aura", he wouldn't think much of her! She hadn't had sex for a couple months. After the sexual harassment she'd suffered at Thurgood Joiner, she grew too pissed off at all men to even consider having sex with any of them. Plus there was the added stress of trying to find a new job.

Jackie emitted an uncontrolled, harsh laugh, startling herself. Good thing she'd masturbated six days ago or Wayne Jones may have refused to talk to her. She didn't masturbate often. It made her feel guilty, and her self-induced orgasms lacked power, leaving her unsatisfied. She thought none of her orgasms – with or without a partner – were very strong as she had no idea what women who were "screamers" felt.

When she masturbated, she used her fingers to rub her clitoris, never to penetrate her vagina. It still felt good though. She wondered why she masturbated at all since it made her feel shame. On the other hand, since it did feel good, she also wondered why she didn't masturbate more often.

If she really wanted to gain "psychic" Wayne Jones' respect she ought to use his monster dildo to bring herself to multiple orgasms. Then Jones would respect the hell out of her! She chuckled and shook her head. Like that ridiculous sword could even fit up her vagina!

Feeling strangely energized, Jackie set the journal on her coffee table and closed her eyes. As she let her mind wander, the image of the strange dildo penetrated her thoughts, again and again. She pictured the dildo's bulbous head nudging against the tight entrance of her vagina, first urging it to dilate, then forcing its way inside until the big rubber cock speared her from head to hilt. Jackie imagined the stretching, the pain, the feeling of being completely filled. How could any woman's vagina survive such an assault? The thing was nearly a foot long! Impossible!

She supposed the dildo could be used to stimulate the outside of a... pussy. Although inappropriate in clinical language, "pussy" seemed the appropriate term in this situation. Jacqueline Thorpe pictured the monster dick parting her pussy lips in search of her clitoris. She imagined her artful fingers flicking the power switch to the first setting on the handle. Gentle vibrations would resonate against her female core, making her pussy walls water and hardening her clit. As she imagined the dildo fucking against the outside of her pussy, her clit swelled and her pussy longed for stimulation. Suddenly her pussy felt sadly empty.

She had to stop this line of thought! It felt like her panties were wet all of a sudden. She reached down and felt the crotch of them with her fingertips. The contact gave her a flash of heightened arousal. The panties were wet. The finding turned her on more.

Perhaps she should finger herself to a little orgasm. Why not? Masturbation was perfectly natural and healthy. She found the idea of orgasming after reading Jones' twisted journal distasteful, especially with the journal lying on coffee table two feet from her right elbow. She imagined the journal, a thing alive with dark thoughts, observing her pleasurable spasms and reporting back to Jones.

So she wouldn't masturbate to orgasm. But she did want to see how wet she really was. It was good to understand. Just check and see.

Her fingers made a few more circles around her clit before slipping between the skin of her lower abdomen and the elastic of her panties. Her fingers trickled through her thick blond bush and lightly traced her pussy lips. At first, she carefully avoided the erect clitoris, but her arousal grew higher and hotter. Feeling inflamed, she brushed a single finger against the clit, thigh muscles jumping, pussy clenching and begging for penetration.

She remembered her purpose. Just check. Just to know. She parted her blond curls and hooked her index finger through her outer and inner pussy lips. She was so soaked that the slight parting of her pussy lips released a small gush of juices that ran down into her ass crack. Her legs reactively stiffened and pushed her pussy onto the finger, her stray thumb brushing against her clitoris. The flood of sharp breathtaking pleasure made her arch her hips, further impaling her pussy on the finger. Her hand independently thrust two more fingers inside the hot wetness and went to work jabbing in and out, her thumb pad pressing ever harder on her savagely erect clitoris.

Oh, she should stop! The lights were on, and she never masturbated with the lights on. Jackie glanced at the actively working mound her right hand made inside her pyjamas and watched her hips struggle repeatedly to lift up onto the hand. As she watched, her left hand joined in, pushing at her right through the pyjamas and wet stretched panty material. For some reason watching the desperate hands inflict pleasure turned Jackie on even more.

The lights in the den seemed way too bright. Part of Jackie still wanted to stop, but the majority favoured continuing. Hell, of masturbating all night long!

Suddenly Jackie felt watched again. She felt sick from the thought though she also felt an unexpectedly severe stab of arousal. What if someone was watching?

This thought turned the tables and she was able to pull her hands away from her swampy crotch. Now that she pulled them away, she would make damn sure they didn't return.

Jackie sat up and smelled the thick scent of arousal emanating up from her pussy. Her juices had soaked her pyjamas all around the bottom of her ass. She vowed to wash her ass and pussy twice in the shower tomorrow. She glanced around the room and felt a little silly for over-reacting. No one was watching her, especially since she was in the privacy of her own apartment and the blinds were down.

Although disconcerting, she was glad for the watched feeling since it enabled her to stop masturbating. She still felt extremely horny, but she was back in control of her actions. For Jackie, passion equated to a loss of control. Losing control scared her.

Back to work. Jackie returned to the desk and grabbed the stack of photos and a couple of the porn magazines. She returned to the sofa wearing a rueful little smile. She was about to browse Jones' porn with a wet, masturbated pussy. She pictured Jones imagining her getting wet because of him, from looking at his nasty photos and porn, not independently from her own two hands. The man's over-inflated perceptions about his importance in kindling a woman's desires were demeaning and misguided.

The full size 8 x 10 photos were graphic. They showed an assortment of women in bondage, in positions of vulnerability, or showing signs of mistreatment. In one a slim brunette bent forwards and pointed her ass to the camera. Her hands spread her ass cheeks to reveal her pink little anus. Beneath her fingers blazing red abrasions decorated both ass cheeks, perhaps a half dozen on each. She looked back at the camera with an open-mouthed, ready-for-the-next-command expression.

Another photo showed a bound ash blond woman lying on her stomach on a cement floor, her hands and feet tied together behind her back. Her full breasts bulged out from her body. Jackie couldn't see the woman's face, but her tongue was extended, the tip in contact with the floor.

There were at least fifty photos. She studied the first dozen with awful fascination, then flicked through the rest before tossing them on the coffee table. All of the photos were equally twisted but all of them possessed a unique twist. Each woman was physically distinct, there were no repeats, although all had well-shaped bodies and all of the faces she could see were quite pretty. How did Jones find and attract so many sexually prime women and induce them to put up with such humiliating treatment?

Ah ha! With a flash of realization, Jackie knew the answer. The women were models and Jones paid some Internet site to mail them out. There were probably thousands of copies of each print. She grinned as she thought of the dozens of men across the nation who at this instant were gripping these photos in one hand and masturbating with the other.

Jackie grabbed the stack of photos again to study them with greater care. Pussy juice still soaked her crotch and pyjama bottoms, and every time she shifted on the couch her pussy lips rubbed against her clit, distracting her repeatedly.

She scrutinized a picture of a lovely, large-breasted brunette sitting on the corner of a carved wood dining table. Jackie noted the woman's hair had hairspray sculpted curves like a 50's housewife. Obviously, from the date stamped on the back, it was a modern day photo, though. The woman's mouth formed a luscious O of intense pleasure, despite the metal nipple clamps dangling from each plump nipple and the orange wax dried all over both breasts and sprinkled across her athletic belly. Jackie spotted a lit orange candle on the table behind the woman.

Jackie stared at the woman's pussy, which the photographer perfectly centred in the middle of the photo, ensuring the viewer would immediately spot the dildo penetrating the woman's slit. At the moment of the photo, the woman's right hand pulled her right pussy lip to the side and her left hand drove the huge dildo halfway up her pussy.

Jackie gasped, her shocked gaze focused on the dildo. She felt a tremendous wave of the 'roller coaster going downhill' sensation. Although half the dildo was in the woman, Jackie clearly saw copper coils winding around the shaft and disappearing up into the woman's pussy. Jackie even spotted the strange hilt with the upward twisting anal penetrator since it was not in the woman's anus. It was the exact same dildo that currently rested on her coffee table.

It couldn't be true! She emitted a weak, relieved laugh. She was being silly. Of course it was the same model, but not the same dildo. The dildo factory made thousands of them. Jones must have seen it in this photo, did an Internet search, and bought it.

Although twisted and shocking, at least the dildo photo did satisfy Jackie's curiosity. Apparently, a woman could cram the monster into her vagina, at least half way up. Jackie wondered if the model was very tall. Perhaps the enormous dildo fit because the model had an especially wide pussy. It was hard to tell from a photo.

She flipped through more photos. She felt tremendous arousal, and each photo viewed threw another log on her bonfire. She felt crummy for letting these twisted photos turn her on. Why should they? She wasn't a lesbian. She tried to reassure herself that it wasn't looking at other women in distress that turned her on, it was imagining herself in each of those poses, each of those situations.

Of course, that wasn't very reassuring at all. She wasn't any kind of sadist or masochist.

Her previous masturbation, ending short of satisfaction, must have left her vulnerable to sexual input of any sort. Maybe an orgasm would free her from her fascination with the photos. Maybe she should not have stopped. As if the thought gave it license one of her hands drifted down to her wet sex. She pulled it away with a shake of her head. She needed to work.

In the next photo, a red-headed model's pale-skinned body glowed against a dark brick wall. Cobwebs covered the bricks and the room seemed dark and cavernous, like an unfinished basement. The woman's arms stretched straight up from her shoulders to big iron manacles set into the bricks. Iron manacles also restrained the woman's pale sculpted legs, stretching them as wide as she could possibly manage

Bright red stripes, raised welts, covered the model's inner thighs. A clothes-pin stuck out from the top of her red furred slit, probably pinching her clitoris. Despite the pain, juices darkened and matted her red pubic hair.

Thick rings impaled the pale pink nipples of the woman's full breasts. Jackie found piercings other than ear piercings to be ridiculous, embarrassing, a sign of insecurity, and an obvious appeal to please viewers at one's own expense. The silver rings in this set of nipples were an exact match for the dozen rings currently lying on Jackie's desk.

Jackie studied the woman's face. She was smiling widely at the camera, obviously conscious of being photographed. Jackie felt a jolt of sudden recognition. It was Monica, the woman who stopped her in the parking lot at the Goethner-Varner Mental Rehabilitation Centre so that her daughter, Kira, could talk to her at her car window.

Jackie flung the photo on the coffee table. Now she knew. These photos were genuine. Their subjects were not actresses in pose. These were real women under Jones' spell, allowing and enjoying the mistreatment. It was disconcerting. It was repugnant.

She wondered if Kira was also displayed in one of the photos, but she didn't want to look. She didn't need to see that.

She needed a break from the photos, unable to deal with this revelation now, all turned on and wet. She was in the wrong state of mind. She needed to be 100% horrified, then set her emotions aside and return with an analytical and clinical mindset to examine the sorts of abuse Jones chose for his "girlfriends" and to derive conclusions about what the pictures indicated about his mentality. Right now her arousal prevented her from being 100% horrified. Right now she was at 80%, maybe only 60%.

She thought about heading to bed, but it was still early and she had more work to do. She turned to a porn magazine to distract herself. Again the material treated women as objects to be used for pleasure. Again the women pretended to enjoy the abuse. But these photos differed from Jones' private collection. Since they featured paid models Jackie didn't have to feel guilty for being turned on while looking at them.

One series of photos showed a man in a suit, perhaps the erstwhile owner of the mansion in the setting, admonishing two auburn-haired maids. Were they supposed to be sisters? The stern man held a riding crop. As the picture story progressed the maids shyly removed their clothes at his demand until they wore only high heels and fishnet black stockings. Then he lashed one's upturned ass as she bent over and licked the other's pussy. As the pictures progressed many more welts appeared on the rears and flanks of both models. The damage appeared to be genuine, but Jackie figured the magazine had good makeup artists. After five photos the women switched places, the licked one becoming the licker. For the finale the women, now sporting blazing red asses, kneeled hip to hip while the man towered over them, sticking his rigid cock in their faces. While he scowled the women teamed up to tongue-bathe his cock. A close up photo caught the moment a thick stream of come shot from his cock, and more photos showed come splashing on both women's faces, then them licking it off each other. The women appeared quite happy with how it all worked out. How realistic was that!

As Jackie scrutinized the pictures, her hand scurried up and then plunged beneath the waistband of her pyjamas and panties. Pushing the soaked material of her panties aside, two fingers made rapid fire shallow plunges into her pussy. Her left hand pressed on her right through the materials helping it exert more pressure, more contact. She was desperate for release. She pulled her oily slick fingers out of her pussy. Her clothes. She needed them off. Now.

She stood, pushed down her bottoms and panties, and nearly fell as she kicked them free. Wearing only a tight white T-shirt and athletic socks, her face reddened with sudden shame, but shame wouldn't stop her. Right or wrong no longer mattered. She needed a release. She needed an orgasm and she sensed a huge one literally within reach.

Jackie flopped cross-legged onto the sofa, her right hand thrusting three fingers up her pussy and her left hand stroking her hard clit. She ground her bare ass and the base of her slit into the material of the sofa. Her pussy juice would leave a stain. That thought spiked her passion further and propelled her fingers deeper and harder. Her potential orgasm kept cresting higher without breaking into surf. She wondered at it, at herself, and in that moment of detached, self-analysis the watched feeling returned.

Her cheeks and forehead burnt with shame but her fingers did not stop their action. What if she really was being watched? What if Jones had some clairvoyant power and even now stared at her hot worked up pussy? The idea of Jones watching her orgasm gave her a massive charge of arousal, and fluid gushed from her pussy onto her active fingers. The idea of someone, anyone, coldly or angrily watching her, taking no action, while she performed a graphic and humiliating masturbation was suddenly a huge turn on. Her newly discovered exhibitionism frightened her. Maybe she didn't really know herself.

Jackie felt out of control. Would watching her out of control actions give her watcher some twisted power over her? In her mind, she pictured Jones watching her at this moment. The flash of his impassive face and crazed eyes filled her with a sick wave of self-disgust, loathing for Jones, and heightened arousal all swirled together. Desperate to forget Jones, she replaced his face with the image of the stern man from the porn pictorial. The one who severely and pleasingly punished the two maids, bending them to his sexual will. What if he were here, punishing her?

He'd have that riding crop in hand. He wouldn't be satisfied just watching, he'd give orders. But what would he order her to do? Bend over to take an ass beating? Kneel on the floor and suck his cock? As she imagined tongue laving the man's hard but soft dick, Jackie's pleasure crested higher and higher, but an orgasm remained elusive. He was imaginary, and her imagination alone couldn't get her off. She needed something more, something real.

A man like that, similar in nature to Jones, would order her fetch the strange giant dildo and shove it up her crack.

She couldn't. No way. But the more she pictured the dildo, the more her fingers plunged into her hot wet personal swamp and the more restless she got. She imagined the stern man observing her, ordering her to fuck herself with the dildo, and whipping her for noncompliance. She craved to submit to the stern man's will. She needed that dildo in her pussy. It would be wildly hot.

As she imagined the man whipping her tender ass flesh, Jackie sensed she could make herself come if she gave herself permission. Her fingers unconsciously slowed their work, keeping her on edge without satisfaction. She didn't just want a great orgasm. She was greedy for the best orgasm of her life. She got up from the couch and paced over to the desk, pussy juice dripping from her pubic mound and disappearing into the carpet.

She hoisted the bizarre dildo by the handle, forced her passion down for a few moments, and washed it in the kitchen sink. There was no way that thing would touch her pussy until she knew it was clean and germ free. She washed it twice, feeling scared at its immense size and trying to talk herself out of it, but the stern man in her head ordered her to fuck herself with it.

She returned to the sofa, blushing at the dark wet patch on the cushion. She had blushed more today than she had in the entire last year. She hated that feeling, flustered, helpless, and vulnerable to events outside her control. She thought she hated it. Pretty sure. She wondered if someone watching her would have noticed her blushes. No, they were probably watching her bare ass.

Jackie laid on the sofa, the wet splotch centred under her tailbone. She spread her legs wide, one small foot on the back of the sofa, the other on the floor. She bit her lip and examined the bizarre dildo held in her trembling hand. It looked immense in the grip of her slim fingers. She trembled, from fear, from anticipation, from sexual intensity. Just looking at the dildo turned her on. How turned on could she get without actually coming?

She burned with need, burned with shame, burned under the imaginary watchful eyes. She held the wicked dildo a foot above her belly, hesitating, intimidated to take the next step. Maybe she should set it down and go to bed. The thought of going to bed without satisfying her need was nearly unbearable. She doubted her fingers could do the trick. She'd orgasm but now she needed more than a simple orgasm. She needed to cross a border into new territory. She would lose respect for herself if she backed away from the challenge now. She would also lose respect for herself if she proceeded. Jones probably used this dildo on hundreds of women and now, for her to use it on herself on the same day she met him was crazy.

She was in a Catch-22. Either way she'd feel shame and think less of herself. But, at least one of those ways she'd come so hard...

The thought was a green light to the hand holding the dildo. It lowered the giant mushroomed head to the lips of her pussy and nudged gently to split them open. The hilt was in her right hand, the shaft stretching from just above her belly button down to the head splitting her swollen lips. Swirls of copper glinted as the wide translucent shaft rolled and agitated her painfully hard clitoris. She wouldn't penetrate herself with this behemoth. The wickedness of using it at all would be enough to satisfy her new need. It obviously wouldn't fit, at least, not without damage. The last thing she wanted was to walk into Jones' room and have him notice she was walking stiffly from a sore vagina!

As she continued to roll the shaft and jog the ballooned head against her slippery pussy, her legs sought to stretch even wider and her ass thrust her pussy up against the monster's head, effectively jiggling her pussy lips against the wicked toy.

She couldn't help but imagine walking stiffly into Jones' room, his mad eyes observing and drawing all the correct conclusions. He would stand over her, rattling off every embarrassing act she performed on herself. She would lower her eyes and reluctantly nod her agreement, unable to lie, knowing he could recognize a lie anyway. She moaned and bucked her hips, her ass rising off the sofa, her hand shoving the shaft of the dildo hard against her lower abdomen.

She imagined what Jones would say when she confessed her naughty personal acts. He would coldly examine her as if she was a thing, a creature inferior to him, but would tell her, "Good Girl."

She rammed her pussy up hard against slippery shaft. Seeking as much sensation as possible, her left hand pressed the mushroomed head against her clitoris, crushing it, brutalizing it. Her gapped pussy released a burst of pussy juices with nothing but sofa to soak it up.

Jackie made a long piercing siren wail and felt distantly amazed that she produced such a sound. She was coming, coming, still coming. Her ass slapped up and down off the sofa like it was having an epileptic fit. She heard the siren wail drop down in octaves to become a deep throaty groaning thing.

Her pulse thundered, her pale legs were gleamed with sweat, pussy juice slicked her upper thighs, pubic mound, and belly. Her pussy continued to twitch and flinch with mini orgasms, but she no longer had the strength to feed her ravenous arousal with more sensation. Her legs stilled and her hands nearly dropped the powerfully built dildo.

Coming to her senses, especially her sense of propriety, she gasped, mortified at all the noise she made. Had her neighbuors heard? Instinctively, her hands covered her mouth as if she could retroactively stifle her wails. A pungent smell notified her that the pussy juice dripping from her fingers now coated her lips, chin, and cheeks.

She sat up and let her hands drop back to her lap. "Oh, God!"

What was that sound? She heard a thump, and then a scraping from outside the blinds covering her big living room window. The glass of the window vibrated with another small contact. Jackie covered her wet pubic mound with one hand and threw the other arm across her tee-shirt covered breasts as she backed out of the living room and into her bedroom. Was someone out there? Could they have seen her through the slits in the blinds?

Oh God, had someone been watching her perform?

In her bedroom Jackie pulled on sweatpants and shoes. She had to find out the truth. If someone watched her masturbate with part of Jones' official medical portfolio she would be screwed professionally!

CHAPTER 8

Just before stepping out of her apartment, Jackie worried she'd find neighbours gathered in the apartment complex hallway, trying to determine the source of the orgasmic wailing. She also worried someone might smell her aroused scent, since she hadn't taken any time to wash off the smeared pussy juice on her face.

She peeked through her keyhole, relieved not to see any of them. She grabbed the flashlight she kept in case of power outages, opened her apartment door, raced down the empty hallway, and exited the apartment into the bitter night air. Why did she have to rent an apartment on the ground floor? Answer: On moving day, she hadn't wanted to carry boxes up flights of stairs. Another good question was why she hadn't masturbated in the darkness of her own bedroom. Answer: She enjoyed the watched feeling, although she believed at the time it was a delusion.

As she started towards the outside of her apartment, she considered the image she would have presented to a peeper. No clothing below the waist other than athletic socks, slim legs stretched wide, her hands pushing the shafted length of the oversize dildo against her swollen pussy. What if he also heard her? Wailing and grunting and grinding. It was awful that even now, out in the night facing the stark possibility of a compromised professional career, her mental image of herself behaving like a mindless sex creature re-ignited her inner pilot light. The orgasm had failed to satisfy her lust.

She went round the corner and flicked on the flashlight. No one was outside her living room window. She was momentarily relieved, and then realized they probably left after she concluded her act and retreated out of the room.

She turned the flashlight's beam down on the snow below her window. Footprints! There was a large trampled area in the snow, like someone stood at her window for a long time. This was terrible. But what had the peeper really seen? Jackie turned off the flashlight and peered through the gaps in the blinds at her brightly lit living room. She saw the entire room. In detail. With a gasp of horror she even spotted the tremendous wet patch on her sofa.

Who had watched? Was it one of the apartment complex residents? Had it been some homeless person, maybe? Jackie turned the flashlight back on and examined the footprints in the compacted snow. They were quite small. Whoever it was wore tennis shoes. In the cold weather they must have had a powerful reason to stand out here so long. Jackie well knew the reason.

Comparing the size of the footprints to her own shoes, Jackie figured there was no way the peeper was an adult man. A small adult female like herself fit the print perfectly. Although still outraged, she felt relieved her watcher was female. A man might make a pass at her, thinking she was a creature of passion. A woman wouldn't do that. She supposed her ideas were sexist and antiquated. Couldn't a lesbian behave similar to a heterosexual man? Wouldn't a sexually perverted woman be equally capable of wrongdoing as a perverted man?

What kind of woman peeped through blinds to watch another woman masturbate? The answer was pretty obvious. It was one of Jones' female followers. Jackie immediately thought of the sick mother-daughter pair Monica and Kira. Had they followed her home from Goethner-Varner?

It made sense. Jones' followers were just the creepy sort who had no regard for the privacy of others. She recalled how Monica and Kira knew she was at Goethner-Varner to visit Jones. How long had they known about her before her arrival? Did they research her background, learn her middle name to pass on to Jones, and also discover her home address?

Though relieved the peeper was a woman, the idea her peeper was also a Jones' fan deeply concerned her, because this could impact on her professional life. A Jones' fan watching her masturbate with equipment from Jones' portfolio was really the worst-case scenario. Would Jones be told? Would he regard her with even less respect and cooperation? Would he tell Wendy Carter, the Director of Operations, at Goethner-Varner?

She reassured herself. Pulling a Peeping Tom was a criminal act so whoever it was had good reason to keep quiet. Besides, no one outside Jones' group would believe anything this whack-job peeper claimed. But, oh God, what if it was Monica or Kira and they told the other fans in the parking lot? She imagined all the female fans staring at her next time she pulled in to visit Jones. What an awful prospect! She felt violated. Invaded. Startled, she realized with unexpected empathy this may be how Jones felt when the police executed the search warrant on his home and took possession of his porn, his photos, his "tools", and his journals.

The tennis shoe impressions led away to the parking lot. Discouraged, Jackie trudged back to her apartment. Infuriatingly, she was still turned on, feeling humming warmth deep in her womb and her still swollen pussy lips slid against each other with every step.

Morosely, she realized she better get that wacky dildo washed, get some sleep, and try to regroup for tomorrow.

The following day, Jackie spent time running errands. Morning at the Goethner-Varner Center involved many structured activities to socialize, draw out, and counsel the residents. Visiting time, even for semi-official visitors like Jackie, was any time after two o'clock. She tried to imagine Jones participating in structured group activities. Difficult.

Jackie still felt dismayed over the events of the prievious evening. As she imagined the peeper reporting her actions back to Jones, anger replaced dismay. What upset her most and made her really angry was the violation of her privacy. Some Peeping Tom, or, more likely, Peeping Tomasina, had taken away her feeling of security and privacy. People like that should pay! There was good reason peeping was absolutely illegal.

Sure she'd masturbated, but she shouldn't feel bad, it was natural. Everyone did it. If it wasn't for the watcher she'd be free to feel proud of herself for stepping out of her comfort zone and achieving the most powerful orgasms in her life. Perhaps 'stepping out of her comfort zone' was inaccurate. She had stumbled into her sexual abandon zone! She wasn't quite sure how to characterize her experience. Amazing, at the very least.

Although her act of masturbation was natural, some of the thoughts she had were decidedly abnormal. Obviously, she was far more suggestible than she initially believed. She guessed most people were. People never thought advertisements affected their decisions, but if they heard a product name enough times, that's the one they automatically gravitated toward in the store.

Later in the afternoon, on her way to the Center, Jackie kept thinking about the peeper incident. She should not be the one feeling ashamed. The peeper should feel ashamed! She hadn't broken the law, they had.

In the outer lot at the Center she looked coldly at the blankly smiling mother and daughter, Monica and Kira. She couldn't tell by looking at them if one of them was behind the peeping incident, though Jackie still clung to her suspicions. The graphic photo of Monica popped into her mind, and a heavy pulse of arousal vibrated deep in her pussy. Simultaneously staring at the real woman while picturing the events in the photo seemed wicked. Ridiculous that she should feel such arousal. She was no lesbian! But she couldn't stop herself from imagining the welts on Monica's pale skin, the clothespin clamped on her furry red pussy, and the thick silver rings hanging heavy from her pink nipples. Jackie reassured herself that her interest was purely aesthetic or stemmed from fascination with the forbidden.

Neither Monica nor Kira knocked on her window this time. They seemed awfully pleased to see he, though. Extremely pleased. Suspiciously pleased. Had one of them watched her last night? If they had, did Jones now know? The idea of Jones' smug triumph made her want to shrink until she was invisible and remain that way forever. She called on all of her courage, knowing facing Jones' unwavering eyes and his personal knowledge of her would take all of her reserves.

The same guards, Hotchkiss and that stooge Wilrey, sat behind the expansive metal desk in Building C. She noted with relief they switched chairs today, so there was no need for her to ask Hotchkiss to watch over her this time. The guys weren't sweaty today, but they seemed tired, and probably not from hard work. They were probably tired from laziness.

As she approached Jones' suite she realized she didn't fear for her physical safety. Perhaps she was naive, but she believed him honest when he told her he wouldn't touch her until she asked for it. Since she'd never ask, she was safe. He'd also said he wouldn't try anything until she made him a free man. Jackie was pretty sure that would never happen either, so she was doubly safe.

She knocked on the suite door, and Hotchkiss buzzed her in. Jones sat at the small table on a chair facing the door, the same one she'd left him in the day before while backing out of the room. For a moment the surreal feeling he'd remained sitting there waiting for her to return for the past twenty-two hours assaulted her. Realizing he wore a different shirt quickly dispelled that feeling. The Center gave residents a dress code of sorts, by only allowing pyjama-style pants and tunics. The males could choose between green or blue, the females pink and yellow. Yesterday Jones wore blue. Today he wore green.

Jackie sat across from him.

"Hello, Mr. Jones, how are you today?"

"I'm fine."

"Good! Here is what I have planned for us today. I'm going to ask you questions about your time at the Center, the people here, your daily activities. I also want to learn about your future goals. Finally, I'll show you various pictures and ask for your reactions. All this will help me to get to know you better."

"You don't need to get to know me as much as you need to get to know yourself, Jackie Rose."

"Mr. Jones, I want to help you, but when you address me inappropriately, you simply add obstacles in the path to your release from Goethner-Varner. Yesterday we discussed treating each other with respect and courtesy. Please remember to call me Dr. Thorpe. We'll both feel better."

"What is freedom if I must stifle my own free will in order to achieve it?"

"I'm your best chance for a quick release. If you refuse to treat me with respect why shouldn't I just walk out? Just leave?"

"Leave then."

"What?"

"I said: Leave then. You offered the carrot and the stick, a possible reward and a possible negative consequence. I am not a donkey who will perpetually attempt to obtain the unobtainable carrot, nor do I reward negatives such as threats to 'walk out'."

"Don't you want your freedom?"

"You cannot offer or deny my freedom. My freedom is already achieved though it has not yet come to fruition. If I allow you to stay you will give me my freedom. If you leave you will be replaced and, whoever your replacement is, she will then give me the freedom I require."

Jackie realized he was serious. Patients had some control over their visitors, and he could refuse to see her. Robert would then be forced to replace her.

"Are you asking me to promise you your freedom? I can't and won't."

"No, Jackie Rose, I want you to give me my freedom of your own free will, because you see it is the right thing. That's why, no matter how much you beg me for sex, I must deny you until I am free."

Jackie snorted, angry now, "Mr. Jones, believe me I want our interaction to remain completely professional. I don't understand why you persist in being so contrary and difficult."

"I am the way I am meant to be. You are not. That is the source of the difficulty. I am meant to be in charge, you are meant to take direction. Resisting this is going against Mother Nature. You are living encased in an unhealthy illusion."

"Mother Nature? I would have thought you would think of nature as Father Nature."

"Of course I don't. Think about it. Don't we take what we need from nature? We plough her fields, plant our seeds, hunt our prey, take advantage of all the fruits she has on offer."

"Mr. Jones, don't let your unhealthy outlook fool you into believing others are here to serve you, simply exist for your personal use, and are somehow less important than yourself."

Jones was silent, pursing his lips in probable irritation. She waited. Let him think on her words, maybe some truth would sink through his shaved skull. After a few minutes of silence she decided it was time to try again. She could barely stand his cold cracked alien eyes staring at her.

"Look, I think you're being difficult because you fear my reaction to your highly personal thoughts, especially your sexual perspective. I know your ideas are unusual. I won't reject you for that. Different people have widely varying fantasies. Look at foot fetishes for instance. Perhaps it's a rare predilection, but most people with foot fetishes function quite happily in society. However odd your thoughts or urges, as long as you aren't a physical threat to yourself or others, I won't condemn you. As far as I know, you've made no attempt to hurt yourself or anyone else. We've been alone twice now and you've done me no harm. Just share and let's see how it all works out. You have nothing to lose.'

Jones gave a slight smile, amused, "Nice speech, Jackie Rose. Again, you make assumptions. I have zero fear of you rejecting me as I don't care what anyone thinks of me. My opinion is what matters to me. In my opinion talking with you at this point is a waste of time. Sharing my "perspective" with you would be like sharing my thoughts with a foreigner who has no understanding of my language or trying to explain emotions to a robot. I cannot help you at this point. Leave and do not return until you can understand my language. You have my file, you said. There you will find my language. Return when you know how to speak it. You don't have to be fluent, just able to understand it. Leave now."

Panic struck Jackie's solar plexus. Jones talked circles around her and had called her bluff by telling her to leave. Bizarrely, she realized she needed him more than he needed her even though he was the one locked up in the Center. Through him she could earn a great career, a solid reputation, a book deal, and even talk show appearances. She actually had nothing to offer him. He seemed to know, perhaps instinctively, that she did not plan to seriously consider his release. Although incarcerated, he still held the winning hand and knew it. She hated this helpless overwhelmed feeling.

She decided to throw him a bone, "Look, fine, I'll respect your preference. Call me Jackie Rose if you want."

He grinned savagely, "I know and I will. Leave now."

She started to say something then realized trying further was futile. Jones' eyes showed an iron will. She stood up.

"Think on what I said, Mr. Jones. I'll be back tomorrow."

"No. Come back in six days. If you are a good student, that should be plenty of time for you to learn my language. Every course has tests to pass before graduation. When you return I will ask you three questions and you must answer all three correctly or I will send you away. Also, you must show me one proof you understand my language. Finally, you will bring me one personalized gift. It must please me, or I will send you away."

Jackie stood still, her mind racing for a solution, trapped in a maze.

"That is all, Jackie Rose. Good day."

Jones stood up as if to see her out. He was naked from the waist down. Her eyes automatically targeted his semi-erect penis. It was wet, covered in a sheen that looked like vaginal secretions but must have been spit or butter from his lunch. Somehow, his nudity didn't shock Jackie. It was as if she'd known all along he was naked under that table top.

Jones watched her, drinking in her reaction, "You see, Jackie Rose, I don't try to hide anything from you. I don't try to conceal, I reveal."

Jackie grabbed her unopened briefcase and left making sure the door electronically clicked shut behind her. She jogged down the hallway and past the guards' desk. She made no comment to them despite their curious looks. She was embarrassed. They must know she failed in some sense to be leaving so soon.

A minute after Jackie left, Jones pulled a cell phone from under his bed mattress. He pressed a pre-programmed number.

"Wilrey, send her back in."

"The Thorpe woman?"

"No. My little fan currently sucking your dick."

"How'd you know? Hey, we turned the air down like you said. It's a lot cooler out here. But Sir, she isn't done yet. Can you wait a few?"

"Wilrey, she is my pawn. You are a fine knight, but I am the King. Tell the pawn to get in here to finish the job she started before Jackie Rose Thorpe arrived. When I am done with her I will send her back to you knights."

Wilrey was no doubt pissed when he hung up but Jones knew he would follow his orders. Thanks to Jones' fans, Wilrey's every fantasy was fulfilled. Wilrey knew the gate to his new world of sex would slam shut the moment he failed Jones.

Within moments Jones heard the woman's bare feet slapping down the hallway toward his suite. This pawn was different from yesterday's. Pretty, always pretty, but with brown hair. Jones had a huge chess board. He had many more than eight or even sixteen pawns. Far more than two knights as well. But Jones knew he was no King. Much more accurately, keeping with the analogy, he was the chess master.

Jackie gripped the steering wheel tightly as she drove. She was angry. She was frustrated. She was worried. She was full of self-doubt. She had to answer three questions, provide proof, and a "personalized" gift? She was doomed.

She felt like striking out, taking her frustration out on someone. An idea built strength in her mind. Maybe she didn't know who yet, but she knew where and how.

CHAPTER 9

A small form bundled in a black hooded parka designed to protect the wearer from both the cold and observation walked through the snow, tracing the brick wall of the apartment building until arriving at a tramped down area. Next to the area of packed snow there was a malformed snow angel from the visitor's clumsiness the previous night.

The lights in the apartment were on and the view through the blinds was just as clear as the previous night. The living room was unoccupied. The view through the other window showed the same items of interest on the desk.

No pretty blonde masturbating. Not yet. Had the pretty occupant heard the clumsiness the night before? The items still on the desk suggested not but the extra prints in the snow suggested it was so.

Returning to the living room window the bundled watcher stopped perfectly still in order to obtain a steady view through one of the window blinds slits. The crunching of snow continued even after the watcher stopped in place. The watcher was preoccupied, considering the humour of staring through a slit in order to see a slit and this caused a delay in realizing the crunching of snow was ongoing and nearing.

The watcher turned and saw the pretty blonde just a few feet away approaching from the apartment complex's parking lot and having cut across through the snow. She looked real angry, real determined.

Not surprisingly, she launched a tight fist straight into the dark oval of the watcher's hooded parka.

Now what?

Little Parka huddled on the ground, snuffling.

Jackie glanced around nervously. No people to or from cars in the parking lot. No busybodies peering out apartment windows. It was safe enough. She poked Little Parka with the toe of her boot, rolling the limp figure, and then kicked her foot in the approximate location of the ribs.

Little Parka's thick wail told her she'd nailed something the owner considered important and sensitive.

It felt great getting payback, but she couldn't very well kick Little Parka to death. Besides, she had more important things to do, like finding out Little's identity, issuing a severe threat to keep her away in the future, and shopping for new blinds. Hell, maybe even shopping for a new apartment.

Jackie knelt and pulled Little Parka's hood back. Little Parka was a man! A very little man but the rough fringe of black facial hair left no doubt. Her watcher wasn't a Peeping Tomasina as she had originally theorized. He was a small man, maybe some kind of oversize Dwarf.

Somehow, the fact it was a man made her furious. That and just as she thought she was really taking control of the situation, she'd been thrown for another loop. Without planning to Jackie slapped his face hard. She enjoyed it so much she slapped him again. Fear of other residents hearing the loud smacks stopped her more than worry over hurting the pervert.

As she leaned in to deliver the threat she'd planned while staking out her apartment from the parking lot, she realized both his lips were split and bleeding, trickles of blood retreating into his fringe beard.

"Listen to me, you asshole! Never come back or I will rip off your head and send the rest of you to prison!" She liked that one. It sounded like a line from an action movie and it simultaneously threatened physical damage and prosecution.

The little guy tried to say something, coughed twice, and then found his voice, "I can explain. Let me explain."

"That's crap. I know exactly what you were doing. Don't try to lie."

Jackie fumbled through his pants pockets for his wallet so she could I.D. him. Hell, she should steal his driver's license. That way she really had the goods on him. As a bonus, it provided the added satisfaction of knowing he'd have to go through the time and trouble of getting a new copy of his license. Not finding a wallet in his pants pockets she rolled him in the snow to get to various pockets of the black parka. He didn't resist but she was highly conscious of how it would look if any of her neighbours saw them.

From a large side pocket in the parka a small camcorder rolled out into the snow. Jackie stared at it a moment, analyzing the possibilities.

"You little fucker! You planned on recording me!"

"Planned?"

"Did you? Did you record me last night?"

The little man caught his breath now, his blood stopped flowing, and his eyes gleamed alert with evil.

"My dear, I'm cold and bloody. Also, my face hurts. Let's warm up in your apartment. We can discuss things in private."

"Forget it. You are not entering my apartment. I'm no fool."

"What do you think I'll do? Raid your panty drawer? I don't want to conduct our discussion in public, so move it inside or I'll leave. Live sex acts are the most enjoyable but sex on video is also fun."

Jackie's mind flicked to an image of the ugly little man in some creepy dingy place watching the events of her masturbation. The little creep would probably masturbate himself to it every night for a year, and then once a week after that. Jackie's face flushed red even out in the cool evening air.

"Like I said, I'm not a fool. No way are we going to my apartment."

"Why fear me? You can see how small I am. You outweigh me and are in much better condition. You already kicked my ass! I could never do anything to you unless you wanted me to."

The little man licked his split lips and the blackness of his eyes reflected the parking lot lights demonically. It looked like his mind was busy imagining her performing sexual acts.

"I don't know you. I don't know if you're dangerous. All I know is you're an ugly little pervert."

"Lady, you already searched me. I'm little. They sent me so you wouldn't be intimidated. I promise you. I will not touch you unless you ask me to. I'll be on my best behaviour. I'm just grateful you stopped kicking my ass and only kicked me once when I was down. Also, I'd appreciate a cup of hot coffee. My teeth are chattering."

Jackie didn't like his reference to being sent by "them". Was he connected with Jones? The way he promised not to touch her without her permission sounded exactly like Jones.

"I don't suppose if I kick you a few more times you're going to spit out who sent you?"

"Are you threatening or are you realizing?"

"I could call the police and have you arrested. They'll go to your place and find any recordings you have of me."

"Do you really want that? The police watching the recording to make sure it is you and it is evidence? Are you that much of an exhibitionist? Calling them is one option, I guess. Of course, I'd tell them I was minding my own business walking by when you assaulted me. I'm the only one with evidence of physical harm here."

Damn. Punching and kicking him, which had felt so rewarding at the time, was being turned against her.

"Finding the video in your residence will confirm my story."

"Sounds risky, Lady. You sure it's even there? Even if it is, I imagine exactly how it'd go down. Reporters read the recaps of every police arrest in search of interesting gems their readers or viewers will find titillating. News nowadays is less about what is actually newsworthy and more about the odd and unusual. It is to modern day what the travelling freak shows once were. I can imagine a good headline: Vigilante Psychoanalyst Captures Midget. Of course, I'm not quite a midget but the news people like their catchy headlines. Good story like that might get kicked up to the networks. It sure would hurt your professional reputation if they published the follow up story: Captured Midget Claims Psychoanalyst Put on Sex Show. I have no reputation so I have nothing to lose."

"How do you know I'm a Psychoanalyst?"

"That's something else I might be willing to discuss. But only in the warmth and comfort of your apartment with a fresh cup of coffee in my hand."

Jackie was stuck. This creep had information she wanted. She wasn't about to call the police. She couldn't stand the embarrassment. She studied him, noting the bad intent brimming in his devious eyes. Poor little guy did look cold though.

Entrance to her apartment and a hot cup of coffee seemed a small price to pay to get valuable information.

Of course, that was not the actual price....

Just inside her apartment the short peeper turned to her, his voice taking on a new confidence, "Lock the door and deadbolt it."

Jackie followed the command automatically and didn't realize she did it without thinking until she turned back to him. She flushed yet again when she saw the triumph dancing in his eyes.

Being alone with him made her nervous. Jackie vowed to remain calm and confident, take charge, get the information she needed, and then kick him out of her apartment. Perhaps literally. However if he did have a recording of her, she'd have to confiscate it first.

The semi-Dwarf held his parka-covered arms straight out from his sides like a living crucifix.

"You may take my parka. Hang it up. I wouldn't want it to get wrinkled."

The nerve of the little bastard! Jackie held her tongue, deciding an angry retort was unhelpful. It was sort of funny, though, seeing as the parka was wet and wrinkled already.

Jackie took the parka off him and hung it up.

"Make coffee, black and strong."

Now the little bastard was more abrupt, his voice serious. Jackie mentally chafed and longed to tell him to go to hell where he belonged. Or she could punch him again. That would be wonderful. That enjoyable thought soothed her, preventing her from saying anything she'd regret later.

He poked around her apartment while she made the coffee in the kitchen. She didn't like that. Maybe the little bastard truly was a panty-snatcher. She kept an eye on him. She saw he kept an eye on her as well. Every time she turned she caught him staring at the curve of her butt, making her wish she hadn't worn such tight jeans. Their durability seemed practical for the stake out. However, she was sure he had no difficulty picturing her bare ass naked. The guy didn't need an imagination, just a memory of last night!

The longer the half-Dwarf remained in her apartment, the angrier she grew. He was slowly changing from a mysterious unknown peeper into a real person. That made the idea of last night's observations all the more embarrassing.

As she handed him a cup of coffee, he unashamedly stared at her chest. Although she wore a bra, a T-shirt, and a pullover sweatshirt, the little freak was still trying to gauge the size of her breasts. Embarrassed, Jackie hunched her shoulders forward. Her breasts

~ 113 ~

were far too big for her thin body. Jackie wished she'd already had breast reduction surgery. Once she had a year making good money as Robert's partner she would have them done.

The little bastard even had the nerve to comment on them!

"You have nice titties. Too big to call them titties really. Boobs or jugs. Why'd you even pay all that money for an education? With those big jugs, tight ass, and prime dick-sucking lips you could have been a great stripper. You wouldn't need to pay for boob enlargement. You could have made at least as much money that you do as a shrink. I don't know why you would waste that opportunity."

"Go to Hell, little man!"

Jackie knew she should not antagonize him, she wanted his cooperation, but she just couldn't help it. His words humiliated her. How dare he speak to her that way in her home!

"Why so mean?" Now he adopted a mock hurt expression, sticking out his split lower lip and innocently widening his eyes.

"You're a lonely little man because you say hurtful, inappropriate things."

"Who says I'm lonely? I'm not. Like I said, I was sent here. I don't just go around peeking in windows at night. Don't get me wrong, I enjoyed your performance but normally I like to participate. I get more tail than you could imagine."

"You're right about that if you aren't a virgin. What's your name anyway?"

"They call me Little Johnson."

Jackie laughed and raised her eyebrows, "They actually call you that to your face?"

Little Johnson looked furious for a second, exposing a wild and unpredictable temper. Good thing he was small and relatively harmless.

"It's in reference to my height and my last name, not a reference to my dick.'

"OK, Little Johnson…."

Somehow learning his name, or the nature of his nickname, or having laughed in his face raised Jackie's confidence.

Frowning, still looking angry, Little Johnson stepped over to examine the Jones' items arranged on the desk. He ran his tiny hand over the huge dildo, appearing deep in thought. Jackie's new confidence leaked away like water dribbling through spread fingers.

She was horribly embarrassed to have the half-Dwarf touch the huge dildo she'd used on herself last night. He picked up the collar, using one finger hooked to a metal loop in the collar to turn the name plate towards him. Little Johnson must think these things belonged to her. She hurried to correct that misunderstanding.

"Please don't touch those items, because they aren't mine. They are part of a work project. They're evidence, part of a clinical case."

"So, you're saying you're not a... let's see... a 'Good Girl'?"

"No, I'm not, I mean..."

"Well, if you aren't a Good Girl, you must be a Bad Girl. Bad girls need discipline, need punishment."

Jackie's mouth fell open but no words tumbled out. Why was everyone, at least men like Little Johnson and Wayne Jones, talking circles around her and trapping her with conversation? She was smart, wasn't she? She saw Little Johnson experimentally grip the handle of the whip.

Jackie's embarrassment and discomfort with the situation flooded higher. For some reason her womanhood was also flooding. She could almost see the scenes playing in Little Johnson's head.

She didn't know if he was messing with her or if he honestly believed she would sexually interact with him. But she did know it was time to put a stop to this line of conversation.

"Stop touching those things. They aren't toys, and they aren't mine. They're evidence. Just leave them alone. Let's move on to why you're here in my apartment. I want to know who sent you and why. Then we'll fetch whatever video you shot of me."

He turned back to her holding the huge exotic dildo.

"What about this fake cock? This is yours, isn't it?"

"No, it isn't. It's just like the rest, evidence in a case. Not mine at all."

"Listen up sexy Psycho-anal-yst. I'd like to help you and I know I can. Problem is, I can't remember last night very well. Did I record your performance for posterity? If I did, where did I put the video? Did I make any copies? If so, where are they? Tell you what, why don't you help me remember? I know what will help. Go change into those cute pyjamas and tight little T-shirt. Maybe if I see you in them again I'll remember."

"You have got to be kidding. No way."

"Correct me if I'm wrong, but didn't you say this big wacky fake dick is part of a case, evidence on a patient? If I did record you using evidence to masturbate with, that would be a bad thing, right? I guess you are a Bad Girl, aren't you?"

Jackie clamped her lips and trembled as she considered the full import of his words. He was toying with the idea of blackmailing her.

"You probably don't even have a video!"

"Maybe I don't. Maybe we'll agree I don't. Then I can enjoy it to my heart's content. Show it to friends. Maybe turn it into cash by showing it on certain Internet sites."

Jackie nibbled on her red lipstick. The fists at her sides sported white knuckles. She needed to be very careful not to say or do the wrong thing. She sought a solution, but it didn't seem to exist. There was nowhere to retreat.

"Indulge me, Pretty Doctor. Go change into something sexy for Little Johnson."

.

Jackie stepped out from her bedroom wearing pyjama bottoms, tight T-shirt, and athletic socks. As she'd changed she'd worried Little Johnson might burst in on her. He didn't, and her stereo started playing loud electronic dance music. She wondered if the music was a ruse to cover whatever nefarious hi-jinks he was up to in the rest of her apartment.

She knew Little Johnson wouldn't see her in the outfit and suddenly "remember" everything, and then answer all her questions helpfully. She didn't want to think about what the little troll had in store for her. She couldn't bear to. She'd cross his bridge when she came to it. Or refuse to cross his bridge she hoped.

She found Little Johnson reclining on the middle of her sofa. He seemed immensely pleased with himself and with her when he saw her wearing the requested outfit. Jackie mentally shrugged. It wasn't so bad. It wasn't like she wore revealing lingerie or like he hadn't already seen her dressed this way before.

He ordered her to stand on the other side of the coffee table. She complied, happy to

put the piece of furniture between her and the perverted little man.

"OK, Mr. Little Johnson. I dressed as you requested. Now, hold up your end of the bargain, tell me who sent you and why. Then I'll change and we'll take my car to get that recording."

"Bargain? There is no bargain here. You want something for nothing. I just want a fair deal."

"What do you want?"

"I want a nice sexy show."

"You already got it last night."

"I was in the cold. I want a nice hot show in the warmth where I can relax. So I can hear you. So I can smell you. I won't touch unless you ask me to, I already told you that. But I want a good show from a Bad Girl."

"What kind of show?" She needed to know exactly what he wanted to best turn him down.

"You ignored a whole possible career path as a stripper. You're sexy, you have a stripper body, and you are passionate as I saw last night. Just let loose and strip all the way, slow and sexy."

Jackie put a hand to her face fingers pinching the top of her nose between her eyes, "That's it then? Nothing else?"

"I don't know. I don't know what kind of performance you'll put on. If it is a great one, good as a Las Vegas stripper, that might be enough. If not, I won't be getting full market value for what you want. I can't say yet."

Jackie considered. How could she take off her clothes and stand in front of this little pervert completely nude? Naked, she reminded herself. Nude was for certain beaches and sexy situations. Naked was for unclothed and vulnerable. She despised this, especially the non-committal open-ended aspect of his part of the bargain. There was no guarantee stripping would satisfy him. Meeting those black voracious eyes, she felt certain it would take far more.

"I bare everything and you give no guarantees on your part. That's a bad bargain, Little Johnson. Let's renegotiate."

"I'm the only game in town. You could say I have a monopoly, meaning I can name my price. No renegotiation. Tell you what, though, I'll give you an option. If you do this one thing for me, you get everything you want."

Jackie dared to be hopeful, "What is it?"

"Simple. Immediately take off all your clothes, come over here, kneel on the carpet, pull out my cock, and give it a nice long deep-throat blow-job. Do that and I'll give you all you desire, I guarantee it."

Jackie was disgusted but not completely surprised. She knew he was a pervert after all. Feeling desperate, she seriously considered the offer. Little Johnson watched her emotional struggle with malicious enjoyment.

"Remember, as with all real blow-jobs, you have to swallow all the semen, every last drop."

Forget it. Jackie had practiced oral sex in the past, but she had never swallowed. Drinking semen was nasty and pointless. It was purely to satisfy the man's fantasies and did nothing for the woman. The entire nature of the act was sexist.

"Nope. Not doing that. Fine, I'll strip and take my chances."

Jackie was nervous, trembling even, but let her anger drive her. She reminded herself he'd seen it all anyway. Better to let him see it one more time than to let countless people watch her on video.

The electronic dance music Little Johnson selected was perfect for the task. Jackie swayed her hips, circling, and then cocking them at angles while her hands caressed both breasts through her white T-shirt and bra. It felt strange, bizarre, to try to come across as sexy to someone who disgusted her. Strippers had to do it every night they worked. Like many intelligent, highly educated women Jackie looked down on strippers. Way down. Now she realized their job was not necessarily easy.

She focused her eyes on furniture in the room or on her own body instead of looking at Little Johnson. Those unblinking, snake-like black eyes unnerved her.

"Allow me to be of assistance. A good stripper looks into the eyes of her customer and really sells the idea that she is into him. She makes him believe every movement she makes is to entice him, and she wants nothing more in the world than his happiness. You need to do that, Bad Girl. Maybe this would help you get in character?"

Little Johnson hoisted the monster dildo by the handle like a crusader ready to take on a dragon. He waved the bulbous head in circles and waggled his thick eyebrows at her.

Jackie burned with indignation. Like he was offering her some kind of treat! Of course, she considered shamefully, he might assume she considered it a treat based on her previous performance.

"No, thanks."

"Maybe you'll reconsider after warming up your pussy."

He smiled, exposing overly large, crooked and stained teeth. She barely stopped herself from swearing at him.

Lacking a sense of rhythm, she had a hard time moving in sync with the music. She knew even less about stripping than dancing. She figured fondling her breasts, tracing her rear, and diving her hands between her legs were pretty effective moves. Unfortunately, these movements also turned her on. Her body awakened sexually from all the touching and that was the last thing she wanted. She changed her strategy and started air-tracing, avoiding actual contact.

She continued to avoid taking any clothing off in the vain hope she might still conjure a great idea and wiggle off Little Johnson's hook.

"Now you're just dancing and not very well at that. I see far sexier dance moves at clubs. Get some of that clothing off. Not all, not yet, just some. Keep your hands on the parts of your body that interest a man and keep them busy doing the work a man's hands would do. Make me believe those are my hands squeezing your breasts, cupping your ass, and rubbing your pussy."

Angry as she was Jackie had to admit the little twerp had a point about her dancing poorly. She'd better strip and strip good if she didn't want his demands to progress beyond stripping. Like it or not her mission was to satisfy that ugly little man. She had to pull this off.

She stared into his eyes, did a little breast shimmy that made her thick cones smack together and then spread her legs wide and pulled her T-shirt over her head. She slid it, caressing and rubbing, down her body, and then unhooked the rear catch of her bra. With sudden stripper inspiration she tossed the bra into Little Johnson's face. When he grinned, she felt a surge of emotional satisfaction from his pleasure. Now she repeated the same breast shimmy with her unrestrained breasts sloppily colliding then plunged both hands down to press into her crotch.

She kept her eyes locked on Little Johnson's beady ones as much as possible. She didn't want to fuck this up. As she sensed his pleasure build, she felt a curious sense of pride. She tried to turn this act into an affirmation of her womanhood. She could be sexy and passionate when she wanted to be, and still accomplish her goals.

Even in this strange stripping territory, she still found a way to be successful.

As she continued her sensual show, behaving in a foreign, wanton way began to exhilarate her. Once again, she realized she must have a streak of exhibitionism. No normal woman would get turned on by an evil Dwarf ordering her around and making her debase herself. Thinking of her degradation only heightened her thrill. Her hands sure felt good on her body, especially when they connected with her sex. She let them wander wherever they wanted to go. They moved to her pussy and remained there, massaging with light pressure, but, unplanned, her hips drove her pyjama-covered pussy up onto the rigid fingers.

She turned to give him a good view of her ass and bare back. She knew the taut, defined musculature and delicate little bumps of vertebrae of her back were sexy. Past boyfriends commented on it, and she wore a backless dress to prom to feature it.

She peeked over her left shoulder, meeting his intense eyes with a sultry gaze. She needed to get her loose pyjama pants down so he could get a good view of her bare butt. She wanted to show him her body, and could barely wait for his reaction after he saw her ass. Her left arm covered her breasts and her right hand popped the ribbon tie at the top of her pyjama bottoms. Because the pyjamas were baggy, two hip wiggles dropped them down to her knees where they only stopped because of her widespread feet. Her right hand caressed her pussy lips through her panties even though Little Johnson couldn't even see it from where he sat.

Jackie saw his eyes zero in on her small round ass, which rotated in figure 8's. Since his eyes were occupied, she stole a quick peek at his groin. She didn't want him to see her looking and misinterpret the look. She just wanted confirmation her movements were effective, getting him turned on. She saw they were because he was.

She thought his penis must be huge, especially for his size. Wasn't that true of 'Little People'? Everything else was small, but their genitals were the same size as regular people? She wasn't sure if that was the rule or if Little Johnson was exceptional, but his cock created a massive bulge in his pants. Any bigger and it would poke out of his waistband. Jackie's eyes flicked to the bizarre dildo to make sure he hadn't shoved it down his pants. Nope, the dildo was right there next to him. She felt a hysterical giggle bubble up when she thought, "The foot-long dildo lying next to Little Johnson is only a foot away from Little Johnson's Big Johnson."

Without her pyjama bottoms, all that covered her butt was a paper-thin pair of pale blue silk panties. Her body was now fully in auto stripper mode, moving sexually without thought. She felt the beat of her pulse in her temples, puffing up her vulva, stiffening the tips of her nipples. Part of her remained outside herself watching and reacting with pleasure to what it observed. Little Johnson wasn't the only one enjoying her performance.

Still on auto stripper, Jackie bent at the waist and looked between her legs at him. Her hair grazed the carpet, blood rushed to her head making her dizzy, the skin of her buttocks stretched to accommodate the position, and her thin panties rode up the crack of her ass.

She tried to achieve the demanded eye contact while shaking her ass and looking through her legs upside down but it was a challenge. She watched the little guy pull his cock out and handle it. The cock grew quite big, swollen dark with blood and almost purple at the head.

For just a second, Jackie imagined that cock plunging into her pussy while she was in her present semi-helpless ankle-grabbing position. She felt a tremendous flush of heated arousal. Her right hand stroked her oily slick panty gusset, throwing oil on the blaze there, while her left hand clutched her left ankle to keep her anchored in place.

Watching his hand pumping the angry-looking cock, she reassured herself she was only getting into her role to turn him on so much he would come from his own hand. Satisfied then, he would give her what she wanted. Her pussy didn't buy that revisionist version of events.

Feeling lost and helpless, her right hand working on its own agenda, she wondered if Little Johnson had noticed how wet she was. Did she want him to? Her consideration of the question turned her on more, and she released a flood of pussy juice that flowed right through the soaked panty crotch and dappled the fingers and palm of her agitating hand.

"I call pause. Stay like that. Don't move except for your hand. Keep moving those fingers. Keep playing with your pussy."

Not understanding what was going on, she automatically followed the little man's commands. For that moment, all she knew in the world was her desire to please him. Besides, her pussy felt so needy and so wet and the last thing she wanted was to lose contact with it. She was grateful he allowed her to continue rubbing it.

Her fingers pushed the triangle of the panties to one side until it cut deep into the tender flesh connecting the top of her inner thigh with her pubic mound. It hurt a little but that was fine, somehow even better than it not hurting. Jackie felt confused and had a hard time thinking clearly.

Her only motions now were her hand working at the wet folds of her pussy and the slight bumping of her hips to drive her pussy into harsher contact with her hand. She couldn't help the small hip movement, but figured Little Johnson wouldn't mind, would enjoy seeing the rippling tensing of her butt muscles as wanton electric currents fired.

She heard the perverted little man laugh. It was weird how she could simultaneously feel so much dread about her predicament and so much physical pleasure. She knew the combination was coincidental, not causal. She regretted that her behaviour perpetuated the myth in Little Johnson's mind that women liked to be demeaned and sexually objectified. She hated affirming his misogyny.

All her senses returned to her current situation. She heard the liquid slurp of her pussy lips, her breathlessness, the pounding of her pulse, and now the sound of pants dropping to the floor and heavy shoes kicked off.

She squinted between her legs, her upside down view confirming what her ears already revealed. Little Johnson's pants and boots were off and his Big Johnson bobbed in the open air, cranked at a forty-five degree angle. He rubbed it as he approached her and she thought he might masturbate on her ass once he got nearer. How could he masturbate without embarrassment, while she was suffused with shame for conducting the same action? It wasn't fair.

As she eyed bobbing Big Johnson, her pussy felt hotter and wetter. Suddenly, it all seemed worth it. The stress, the embarrassment, the loss of control, and the humiliation had all led up to this point in her life. Now she lived in the moment, only looking into a future as far away as a climax of epic proportions. Her clit throbbed and she knew orgasm was not far away. Feeling reckless, she wondered if she could shove all four of her fingers up her pussy. She was sure Little Johnson would love that. So would she.

She opened her passion-clenched eyes and look through her legs at Little Johnson. Inanely, she worried he might come on the coffee table her mother gave her last Christmas. Wherever he ejaculated she knew she better see it so she could clean it up later. But she also wanted to see him. Though he was an ugly little shrimp and he bossed her around it excited her to see him hard, rubbing that too-large cock, and staring at her ass and pussy. The watched feeling was highly arousing. It made her picture herself as well and that made her even more excited. Her unleashed thoughts stimulated a pulse of vaginal fluid. God, she must have a bucket of it stored up in her womb! A thin streamlet of pussy juice ran down each of her legs.

Little Johnson moved even closer! He stepped up until the head of his penis hung only about a foot from Jackie's pussy. Jackie was suddenly worried about that cock and grateful her hand was there working at her pussy folds. The hand would protect her. He wouldn't be able to stick it in. A cock penetrating her wasn't the worst thing she could imagine. It might be the best thing. Her fingers squeezed her pussy flesh trying to bring herself back to reality but the intermingled pain and pleasure drove her further out of her normal mind.

Her mind was on the possibility of that cock shoving into her steaming pussy. Doing whatever it wanted to her. It would split her and glide through her vaginal folds. Her mind was trying to wrap around the idea of that cock pleasuring her, the same way her pussy lips would wrap around it. She knew there would be no physical or mental resistance once her hand was out of the way. Everything was so slippery the smallest brush from his small hand would knock hers away. She was even more breathless now, expectant.

She eyed that dark swollen nasty cock and it looked wonderful to her at the moment. That is, she tried to convince herself, it would if the cock was connected to a decent normal-looking man who loved her and treated her with respect. She desperately reminded herself that the current situation was the exact opposite of her ideal sexual fantasy, closer to her worst case scenario.

She closed her eyes and waited, listening to his harsh breathing above her. Her fingers continued to squish her labial folds and the side of her thumb pushed at her erect clitoris which seemed to push back for more. She wanted to stop, stand up, and move away from the little monster but her body insisted on continuing her current activities. Little Johnson was very close, but he still had not broken their bargain. If she stopped without permission she'd be the one at fault and all these embarrassing and arousing acts would be for nothing.

With her legs spread, muscles tense, and her hair brushing the floor like she was trying to sweep it, she no longer looked back at Little Johnson, she looked up at him. Mostly gazing up at his cock and wrinkled scrotum which teamed up to block view of his face. She wanted to see his face in order to gauge his intentions.

Considering that cock alone, without the human garbage attached to it, sent a thrill through Jackie. The thought he may masturbate until he came all over her ass sent another thrill piling into her. But the thought he may just knock her tiny slimy hand aside and plunge that purple-headed cock all the way down her channel sent an absolutely massive wave of forbidden need.

She tried to shake the nasty thought out of her blood-swollen head but it remained in place. She actually felt like asking him to do it. She knew he would. Jackie bit her lower lip viciously using the pain to bring herself back to her senses while also trying to stop any regrettable words or requests from coming out of her mouth. If she talked, no matter what she meant to say, she knew there was some small chance she'd ask him to fuck her.

Little Johnson finally spoke, his dark eyes moving from her exposed ass and sex to look down at her face.

"Take your hand away from your snatch. Put it on your other ankle."

Jackie reluctantly pulled her hand away and moved it to clamp on her other ankle. Her poor hot pussy had nothing but cool air now. But her need did not diminish now that her fingers were not poking around in the oven. Somehow, the flames grew higher anyway, creating an anguish of need.

"Would you like permission to return your hand? Would you like to keep diddling yourself bent under a stranger's cock? Like a little slut?"

Jackie kept biting her lower lip. It might be bleeding now. God help her if she allowed her mouth to open. She might hear herself asking for permission to masturbate herself!

"You can answer me or you can stay like that all night. That's up to you. It's a simple yes or no question."

Now Jackie knew she had to answer. Part of her worried that if she said no he would take that to mean he should shove his cock in her. Mostly she realized she had to tell him the real answer. Somehow, she wanted to tell him. She'd been so humiliated and embarrassed for the past twenty-four hours since she discovered she'd been watched. She'd fought hard to avoid further shame but instead the shame factor multiplied. It was like he flipped a switch somewhere deep in her mind. Suddenly she wanted to be shamed and humiliated, wanted to be mistreated in a hundred ways.

Telling him she wanted to return to masturbating for his enjoyment, that she was a little slut ready to make a spectacle of herself, would be an Earth-shattering meteor strike to her self-esteem. Bizarrely she wanted that, felt she deserved it.

"Yes." Jackie's admission was barely audible, just a squeak really.

"That wasn't very convincing. Convince me."

"I do want to. What you said. The answer is yes."

"Not at all convincing. Maybe we should just get dressed, watch some TV. Maybe you could make us some popcorn."

"No. I need to. Please, let me... let me finger my pussy. You'll like it, I'll do it good, and I'll give you a good show."

"All I've seen is you selfishly taking pleasure. You're only experiencing that pleasure because I made you give it to yourself. You should be grateful. Didn't your Mother ever teach you to share? What would Mom and Dad say if they saw you being so self centred?"

The reference to her parents mortified Jackie. Here she was wiggling her ass and grinding her soaked pussy against empty air, and Little Johnson forced her to think about her loving parents. They appeared in her mind, staring at her with mouths open in shock. If they ever saw her like this! If they ever knew she was such a slut! How could her arousal continue unabated even as she thought of her parents seeing her like this? She wished her parents would serve as a mental slap to bring her back to her senses, but she still felt sexually crazed. She had to get him to let her masturbate again!

"I'm sorry, Little Johnson. I've been rude. I do thank you for all you've done for me. Please, may I touch my pussy again?"

"Instead of your worthless short fingers, would a slut like you like my thick cock up her wet pussy? Remember, I've agreed I can't even touch you without your permission. You have to give me permission if you want my cock up your slutty snatch.'

Jackie bit her lip again, feeling fresh pain. She wondered if her lips looked as bloody and ragged as Little Johnson's. She was about to blurt out "Fuck me", and, being honest, that's really what she wanted. But she knew it was wrong and knew she'd regret it forever if she allowed something like that. She tried to calm herself and muster her will.

"Mr. Little Johnson. Please let me use my fingers. I really need it and would be so grateful."

"You reject my cock? I've been kind enough to offer it to a filthy slut like you and you reject it?"

"Little Johnson, I don't mean any offense. I'm sure you're a great guy but we are just not compatible. Please, let me masturbate."

"I understand you slut. I'm not a sore loser, but there should be some compromise. Do you agree?"

Jackie was silent, her mind preoccupied with the anticipation of returning her hand to her pussy. This time she would shove as many fingers as she could in there!

Little Johnson leered down at her, "You don't want my cock, but I want to see a cock stuck up your stuck up pussy. I think we should both get what we want.'

Jackie froze like a rabbit, even her ass stopped wagging. Little Johnson lifted the huge strange dildo she masturbated with the night before. He'd stowed it against the side of his leg the whole time. He knew there was a chance she would refuse his cock, so he formulated a Plan B. He gripped the dildo hilt and brought the mushroomed head towards her stretched and defenseless pussy. It hovered only an inch from her wetness. Jackie longed to break her wide open vulnerable position. She wanted to flee. But she remained frozen in place, blazing hot with need.

"You said I only had to strip." Her defense sounded bizarre to her own ears. Even an hour ago, she never would have imagined saying anything like that. She knew, just knew, he would knock aside her arguments as easily as he could her hand if she attempted to protect her pussy.

"I said we'd have to see. I said I would get my full market value.

You're nowhere close. You tried, I'll give you that. How can you stripping, even masturbating one night compare to a video of you playing games with a big wacky fake cock? At the very least, it's only fair you use the thing right here in front of me. Same shame."

God help her, in the new world she now inhabited, it did seem fair to Jackie.

Little Johnson's will coalesced in his dark eyes, his arm tensed, and the giant head of the fake penis prodded her swampy pussy.

This wasn't fair! Still longing to please him, Jackie held her spread-legged position, but concocted one last panicky appeal. Little Johnson would obey his own rules.

"You said you wouldn't touch me without permission!"

"I'm not."

As he spit out his denial, he shoved the plastic nectarine-sized head of the dildo past her pussy lip gates, sinking it down into her channel at a slow even rate. After a few inches, her pussy walls clenched and resisted. Instead of stopping, he jiggled the hilt and crammed harder, forcing it down into her feminine core.

"Ohhhhhh, you fucker!"

Jackie yearned to call him more names, but heard herself grunting over and over while gripping her ankles furiously. Her inhuman grunts sounded like a pig in mud.

"Correct, slut. I am a fucker," Little Johnson said. "I'm The Fucker, you're The Fuckee. I'm your Lord Provider of Pleasure and you are just another slut. A slut too stupid to recognize and embrace her true slutty nature. Well, you're embracing it now."

He rammed the dildo harder, pushing her stretched ass forward until she almost lost her balance. The invaded feeling and tactile sensations made her lose her mental balance. Moaning throatily, Jackie shuffled her feet forward to avoid falling, despite her hands still shackling her ankles.

Little Johnson laughed and twisted the beast of a dildo down her upended pussy. Drilled two thirds of the way in now, the dildo met even more pussy resistance. He worried that increasing the pressure further would force her to fall. He had a very specific plan which accounted for every eventuality. Although pleased with their progress, it was time to initiate the next crucial step. He hungered to pile-drive his own cock in that choice pussy immediately, but knew he must practice patience.

He was very careful not to directly touch Jackie. He was a man of his word. More importantly, he liked a good challenge. A great man once told Little Johnson ground rules serve to accentuate and propagate the game. Breaking those rules resulted in self-defeat and invalidated the game.

"Slut, get your hand on this goofy fake cock. Keep it shoved deep inside you, and move over to the sofa. I want you up on that couch with your ass sticking in the air. You'll be more comfortable. See what a considerate fellow I am?"

Jackie felt relieved to have commands to obey, but couldn't understand why that would be. She straightened with one hand wrapped around the lower shaft of the dildo. The change in altitude for her head sparked silver stars in her vision. Little Johnson didn't rush her. Once the dizziness retreated, she shuffled to the sofa, pushing the dildo firmly in place up her slit.

She obediently manoeuvred into the ordered position, hiding her face in the sofa material, sticking her rounded ass into the air, and keeping the dildo stuck deep in her. She even managed to secretly rub her stiff little clitoris. At least she hoped Little Johnson didn't notice what she was doing. Why did she bother trying to keep anything hidden from him? Perhaps she did it to rebel in some small way.

When Little Johnson spoke next she listened closely. She was relieved he hadn't stuck his cock in her and wanted to show her gratitude with pure obedience. Obedience was important to him and she had to please him.

"Slut, use that dildo to satisfy your slutty snatch. Your goal is to force it all the way in. Cram that fat round sword up your snatch until the hilt grinds into your labia. Keep your eyes closed or you fail. I won't talk anymore. I plan to just watch and listen. That means you have to do all the talking. While you fuck yourself describe your actions, how they feel. Tell me what a dirty slut you are, tell me you're a real bad girl who wants and needs punishment. When you're about to come sit up and fuck that pussy hard as you can. When you do come open your eyes and tell me you're coming and what a slut you are for coming."

His detailed fuck-structions were a lot for pleasure-distracted Jackie to remember, but they sounded doable, even desirable. The idea of finally earning the satisfaction of an orgasm sounded great no matter what the circumstances.

Jackie slid the dildo out a couple inches and then jammed the dildo in several inches. While her right hand stretched behind her to clutch the hilt and drive the dildo up her slot, her left hand snaked under her body to tweak her clit. She kept her eyes tightly closed. Following directions was her job now.

Jackie knew Little Johnson wanted her to talk. What did he want to hear? He called her nasty, derogatory names like slut earlier. Apparently he enjoyed that.

"I'm fucking myself with this huge dildo because I'm such a slut. My ass is in the air because I'm a slut. I'm a dumb worthless slut!"

She thought calling herself a slut would feel like acting but she was so turned on the words sounded genuine. She felt tremendous physical pleasure as she manipulated the dildo, and tremendous emotional pleasure from thinking about her shameful statements. She crossed a line without being aware of it. It was one thing for Little Johnson to call her names, but much worse to self-inflict those same names, especially since she believed them. Thinking about the nasty admission aroused her. It was an admission! The names weren't insults, they were the truth.

She panted, groaned, and sharply gasped at times, but tried her best to enunciate the words for his enjoyment, "I'm pushing it into my slut pussy hard as I can. I don't care if it hurts. I even like the pain of it. I can't believe something this big fits inside my come chute. I love it!"

She never imagined sticking an enormous object in her pussy could feel so glorious. She wished she'd owned one of these supersized dildos for years. When she completed this assignment and returned the unusual dildo, she would buy one like it for herself on the Internet. Buying a massive fake cock in a sex shop would be so embarrassing!

It was embarrassing just to think about her work assignment while cramming the piece of evidence in and out of her gripping gutter pussy. While focused on her shame, trickles of her secretions dribbled across her pale muscular abdomen.

The heady combination of embarrassment, arousal, and sensation resulted in exquisite pleasure, making her realize she sexually craved embarrassment now. She wished to be shamed all the time. As she shoved and whined, she purposely imagined her most prudish friends and relatives watching her whorishness unleashed. She envisioned them watching her obey Little Johnson's orders, and it thrust her lust to new heights.

"I'm fucking myself. I'm shoving a plastic cock in me. I'm a bad girl. I need it."

She fervently hoped her performance pleased Little Johnson. It felt strange to be trying so hard to please a creep that disgusted her. It also felt right. She had to give him credit for leading her towards such a bounty of pleasure. Inappropriate gratitude replaced her anger. She really was grateful, even delighted by her own corruption.

"It's so good. It feels so good, and I'm so bad. I'll do anything I'm told to do."

Pain and pleasure intertwined in her body as she pummelled her raised pussy and pinched her slippery hard clitoris. She pinched it far too hard, the pain overwhelmed her, but it still wasn't hard enough for a dirty disobedient slut like herself. Oh, she was so near. What had Little Johnson told her to do when she came close to coming?

Jackie rose up and flipped around like a good little slut. Eyes still clenched shut, she positioned her feet up to her ass, her knees wide and nearly straight to either side of her body, her ass in contact with the stained sofa cushion, and her back pressed against the backrest of the couch. Now both hands teamed up to shove that ridiculously wide plastic cock up her impossibly stretched pussy.

It was as difficult as shoving a square peg through a round hole, but determination, the new angle of penetration, and the rhythmic bouncing of her slight body weight finally drove the cock sword in to the hilt. Jackie grunted and wailed in agony as the bulbous head smashed against her cervix.

The agony was necessary to prolong her pleasure. She would have come long before if not for the pain, discomfort, and embarrassment restraining her orgasm. Instead her pleasure crested ever higher, the pain preventing it from crashing into surf.

Grinding her pussy lips against the hilt, she remembered the upward curved hilt extension meant to tease and shallowly penetrate the anus. In the throes of lust, the alien idea of anal penetration seemed... desirable. She wanted it and knew Little Johnson would approve. Suddenly there was no reason left in the world not to stick the anal probe up her ass.

Jackie struggled to twist the hilt around, her slippery fingers and the tightness of her pussy resisting motion. Determined, she tugged and twisted until the anal penetrator portion lined up with her little puckered asshole. She raised her ass half a foot off the cushion and made sure she felt the probe tip in contact with her pussy juice soaked anus. She knew this would tear her virgin anus. She wanted the pain. A bad girl like her doing a bad thing like shoving a dildo up her anus deserved some pain. She released her weight intentionally, the heavy force ripping the probe through her tight ass ring. Jackie immediately felt her orgasm breaking.

"I'm a dirty slut! I just shoved it up my ass too! It hurts and I love it! I'm coming!"

Somehow remembering Little Johnson's directions she opened her eyes as she climaxed, fluttering her eyelashes from the bright light and the overwhelming sensations. As she rode the shaft, using both hands to increase its impact, she noticed Little Johnson standing nude, his body covered in black swirled hair. It was like the half-Dwarf's pubic hair spread to infest the majority of his body.

She registered through multiple orgasms that he held the camcorder she confiscated from him earlier. She'd set it on the kitchen counter after they entered the apartment. Little Johnson bent forward, focused on capturing every detail. His cock was hard, but he neglected it, using both hands to hold the camcorder steady.

This was outrageous! It wasn't fair. She was fucking herself to get a recording from him, not to make another one! He was taking advantage of the sensual storm he'd created and was recording the storm wreckage on video for his own gain.

Jackie longed to stop grinding that two-pronged dildo into her pussy and ass, wanted to make Little Johnson stop, wished to protest, and wanted to kick his ass. But her hunger for pleasure dwarfed the Dwarf, she wanted to continue to ride the orgasms as long as she could keep producing them. She was a shameless slut whose only priority was pleasure even at her own expense.

Unable to stop herself, Jackie looked straight into the camcorder and aided her defeat by performing for the soul-stealing camcorder and the thousands of strangers it represented. Imagining the strangers watching her come, her orgasms climbed in strength. Bigger, longer, better.

"Watch me! Watch me fuck and hurt myself. Watch me stuff my pussy and ass with this plastic cock. I'm a stupid slut. I'm just a hot cunt!"

Her voice sounded hoarse and high-pitched. She wailed through more orgasms, her legs trembling and hands twitching. Her flexing pussy muscles eventually pushed the monster dildo out of her writhing body. It rolled off the sofa onto the carpet. Jackie flopped onto her stomach, her body still except for sporadic, twitching aftershocks.

After long minutes, she turned her head and looked at Little Johnson. He stood naked and incredibly hairy, but there was no sign of the camcorder. For a moment she thought maybe she imagined it.

Then he spoke wearing a cat-that-ate-the-canary look on his face, "The End."

"You fucker," she mumbled, exhausted.

Little Johnson sat at the end of the couch nearest her face. He was naked, horny, and bursting with gloating self-satisfaction. Through her post-orgasmic weariness and the scent of her own arousal, she smelled the awful little man's body odour.

"You're in almost the perfect position, my dear Slut-In-Training. Now get up on your elbows and shift forward so you can suck my cock."

She pushed up on her elbows to see if he was serious. Of course he was. He hadn't come yet. His face showed confidence and a little impatience.

She opened her mouth to refuse, to negotiate, to at least protest. He spoke like she was some loose whore he owned. As his dark eyes drilled into her, an insidious thought wiggled through her mind. You are what you do, not what you say you are. She just behaved like a total slut. Naturally, Little Johnson viewed her as a slut. She was a slut, so his order was appropriate. What should a slut like her do in this situation?

Her body obeyed the only possible answer. Mouth still open from her aborted protest, she rose up a bit higher, elbow-crawled a foot closer to Little Johnson, and then carefully lowered her parted lips toward his erect purple-headed cock.

She stretched her mouth as wide as possible until her mouth

surrounded the cockhead and an inch of shaft. She paused, her upper lip brushing the top side his shaft.

It wasn't too late. The rational part of her mind still struggled to be heard and ordered her to stop this.

Jackie knew resisting Little Johnson was useless. He handled her expertly at every turn. If she refused him, he'd convince her, blackmail her, or trick her into doing it anyway. Why bother to resist at all? Her exhausted body was still horny. Against all odds she even wanted to taste his cock.

Committed, Jackie wrapped her lips firmly around Little Johnson's too-large cock and flicked her pointed little tongue against the sensitive underside. She tried to get as much of the shaft into her mouth as possible. She tasted him, unable to tell if his cock was clean or dirty, but started giving it a tongue bath. Her own enthusiasm surprised her, and she heard Little Johnson grunt in satisfaction. His satisfaction was important to her, more important than her own wants and needs. The angle was difficult and her tired arms trembled with the strain of propping up her torso, but her discomfort was insignificant. She needed to make Little Johnson come. She needed to please him. Failure to get him off would crush her.

A new goal, becoming the most satisfying slut possible, replaced her previous goal of avoiding a loss of control. Jackie swirled her tongue, lapping his leaking pre-come, and she revelled in tasting his seminal fluid. The act of tasting his spunk, not the taste itself, so wickedly delighted her.

Her realization spawned the sting of arousal through her groin. Motivated and enthused, she stretched her mouth and bounced the head of Little Johnson's cock against the back of her mouth and mashed her tonsils. Even as she choked a little and almost vomited, she vowed to deep-throat the evil Little Johnson.

Bobbing her head up and down, a new flood of pleasure broke loose, both of sensation and liquid, in her pussy. She tilted her body and stuck her right hand down into her swampy mess.

"Bad girl! Did I give you permission to whack yourself off?"

Jackie's hand froze, but her mouth continued its quest to satisfy. She knew he expected absolute obedience. He would not tolerate independent action from her. In his presence, her independent decision making process became antiquated and useless.

He obviously expected an answer. She extracted his cockhead from her mouth. A thick string of drool plopped out of from between her parted lips before she could snap them shut and swallow.

"No, Little Johnson. I'm sorry."

"Do you want to masturbate while sucking the cream out of Little Johnson's dick?"

She nodded.

"Then you should ask politely for what you want. If you ask nice enough I may even allow it."

The flotsam and jetsam of Jackie's shipwrecked self-esteem floated to the surface. Didn't she have any self-respect left? But what did it matter? He already knew she was a slut. She had nothing more to lose.

"Yes, please. Please allow me to shove my fingers in my pussy and rub my clit while I suck cock. I'll do a good job for you."

"Yes, but you are a bad girl, aren't you, slut?"

"Yes, I am," she said simply. She wasn't prepared to deny him anything.

"You may pleasure that hot little pussy while you suck me off, but there are three conditions. One, you must raise your ass up and give me permission to spank and pinch it as much as I want. I still plan to honour our agreement, as I'm a gentleman of my word so I will need your permission. Two, you may only come when I come and must do it at the same time. Three, as mentioned earlier you must swallow all my semen."

Jackie flushed, feeling infinitely foolish, remembering earlier when she refused to resolve the situation by giving him a sperm-swallowing blow-job. Had she initially agreed to blow him, the situation would already be settled. Little Johnson possessed his own demented sense of honour. He would have held up his end of the bargain. Now he was about to receive what she had earlier refused him, and he'd already gotten a whole lot more. Her defeat was complete, his victory total.

"Yes, I will do all those things. I won't come until I swallow your come. I give you permission to spank and pinch my ass as much as you want, any time you want. Do whatever you want to my butt. I'm a bad girl. I deserve it."

"Very good. Agreed. Continue."

She raised her pale ass by getting up on her knees and leaning forward and down onto his dick. She hoped her ass made a good target for him, easy to reach despite his short arms. She sucked his air-cooled cock back into her mouth, warming it with flood of saliva. Her right hand returned to the wet folds of her pussy and started stroking and tweaking.

She wondered if he would really spank her. She'd never been spanked, not even as a child. Her parents were conservative and well-educated, not believers in physical punishments. She'd always been a good daughter anyway. Surprising such a good daughter could turn into such a dirty slut. The humiliation of being spanked scared and thrilled her. Every time she thought her humiliation level peaked, something happened to drive it higher.

The crack-slap sound and the red flash of pain from her backside answered both her questions. The little man really spanked her. It hurt a lot, more than she'd guessed but also felt much better than she'd hoped. The pain spring boarded her dripping horniness, making her want to shove her whole little hand up her savaged and stretched pussy.

The spanks rained down in time with her pumping mouth and throat. When her mouth came up and her tongue fluttered against the fluid-leaking head of his shaft, the little hand sliced down with a harsh impact. Waves of pain built and expanded from her bright red ass. As her mouth lowered to engulf his shaft as far as her throat could manage, his hand raised up, reloading for the next strike. She didn't dread the spanks like she should have, so she never delayed drawing her drooling lips back up the shaft. She did nothing to prevent or delay the blows but accepted them as a bad girl's due.

Getting spanked was natural and right. Only a slut like her would enjoy her pain and punishment so greatly. She hoped Little Johnson enjoyed it too.

Her fingers rubbed back and forth over her hard and hot clitoris. Now she struggled to delay climaxing. She wanted to come now, but wanted to obey Little Johnson even more. Making him shoot his load was her mission in life. Then she could move on to the next mission, swallowing his wad. She wanted to swallow every last squirming egg-seeking sperm. The sickening thought brought her a finger stroke away from a mind-melting climax. Her finger hovered an inch below her clitoris, her mouth struggling to please, as her ass absorbing its fiftieth spank.

Little Johnson grunted a death groan and came, streams of semen pulsing into her mouth. Immediately she clamped her lips tight as possible around his shaft so none of his spend would escape her scooping tongue. Her throat muscles worked to swallow, and the throbbing swallowing sensation on the sides of his cockhead added to his pleasure. Jackie's finger stabbed viciously at her clitoris as if it wanted to punish herself to orgasm. Despite her ass feeling like a bubbling lava field of pain, she came so hard for a moment she lost both her vision and hearing. The only senses remaining were pleasure and pain, which were all she needed.

Jackie succeeded in swallowing and licking up all of Little Johnson's sperm. She felt revulsion and pride, another curious mix.

"How did the slut like that drink of Little Johnson?"

"Good. Tasty." She told him what she thought he wanted to hear, but it wasn't really a lie.

"My little fishes are swimming in your stomach. You know what your Mom would say? You are what you eat. Like all women, you are a slut. Calling you slut is like calling you "Girl". It's too generic. Bad Girl and Good Girl are also too common. All women are one or the other, usually both. You need your own name. You have earned a name. Based on your diet, I dub thee 'Fishy'."

Jackie was too exhausted to muster any emotional reaction to the name.

"Was everything else good? How did you like the spanks?"

"I don't mind getting spanks." She'd meant to say she "had not minded the spanks". "Don't mind getting" made it sound like there would be future spankings from Little Johnson. A quickly recovering Jackie hoped there would be no future spankings. She shuddered. Suddenly she realized something.

"Hey, you never did pinch my butt."

Little Johnson giggled like a circus clown, reached over, and harshly pinched her right butt cheek. Jackie squealed with pain. On her spank-crimsoned ass the pinch was shockingly painful.

He pushed her head and shoulders off his lap, stood up from the sofa, and walked away. One hand cupping her swampy pubic mound and the other cupping the pinched ass cheek, Jackie marvelled that the painful pinch stoked more flames of arousal. Was there no end to her sluttiness? Every orgasm seemed to make the next one easier and more necessary.

When Little Johnson returned, he carried the leather collar sporting the name tag that read "Good Girl". He snapped it around Jackie's neck and locked it closed with the little padlock. Although dismayed by the act, Jackie showed no resistance. At the moment, resistance seemed fruitless and impossible. She was surprised the collar, though built to be uncomfortable by jamming against the base of her neck and chaffing her jawbone, fit perfectly in circumference. The collar was a perfect fit in more ways than one.

Little Johnson spoke, "We had this collar custom made for you. Though it says "Good Girl" we both know you are really a bad girl. Soon, you'll live up to it, Fishy."

Little Johnson stepped away again leaving her fingering the collar and marvelling at what fate may have in store. He returned a few moments later with a blanket from her bed which he threw over her naked, cooled, and collared body.

"Time for me to leave, Fishy. Get some sleep."

After he dressed and just before he left he told the drowsy Jackie, "Fishy, the key to the collar's lock is on your desk. Don't remove it until morning. We want you to get used to it before wearing it full time. I serve Wayne Jones. Since you, in turn, serve me, you now serve him, though in a very different capacity. Welcome."

She wasn't really surprised. She guessed it all along. She easily fell into a deep sleep.

CHAPTER 10

In the morning, Jackie hoped it a nightmare. But she lay naked on the sofa with a blanket thrown over her. And dried secretions stiffened her pubic hair. And friction from the leather collar abraded her neck and chin. There was no denying it. Everything had happened.

Jackie's mind tried to avoid lingering on the events. Instead, she focused on her incredible thirst. She moved to the kitchen and drank five glasses of water at the stainless steel sink.

Jackie found the key to the collar on her desk. After unlocking and removing the collar, she turned it in her hands and brushed her fingertips over the brass nameplate. "Good Girl". She'd always wanted to be a good person, a good girl. But not a good girl who wore a padlocked collar. A collar a dog would wear. She wasn't a dog. She was a human being. She wanted to feel love, not used. These thoughts rekindled some of her old outrage, though the feeling was definitely weaker than it would have been the day before.

Jackie showered, sudsing everywhere twice. Soaping her spanked butt, sensitive nipples, and tender pussy in the cleaning process produced a mix of feelings. Passion, guilt, eagerness, shame, arousal, anger, pleasant soreness, and renewal reacted together to produce confusion. Last night's events played in her mind like a movie. Oh God! That horrible little man had recorded her. He recorded her working that goofy dildo up her pussy while she talked nasty. She'd even looked straight at the camcorder and talked to it! In the throes of lust she basically helped blackmail herself.

Jackie resisted masturbation in the shower, though her pussy throbbed for contact. Her body was highly attuned to any sexual contact at the moment. In the past, after sex, she'd been sated – or, truthfully, very often left unsatisfied – but never left in a state of ongoing humming arousal. It buzzed at her insides insistently, but she still refused to masturbate. She knew she'd see images of Little Johnson and his big purple cock. It would be an unbearable transgression to masturbate to that.

Even when drying herself, her towel-covered hand lingered at her sex, pressing at it through the rough cloth, rubbing well after the water dried. Instead of drying her pussy, the towel contact made her wet again. It felt so good she wanted masturbate on the bathroom floor. She resisted and moved the towel lower to dry her legs.

Jackie had the feeling neither the towel nor her hand could do the same quality job of the bizarre dildo. Not even close. She might need her own bizarre dildo, of similar size and with an anal probe, from now on to achieve satisfaction. She couldn't decide whether the dildo spoiled her or ruined her.

She glanced in the mirror. Although she'd undergone a shift in perspective, she still physically resembled the same Jackie. Much of last night's twisted pleasure was unrelated to the physical sensations leading to climax. The name-calling and the humiliation mixed with the loss of control and free will generated the most intense sensations. Her utter loss of free will led to more climaxes than she'd ever experienced. More than she had thought possible in a month let alone a single night. This kind of orgasm was both a curse and a blessing. They drove her need higher, made sex a new priority. Despite the number and power of her orgasms, she still hungered for more pleasurable abuse. She wondered if she could ever be satisfied, and her eyes in the mirror grew haunted.

Wrapped in a towel, Jackie returned to the living room. When she saw the disarranged, stained sofa cushions her eyes jerked away. The room reminded her of a crime scene, a crime against her humanity.

She had nearly a week to figure out how to meet Wayne Jones' demands. If she found the fortitude to return to Goethner-Varner, she needed to be prepared to answer three of his questions. What else? Provide a proof that she understood Jones' language and give him a personalized gift. She had no idea how to accomplish her assigned tasks. It was repellent that she would have to try.

Jackie was a little curious as she looked down now at the naughty items on her desk. Wouldn't it be amazing if she could complete Jones' quest? For a surreal moment she pictured herself in Jones' room at the Centre seconds after answering all three questions and completing the two tasks. Jones coldly telling her she was a good girl and a surge of submissive victory that she had pleased him. She could feel and sense every detail of the moment and felt something like reverse déjà vu. She was experiencing something that she sensed would happen instead of feeling like she had lived a current moment previously. It made her dizzy. The thought of Jones' stern approval made her sex flood.

She stepped away from the objects on the desk top like they were armed explosives. She had nothing to do today and that was dangerous. Idle hands were the Devil's playground. She knew she could not bring the situation to the attention of Robert. There was nothing he could do. He would judge her and certainly reject her. Her golden opportunity would be gone. She could not just give up and walk way. But she was on her own.

Trying to cooperate with Wayne Jones and his jester Little Johnson was unthinkable, a formula for failure. She sensed that path could cost her far more than a mere opportunity at success and fame. These two could cost her very soul.

Jackie needed a third option. Slowly a plan materialized. A plan that could work! Hope rejuvenated her and pushed her buzzing arousal into the background. After a shopping trip and some work around the apartment, she felt like an old time fur trapper. She had set the jaws of a spring-loaded trap and disguised it. Now it was time to wait for the bear. Lord knew Little Johnson was as furry as a bear. The little bear would return, as it considered her apartment, her body, and her mind part of its territory.

It was a Wednesday when Wayne Jones instructed her not to return for six days. Jackie had until next Tuesday before her audience with the King.

Thursday she spent shopping and setting up her apartment. Then she cleaned. She waited Thursday evening and night for Little Johnson to show up. She was nervous but anxious to put her plan into action. Her plan involved some self-sacrifice which was necessary for success. She knew part of her eagerness was for the wrong reason. That Wednesday night of debauchery, being pushed beyond her limits, had made her curious to experience more of the same.

There was no sign of him Thursday. She imagined Little Johnson out there somewhere playing sexual games with Jones' followers. Maybe he was playing with slim enthusiastic Kira. Perhaps he pummelled Monica with his cock. The same cock she'd had in her mouth might be in some other girl's pussy. Jackie felt a little jealous. Obviously it wasn't jealousy, just anxiety about her plan. She just didn't want his sexual antics with other women to delay him.

Friday afternoon Jackie made the mistake of wandering past her desk and spotting the graphic glossy photos of sexual torture. She eyed them, her hand spreading them out. The images of sadistic torment and masochistic enjoyment sent a plunging free fall feeling of sick revulsion through her stomach. That feeling continued to plunge until it swept through her sex. As her mind processed the images, her labial lips filled with blood and her pussy flooded with juice. One hand palmed her pussy as if to dam the flow of juices. Jackie halted her fingers just before they found her clit. Trying to dampen her passionate response to the photos by masturbating was as bad as trying to satisfy a poison ivy itch by scratching. It would just make it worse. She must resist.

Jackie also possessed a strategic reason for resisting satisfying her longing with an orgasm. She'd be most convincing in the role she'd chosen to play if she was horny and unfulfilled. She just hoped she could concentrate on her mission without becoming completely distracted.

Finally, at nearly ten o'clock on Friday night, a knock sounded at her apartment door. Jackie knew it was Little Johnson.

She was correct. When she opened the door, he leered up at up her, exposing stained teeth. For a second she froze and stared at the awful little guy. She'd forgotten how ugly he was. And how short! And she'd sucked his cock and let him fuck her with the giant dildo!

"Won't you invite me in?"

At that moment, one of Jackie's neighbours stepped out of their apartment and into the hallway. Her neighbour Melissa, a college girl who enjoyed dressing fashionably, paused and looked at them. Melissa was a bit spoiled, since she didn't work and her parents financed her expensive apartment, but she hadn't let spoiling parents spoil her sweet nature. She regarded Jackie as a role model, asking her for advice on college life, her future career plans, and men.

Not surprisingly Melissa seemed startled by Little Johnson. Like usual, Melissa was all dolled up, her skinny jeans fashionably tight, her makeup dramatic, and her blond hair gelled in structured swirls.

"Hi, Jacqueline." Melissa's greeting was warm and sweet as usual, but she frowned with concern at the ugly bearded half-Dwarf that was Little Johnson.

"Uh, hi."

Little Johnson turned and smiled broadly at the college girl, as pleased to see her as Jackie was mortified. He reached out his little paw, which the girl reluctantly shook, "Nice to meet such a pretty neighbour, my dear."

"Uh, this is Melissa. Melissa, this is... John." Jackie's cheeks flushed bright red with embarrassment as she realized she didn't even know Little Johnson's full name. What must Melissa think of her Friday night visit from this odd little man? Jackie opened her mouth to say Little Johnson was her uncle, but he beat her to the punch.

"You have such a warm hand. What are the chances of two such sexy young ladies living next door to each other? This must be a new city zoning plan. I like it! I approve! You look like you're in a rush to be somewhere so let's not keep your night's destiny waiting. Jackie and I are having a stay in date. Those are the best kind, aren't they?"

Little Johnson had the nerve to wink lasciviously at Melissa while grabbing Jackie's stiff hand. He jerked Jackie to stand at his side, her curved hip contacting his upper ribcage. His hand snaked around Jackie's waist and squeezed the far side of her ass. My God, thought Jackie, he's doing this on purpose to embarrass me!

Melissa paled despite her even tan and she took a few steps back, shocked since she'd always admired Jacqueline Thorpe, who seemed so wise, so composed. Now she'd been demoted to "Jackie" and had some kind of ugly Dwarf pawing at her. It was too much to believe!

"Well, have fun. See you guys."

Melissa returned down the hallway to her door and made sure her door lock had snapped in place, before starting for the apartment exit. She wasn't normally suspicious of people, but Jacqueline's new "friend" John looked as crooked as his teeth. She pictured him burglarizing her place. He wouldn't steal and fence her computer. He'd raid her panty drawer!

As Melissa walked down the hallway, she felt his eyes crawling over her body. She heard him comment to Jacqueline, "Nice firm tits on that one. I'd like to see the nipples. Every woman's nipples have personality.'

Even with her front door closed and bolted shut against the outside world, Jackie felt uneasy because the biggest threat, the insidious Little Johnson, was locked inside with her. Jackie did not wonder what personality her nipples had. She wondered if she was going to be able to carry out her plan or if her fury would cause her to beat up Little Johnson.

How she wished she had never met him. Wished she had kicked him unconscious with her boot in the snow Wednesday night and left him there.

"Look, you jerk, you better never pull a stunt like that again! That girl respects me. Or she did respect me. She's my neighbour! I have a career to think about! Whatever we have between us, you need to be discrete. I'm not your girlfriend!"

Little Johnson threw his black parka on the floor and moved through her apartment to the array of twisted goodies from the Jones file.

He turned back to her, one side of his mouth crooked into a smile, "No, you're not my girlfriend. You should be so lucky. You're my slut. You're one of my many sluts."

"I don't want friends, or neighbours, or family meeting you Little Johnson!"

"That makes no sense. How can you and I have a three way with Melissa if I don't meet her first?"

"Don't even think about it, asshole. Melissa is a nice girl. Trust me, she isn't interested in you."

"Don't be jealous, Jackie. You must learn to share Little Johnson. Wouldn't you like a companion to share in your new joys of submission, punishment, and obedience? A nice sexy friend to share your pains and delights?"

"No, sicko! She's a nice girl."

"Hmmm. A nice girl and a good girl. Seems like a matched set. You wearing your GOOD GIRL collar and she with her very own NICE GIRL collar. The three of us could be the Good, the Nice, and the Ugly. I think a leather collar dyed pink and covered in big rhinestones would look marvellous on her. What do you think? Picture it...."

God help her, Jackie pictured it for a fraction of a second. She envisioned Melissa down on her knees in Jackie's living room wearing nothing but a rhinestone-studded pink collar, waiting for orders, anxious to absorb punishment. The forbidden picture sent a blazing comet of lust crashing into her pussy.

"Leave her alone and try not to embarrass me again. By the way, if we ever do run into anyone, call me Jacqueline, not Jackie."

"Just be grateful I didn't reveal your real name, Fishy. I have another agenda for tonight, some quality educational time with my Slut-In-Training. You're still a bad girl. We need to work on that. I'm sure you want to live up to the Good Girl nameplate on your collar. Speaking of your collar, put it on. I'm sure you're anxious to have it back in place."

Little Johnson held the collar in one hand and the padlock in the other. Wetness and warmth filled her clenching vagina. This wasn't part of her plan. She needed him to move into the living room.

"Let's sit down and talk in the living room. Just for a few minutes. I just need to understand things better.'

Little Johnson continued to hold the padlock and collar out, "Sluts obey directions immediately and happily. Obedient sluts are sometimes rewarded with smart answers to their silly questions."

Jackie sighed, her heart heavy. Little Johnson obviously refused to take no for an answer. She took the heavy wide leather collar and padlock from Little Jackson, who calmly observed her wrap the collar around her neck, slip the padlock through the silver rings and secure it, and twist the collar until her name plate faced forward. Her breasts felt hot and heavy. Her nipples swelled, threatening to poke through the flimsy material of her bra. As she looked into Little Johnson's night-black eyes, she felt foreboding and offbeat eagerness.

Damn, she really was horny. Maybe she should have masturbated with her fingers or the huge dildo. Maybe she should have continuously masturbated over the past two days like she'd wanted. Masturbated until her body was sick and over the pain and pleasure. Like a smoker smoking non-stop to burn out their addiction. She realized she made a big mistake and it was too late now. In denying her needs, she kept herself primed and ready for the evil little man. She already felt her control slipping away.

"Good slut. By all means, let's go to the living room. I'll happily answer all your questions."

Jackie felt thankful he hadn't commanded her to drop down and give him head or commit some other obscene act. It wasn't part of her plan, but she would have submitted to play him along. She was also relieved to move to the living room, since Little Johnson already violated its sanctity. She didn't want to spread his infection to other rooms in the apartment.

As she turned to move to the living room, Little Johnson stopped her.

"Wait. Fishy, you must select one of the items from the desk to play with. Your choice."

Jackie studied the array of items, knowing she had to choose one. Which was the lesser of the evils? The huge hilted dildo she'd forgotten to clean. The silver rings used to pierce nipples and other places. A butt plug. A whip. A ball gag. A leather hood. Teflon cords. Two handcuffs. A wooden paddle. Her hand drifted over the items. Her pussy already dripped juice, apparently anticipating and preparing. What was wrong with her?

The leather hood seemed easy but she couldn't choose it. The last time she couldn't see – because she had stupidly followed his instructions – he recorded her climaxing violently. She couldn't risk yet another recording. Two were already two too many.

The ball gag wouldn't be hard or painful. But she couldn't choose it. What if he immediately ball-gagged her? She couldn't take that risk. She had to engage Little Johnson in conversation.

Teflon cords or two pair of handcuffs? She could not afford to be restrained and helpless around this demented little man. God knows what he would do if given complete free reign. Besides, her plan called for some freedom of movement.

The whip and the wooden paddle looked painful. She wondered

what they would feel like... but no way! She wasn't a masochist. It might assist her plan if Little Johnson used them, especially the whip, but she could not bear the thought. Her pussy released more warm wetness into her panties. Apparently, her pussy had no qualms about Little Johnson using the two instruments of pain against her.

What about the butt plug? Gross.

The silver rings were, of course, completely out of the question. The very thought made her nipples harden. Defensively she was sure.

That left her old friend the bizarre pronged dildo. She shivered when she realized it was her "logical" choice. The idea of the dildo revisiting her pussy, returning to the scene of the crime against her will, filled her with dread and anticipation. She knew the dildo itself would fill her far fuller.

She hefted the huge thing in her slim hand, "Little Johnson, I need to wash it first."

"No. What's the point? You're just going to get come all over it anyway. That's your choice. Now I'll make my own choices."

Little Johnson grabbed both of the handcuffs, the ball gag, and the coiled whip. He obviously knew exactly which items he wanted and probably had a clear picture of how he would use each one. Jackie felt a pulse of terror ripple through her when she saw him uncoil the whip. She had to stop this!

"You told me to choose one and I did."

"Yes, and then it's my turn. We have to be fair."

"But I only got one and you got three. It isn't fair!"

"I see your point. Go ahead and select two more."

She clamped her mouth shut in frustration. His black eyes and blacker soul snickered at her. Helpless, knowing he would outmanoeuvre her every time she argued with him, she gave up. Her shoulders drooped, and she trudged to the living room with Little Johnson following like a sheep dog. She was the sheep waiting to be sheered by its owner, perpetually herded and bossed by the barking sheep dog. Her only hope was her plan. She had to successfully execute it, no matter what. But she knew she would pay a severe price before emerging from this mess. When Little Johnson grabbed up those handcuffs, she realized she'd have to do this the hard way whether or not her plan worked. She'd have to do it the real hard way judging by the leather whip.

CHAPTER 11

In the living room she sat on the sofa. She felt so dirty sitting on it. Especially since she remembered what she'd done and what had been done to her on that sofa. She felt especially dirty since she was holding the unclean dildo in one hand.

Well, she better start asking her questions before he shoved that ball-gag in her mouth....

Little Johnson was standing in the middle of the room swinging the uncoiled whip like some kind of leather pendulum. He held the handle over his head so the whip tip barely grazed the living room carpet when it swung to its lowest point.

"Can you tell me what your plans are and where all this is going?"

"I can." He continued to swing the whip, watching it and not her. He was obviously trying to get her to focus on it to get her scared. She knew he'd never use it in her. That would definitely be going too far and even he must know that.

"You're blackmailing me, right? Forcing me because you have that video. Or videos. I don't even know if it is one or two. You're using them to blackmail me."

"No one is forcing you to do anything. You are finding your true calling and you love it. I am just helping you get what you want."

"Come on, Little Johnson, let's put the cards on the table and be honest. You are blackmailing me. If I don't do as you say you're going to put that video on the internet and you'll ruin my career. Just be honest. I need to know clearly what is at stake, that I have to do this, or I won't. Because I am not willing to have sex with you and I am not willing to let you hurt me. I will not do anything if I don't have to. If you just give me those videos I'll never want to see you again."

"I told you, Fishy, we only do the things you really want to have done. You've been living a lie. You're not a career woman. Few women truly are. You're a slut in need of use and abuse. I'm happy to help."

"But you're blackmailing me, right?"

"No."

Jackie was frustrated. She felt like crying. Why wouldn't he say it? Did he suspect?

Little Johnson continued, "The other night when we 'fulfilled each other's needs' as they'd say in the romances, how many orgasms did you have?"

Jackie was silent.

"You're not answering because you don't even know. You came so many times who had a chance of keeping count? What about the quality? Have you ever had that quality of orgasm before? Don't lie; I'll know if you do, because I already know the true answer."

Jackie was disheartened. He wasn't being fair again. He wouldn't give her straight answers but he was requiring her to provide one. And he was going to make her talk about and recognize her own enjoyment of the defiling two nights ago. This was the last thing she wanted because of the embarrassment, because she did not want to look herself in her own moral mirror, and because it was partially defeating her hidden plan. She'd better keep her mouth shut.

"I bet when you've had sex in the past it was always on your terms. The time, the location, the person, even the details of what sexual acts were allowed. I'd suspect not much of a spectrum and a very low frequency."

Jackie blushed. This was ridiculous. She'd heard of women ashamed of having too many sexual partners but he was actually making her feel deficient for having so few.

"All those times you were in control and limited and arranged what happened. You probably had few orgasms and never powerful ones. When I watched you that first night getting intimate with that dildo you're holding, I saw you lose control. You lost control and you enjoyed yourself. That was probably the best orgasm of your life up to that point. You went from control to loss of control. That was a big improvement. But on Wednesday you improved your improvement. That was all thanks to little old Little Johnson. Wednesday, you entered the world of giving control to someone else. Following someone else's orders and letting them lead you. How did that turn out? No doubt it was the best night of sex in your entire life. I didn't even fuck you though you would have loved it if I had."

Jackie felt she had to say something to derail him, "No! None of that is true."

"Was Wednesday the best night of sex you've ever had?"

"No, it was awful. I hated it. I only did those things because you forced me."

"There was no force, slut, other than the force of your lust. Go ahead, tell me in detail about sex you ever had that was better than that."

Jackie opened her mouth but no words came out. Her mind looked around for anything, any memory near as hot as the other night. She thought of many romantic interludes but had to discard every one as not even a faint shadow of what happened Wednesday. She knew her mouth was working open and closed like a sick fish washed up on a beach. There was nothing that she could say to deny that would not be a lie. He would know. More importantly, she would know.

With awareness that she'd enjoyed what he had done to her and what she did for him she felt a horrifying burst of self-realization.

"I gave you the best sex of your life. You probably can't even conceive of ever matching it. You'll more than match that. I'll take you far beyond that."

Even just contemplating the actions of the other night released a shudder of lust and her juices flowed freely, nipples hardly almost painfully now, and her breasts felt swollen, too heavy for her bra. Anticipating the possibilities of the current night, especially Little Johnson's threat/promise of taking her "far beyond", sent a vicious spike of need into the core of her sex.

Jackie's eyes followed the swing of the whip back and forth. She shouldn't look at it. She needed to focus on her plan. Watching the whip, though, it was only natural for her to envision it flashing down to strike vulnerable areas of her body. It should scare her and it did. It should horrify her and it did. It should not turn her on and it did.

When she tore her eyes from the whip and looked up Little Johnson's dark eyes were studying her, "I've answered your question, we both know it. Everything that has happened and will happen you desperately want. As we move along it is my job to culture your want into need. Further questions and answers you must earn, Fishy. Kneel, knees as far apart as you can, and put that beast back to work up your cunt."

Jackie moved to the centre of the living room and dropped to her knees to the section of floor he pointed at. Her plan wasn't going at all well. She shifted her knees as far apart as possible. She wore a loose belted robe and a matching panty and bra set so clothing didn't limit her ability to stretch her knees apart and comply. The rough carpet scraped and burned her knees.

She had to draw Little Johnson out with more conversation. She needed as much information as possible. He expected her to follow orders at the moment and would crush any attempt to keep chatting. But she hoped if she followed a few commands it would lull him and he may respond to questions then without thinking she was defying him.

"Show your little Fisherman what you have for him."

It was intimidating to have Little Johnson swinging that whip around while she slipped the silk robe off her shoulders and dropped it to the floor behind her. She pulled her forest green panties to one side, hoping Little Johnson would not notice the much darker green spread over the crotch area that completely gave away her horniness.

Looking up at him she knew he saw. The coloured puffiness of her labia lips, the dew pressing down her revealed pubic bush, and her thick scent of sexual readiness all gave her away anyway, she thought forlornly. Her own scent was even turning her on. There was nowhere to run, nowhere to hide.

He better not try to use that whip on me or I will stand back up and kick his ass, she thought resentfully. She knew the little man would have no chance against her if she decided to beat him up. She'd already done it once. She'd shown him far too much mercy in the snow outside her apartment window. A dangerous amount of mercy, she now knew.

Jackie angled the massive head of the dildo to the entrance of her sex and realized she would not need to prepare herself to accept the monster into her vagina. She was so wet even this monster was going to slide right in if she gave it enough force. She was such a slut! She'd no idea she could get so wet so quickly with no contact.

Jackie realized she better speak now before the pleasures induced by the dildo

led her too far away from the plan.

"Please, you said you would answer my questions. What is this all about? What is the full plan? I need to know all of it. Tell me everything and I'll cooperate fully. You work for Wayne Jones. Why and what is your mission? Who all is involved?"

"So many questions asked all at once suggest you ask them because you feel you should but that you don't even expect me to answer. You're much more interested in tonight's upcoming events. I will answer them all just to keep you waiting. I'll tell you because I want to not because we seek your cooperation. We already have that though you don't even know it."

Little Johnson tossed the ball-gag and two sets of handcuffs to the carpet in front of her. She looked at them and felt a thrill of fear in her tummy.

"First of all, I do not work for Wayne Jones. I serve him as an admirer, a student, an assistant. I am not paid monetarily though he repays my loyalty many times over. You have also joined Jones' service though in a role suited to your nature; submission slut and pain whore. You have barely begun your endless journey," Little Johnson gestured with the whip handle towards items on the carpet before her, "We were kind enough to help you pack for your journey. Out of kindheartedness I've agreed to help you attune to a selfless loving state of pain-filled slutty service to Jones. That is your own heart's most secret but fondest wish."

Jackie thought Little Johnson's demented perspective was intriguing, though only from a professional standpoint. Was that story something those female followers swallowed? It was amazing to her that some women could be into that kind of thing. They found it arousing to give up everything good, accept everything bad done to them, and get nothing in return. How could that be... such a turn on?

"What are you doing? Don't shove that plastic cock in your cunt yet!"

Jackie was surprised she had managed to slip the massive head of the dildo into her vagina without even noticing she was doing it. It felt good, like a perfect fit! Reluctantly, and with difficulty, she pulled the head back out.

"Never take independent actions," he chuckled, "unless I order you to do them."

Jackie looked again at the ball-gag and two handcuffs. That was good. He hadn't ordered her to put them on. She could just let them lay there. She felt a totally inappropriate gratitude all she had to do was follow his orders. It made a lot of things easier though it did nothing for her plan.

"Take things in proper order. First, insert and secure the ball gag. Second, cram your dildo lover where you know he belongs. Third, I'll tell you what to do with the cuffs when we get there."

No way could she put that ball gag in her mouth and throw those handcuffs on. She could not allow herself to do that! She needed to carry out her plan. Those items would render her unable to ask questions and unable to defend herself. Besides her desperately weakened plan, what if he did decide to whip her? The idea was zany. Obviously the whip was a prop just there to make a psychological impact. A symbol meant to instil fear in her. The whip must also serve as a flag for his delusions to rally around. Still, he'd spanked her the other night and he was a pervert. What if he had the idea women could be whipped? She picked up the ball gag and looked up at Little Johnson, hating that her eyes were pleading with him instead of telling him to forget about it. She didn't speak. It was like she was already gagged.

"Go ahead; shove that in your mouth. I'll keep talking. Trust me; I will satisfy your curiosity before I satisfy other parts of you. Ball gag first and be sure to strap it tight at the back. Then slide that plastic cock completely up your cunt. Finally, you will experience the handcuffs. Do it now."

One look at Little Johnson's mean little eyes and she knew she'd have to do as he said if she wanted him to continue confessing his and Jones' twisted plots.

The "ball-gag" wasn't really a ball at all. The mouth insert was shaped more like a rubber cone with a rounded outer end that stuck of the mouth like one half of a ball. However, when inserted it completely filled her mouth, stretching cheeks and jaw nearly as wide as the dildo could her pussy. The end of the mouth insert tickled the top of her throat. The feeling was nearly claustrophobic but Jackie toughed it out as she attached the double set of hooked leather straps at the back of her skull.

Seeing she was following his instructions, Little Johnson continued to unfurl information, "Wayne Jones is not insane. You must already know this or will soon accept it. Like many brilliant men who are advanced beyond their time he is misunderstood. He brings gifts of understanding some perceive instead as attacks. A man like Jones does not belong incarcerated. He must be free to move about, to test his brilliant theories, and spread the news of discovery. He is like a modern-day Galileo with the leaders of this community like the church in the dark ages."

Now that the gag was strapped in place, her cheeks bulging around the leather straps, Jackie's hands returned to the monstrous dildo and moved it to her percolating pussy. With lusty determination she got the dildo head past her stretched labia and then forced it all the way up her welcoming sex. It was uncomfortable because the head was pushing harshly at the end of her channel. She felt skewered. It was too huge but still felt like it belonged cooking in her personal oven. At the base of the shaft, just before the hilt, she noted it widened and then narrowed precipitously. This allowed her to clench her pussy walls around it and easily keep it inside her pussy even if her hands did not hold the handle. She guessed this was going to come in handy once she was handcuffed. The pleasures and discomforts, mental and physical, were making her eyes water and blink.

Little Johnson watched her struggle with insertion and her resulting victory/defeat with beady-eyed fascination. He abruptly laughed, "You currently have Jones' version of Galileo's telescope up your cunt, Fishy."

He sobered and ordered her to move on to the handcuffs. Filled with dread but unable to escape this evening's events Jackie picked up the sets of handcuffs and frowned in confusion. She was resigned to wearing them but didn't know what he wanted, why there were two pairs of handcuffs. She looked up at Little Johnson for 'help' but he was momentarily lost delivering more of his evil monologue.

"The incarceration of Wayne Jones is an error. Actually, it was an intentional wrong. You will help correct the wrong. That will be very noble of you." Little Johnson sneered at the comment, "All that is needed is your clear-minded objective report Jones is no danger to himself or others. He isn't. In fact, many women now completely depend on him so his imprisonment is harming them as well."

Little Johnson noticed the handcuffs were unlocked and dangling from her open fingers, "Fishy, you're out of your depths aren't you? You obviously have no idea why there are two. Here's what you do; Lock a cuff of one on one wrist and lock a cuff of the other on the other wrist. Then lean back and reach down to your skinny ankles.

The remaining open cuffs belong locked around those ankles. Won't that be lovely?"

Jackie paused, digesting the instructions, and picturing how she would look once she was fully cuffed. She pictured herself a long time then snapped out of it and moments later snapped the cuffs on each wrist. The left cuff she tightened too far and it squeezed her wrist bone painfully. She discovered the cuffs could be tightened, but, once clicked further, could not be taken back without a key. She sincerely hoped Little Johnson did have a key. She arched her body back, her stomach tightening flat, her thighs and shoulders straining to bring the remaining open cuffs back to her ankles. She felt clumsy and vulnerable. Her ankles were slim but much thicker than her wrists so she only had to tighten each cuff a couple clicks.

"You are the last piece to the puzzle. It takes the recommendation of three accredited Psychologists. The first two ladies have already submitted signed and notarized reports endorsing Jones' release. Carol Milligan and Shara Tillings were so helpful they wanted to do even more for Mr. Jones. Besides submitting those reports they also submitted themselves. They travelled the same path you are travelling down. They were given the knowledge of their need to submit, need for a Master, lust for pain, and delight in humiliation. So much so that once they completed their usefulness to enable Jones' ultimate release they volunteered and Jones allowed them to join him in Goethner-Varner. They are committed and cannot affect their own releases. They have handed over the keys to their lives to Jones. They are in the same ward as Jones in order to help fulfil his whims. They wanted to show support by enduring imprisonment with him. In fact, they won't be released until he is, if then. That will be up to Mr. Jones."

Jackie tested the strength of the cuffs. They were solidly in place; the thick chain between them was just a few links and allowed very little movement. She marvelled to be in this predicament, that she secured the cuffs with her own hands. She had fallen for the promise of revelation. But knowledge was not the only lure in the water. There were the lures of compliance, bondage, arousal, and threatened pain. With so many lures it was obvious to anyone but Jackie that she would fall for the bait.

"You see, Jones' brilliance is recognized by nearly everyone who meets him. As a result, he practically runs Goethner-Varner now.

It's his private wonderland. He's enjoyed his retreat but wants his freedom returned. More than that, he wants revenge. You're going to help. That's why you're a "Good Girl". We'll see to it that you sacrifice your freedom in order to give Jones his. Not by force or blackmail but only through your own free will. We have standards, we don't cheat."

Jackie already felt like she no longer had freedom. The handcuffs / leg shackles were making her feel incredibly imprisoned. She felt so helpless. She sweated anxiously and her pussy juices ran. Her position was muscle-straining and her ankle bones ground against the unforgiving metal of the cuffs. She needed for something to happen. She either had to escape this horrible discomfort or she needed hard sex, one or the other. She couldn't stand it if she didn't get one soon.

Little Johnson narrowed her eyes and studied her up and down as if he was trying to memorize her in every detail. He just stood there patiently watching. He was waiting for something.

The dildo planted deep in her and gripped in place by her slick labial lips kept her on edge sexually. It was just up her at rest. She needed it thrusting in and out, the harder the better. She had a hard time concentrating on Little Johnson's unfolding of the evil plot and a more difficult time adding up its consequences for her. It all sounde bizarre, far-fetched, and demented. But... it did not sound like a lie....

Little Johnson set the whip on the coffee table. Good, she'd known he wouldn't be crazy enough to use that thing on her. Little Johnson took off all his clothes though he was still cloaked in his thick pelt of body hair. Once nude he picked up the whip again. Oh no.

Little Johnson stepped over to stand before her with his semi-erect penis only half a foot from her gagged mouth. Already her mouth felt sore from the gag, especially the stretched corners of her lips. One more discomfort added to the list. Still, she was grateful for the gag since it meant he couldn't shove his dick in her mouth. But it did force her to breathe through her nose. She wasn't sure if he'd even showered since his last visit. He smelled then and smelled worse now.

As Little Johnson dangled his smelly equipment inches from her face she did a mental checklist of her status. It wasn't good. Her mouth and pussy were both sore from succeeding in accommodating overly large objects. Her legs hurt and trembled from supporting her weight while spread so wide. Her knees also hurt from the carpet fabric digging into them.

Jackie had a stomach-sinking downhill roller coaster feeling all of a sudden when she thought these pains were as nothing compared to what Little Johnson looked like he would inflict. How had she gotten herself into this situation? She marvelled at it. She felt sure this must be the worst moment of her life. For some reason her dripping pussy and hard-tipped swollen breasts disagreed with her. This really was new and very exciting to them. She felt outnumbered even just within herself.

Little Johnson let the suspense build and made sure her widened nostrils sucked in his scent before he spoke, "What I do to you tonight you will remember for the rest of your life. It will change you. After this, vanilla sex will never serve to even partially fulfil you."

He reached down to the hilted handle of the huge dildo in her. Galileo's telescope, she suddenly remembered. His little fingers were immediately slippery as they fumbled around the handle. The slight bumps caused echoing ripples of pleasure in her. On the side of the slick handle he managed to nudge the flat switch one notch forward. A humming erupted from her crotch and vibration rolled outward from the wide cylinder.

"Mmmm... mmmm... Hmmm... mmmm... Mmmmmm!" Jackie did not know if she was trying to protest or just release some of the power of the tremendous sensations. It may have been the vibration itself manipulating her throat muscles. Her gag kept the noise under control. Without the gag she might be screaming.

Little Johnson found the desperate breathless noises as soothing and enjoyable as always.

He stepped back and watched Jackie redden, not just her face but all over. She still wore the forest green matched bra and panty set so the overall image reminded him of Christmas. He felt like a kid on Christmas morning.

Jackie's hips thrust and danced in little circles. It was impossible to tell if she was trying to shake the dildo out or if she was trying to screw it. Probably both. In moments her thighs shined with pussy juice. Those forest green panties just couldn't suck it all up.

Sometimes Jackie's eyes darted around as if looking for an avenue of escape or watching for the arrival of a rescuing knight in shining armour. More often she was blinking and her eyes were unable to focus on anything.

The more sexual anxiety the women felt the more relaxed he was. Little Johnson delighted in viewing Jackie trying to cope with all of that lovely sensation. Long minutes stretched and he knew each of his minutes felt like an hour to Jackie. She was in a state of continuous orgasm. He knew she could not manage her pleasure any more. He had seen quite a few women broken on this particular rock. Carol Milligan and Shara Tillings included. Damn, Psychoanalyst chicks were hot bitches! Breaking them was fast becoming his specialty.

"Mmmm... mmmm... Hmmm... mmmm... Mmmmmm!"

The Thorpe woman was a fine specimen. She put on quite a show. Little Johnson felt like watching her for hours. The giant vibrating dildo would show her again she was helpless to control her pleasure. That lesson's first class was the other night. She'd already been taught that lesson once though he doubted she took it to heart. She needed to enrol in another class tonight.

Little Johnson approached her again. He turned the massive tube until the curved upward side of the hilt lined up with Jackie's anus. She squealed in protest or increased sensation as he pressured it up her back passage. Once it was deep and secure he pulled his little paw away, wiping it on her left bra covered breast. He liked that she hadn't tried to move her legs or leave her ordered position. She verbally protested with muffled damsel in distress sounds but she had not actually resisted. She was marching down the path he intended for her quite nicely. She was a good little soldier. Little Johnson giggled. This army had a lifetime enlistment.

He stepped behind her. He took time to admire her lovely back and twitching ass cheeks. He unsnapped her bra and tossed it to the floor. He wanted to see her tits, but, just as importantly, did not want the straps to get in his way. He reached down and pulled her panties viciously up her ass crack. The panty was to one side of the dildo but it did stretch across the portion up her ass. Pulling up the panties humiliated her further, kept the anal intruding section of the dildo firmly up her ass, and revealed the slim perfectly rounded globes of her sexy ass cheeks. He saw they blurred slightly at the edges due to the heavy vibrations travelling to them from the dildo. Little muscles in each ass cheek randomly spasmed ass nerves fired in confusion.

Giving Jackie that wedgie also meant the panties would no longer provide even minimal protection to that adorable ass.

He stepped back and braced himself to begin, taking one last look to drink in the scene.

"Mmmm... mmmm... Hmmm... mmmm... Mmmmmm!"

Little Johnson's cock was hard as could be now that the crucial moment was arriving. That beautiful unblemished back! That narrow incredibly pale ass! He was looking forward to this.

From behind and to her left he brought the whip up plotting a path to obtain the maximum impact area.

*****

Jackie was so lost in sensation she had no idea what was about to happen. Even without active thrusting, the intensely vibrating dildo sent radiant spirals of ecstatic pleasure in waves through her body to pool in her mind.

Within the continuous orgasm she just began a massive orgasm when the striking whip wrapped around her waist across her back from hip to hip. Her orgasm was so profound the horrendous pain was actually a secondary sensation. The pain was too late to dam the orgasm. Instead of stopping it the pain joined it and magnified its force.

*****

Little Johnson had timed it perfectly. He enjoyed the moment as she doubly shook with the orgasm and the shock of pain. He noted the pleasing red stripe across her lower back. It was the first brush stroke in the masterpiece he planned to paint. Jackie was making nearly the same moans and groans as before but it was as if the volume was now turned up to maximum.

If her mouth was free Little Johnson knew Jackie would be yelling loud enough to wake the entire apartment complex. She hadn't learned yet to deal with pain, to enjoy it. She would. He was here to help.

Little Johnson brought the whip down again, this time lower. A woman's rear really was ideal for absorbing punishment. Lovely padding but still extremely sensitive, a secret area few ever see, and just on the other side of the central sexual erogenous zones. Sometimes Little Johnson thought a woman's ass was designed more for abuse than anything else. The whip scored across the middle of both ass cheeks.

*****

Jackie was trying to make sense of all the intensity. So good, so awful. She struggled to figure what was happening. The pain struck across her ass three more times all the pain combining and adding together. Her pussy was blazing with pleasure as the dildo mindlessly buzzed. It was dragging her down to her own state of mindlessness. Too much pain, too much pleasure.

Jackie wanted to scream but couldn't. Jackie wanted to orgasm again... and could. She came again simultaneous with a fifth stroke of fire across her shoulder blades.

More pain. More pain! Jackie finally twisted her head and looked behind her. There was Little Johnson with whip in hand. He was whipping her! Even as she looked she saw it come down again so fast her eyes could not trace its path. The pain from it traced another path across the top of each side of her horribly pain-filled ass cheeks.

Jackie turned away as the whip rose again and tried to bring her knees closer together. The whip struck, the pain slashed, she heard a high-pitched squeal that must have come from her throat. Weak-kneed from the orgasms, she was barely able to get her knees together as the whip scored again. She wondered if she was bleeding. She wondered if she would be scarred.

Not knowing where she could go with her hands cuffed to her ankles and with no exact destination in mind, she tried to walk forward on her knees. She felt no carpet burn pain in the knees. The pain from the whipping put her well beyond the ability to sense such minor pain.

As she shuffled the whip struck again and again and she knew Little Johnson was easily keeping pace with her. There could be no escape. He had her right where he wanted her and she knew he must be enjoying her silly escape attempt. All she was doing was entertaining the little bastard. That made her want to stop her hopeless escape just to defy him but holding still for a whipping was a pitiful form of defiance.

She wanted to escape the pain but it wasn't as simple as that. She wanted to escape the pleasure. The strange vibrating dildo was lapping unreal pleasures from her swollen slippery labia lips, up into her womb, and all through her entire body. The anal prod was vibrating a lot of sensation back there as well. The pain was awful but the pleasure was really too much. The two in combination were the perfect tag team. She had about as much chance of defeating them as an actual wrestling tag team.

They were combining to become a force much greater than the sum of its parts. Physically, she was at both ends of the spectrum, ecstatic pleasure and hellish pain. The pain and pleasure reached past her physical form and seemed to poke a hole in her will, in her soul. It was like air running out of an inflatable beach toy.

With every second of mind-bending pleasure and every wicked strike of the whip she felt less like a person and more like just a bundle of nerve-endings lusting for extreme sensation.

Jackie came again or her non-stop orgasm crested particularly high for long seconds and, at the end of it, she fell forward her cheek resting on the carpet. The striking whip never slowed. The new position stretched the skin on her ass and made her even more vulnerable.

The whip came again and she came again. When the whip struck again she had not finished coming and a new orgasm struck overlapping and joining the first. This continued strike after strike, orgasm after orgasm. It was the whip and waves of pain that were making her orgasm, not the powerful dildo.

*****

At some point, Jackie realized the whip strokes ceased. She didn't notice immediately because the pain and orgasms continued. Every several seconds, face still in the carpet, her ass would shake and pump and she would come yet again. Distantly, she noticed that at the peak of each come she was consistently levering her butt several inches higher in the air as if it was seeking the next strike of the whip.

The whip blows were over but the waves of pain from the whip's work continued. That was what caused the ongoing orgasms though the dildo continued buzzing angrily. Jackie knew that for certain when Little Johnson's pawing fingers shut off the dildo. The orgasms did not stop.

Over minutes as the whipping pain simmered down the orgasms slowed, diminished, and finally stopped. Jackie's field of awareness began to cautiously expand outward from the bounds of her own skin.

Jackie could Little Johnson's nearness, sense his enjoyment of her present state, and could maybe smell his lust. She was relieved the worst of the pain was over. She was relieved the best of the orgasms were over. Or was it the other way around? And did she miss them a little?

Only now that she was recovering from it did Jackie understand that she'd been in some kind of alternate state. For an unknown number of minutes he'd been in a state beyond thought, beyond fear, and even beyond any sense of self-preservation. These abilities were slowly returning. She was evolving from a pure sensation-based animal back into a human being, attempting to crawl out of the water and up onto shore.

"Look at me, Fishy."

He was behind her to the right instead of to the left as when he whipped her. Jackie looked over her shoulder and saw all of nakedly aroused Little Johnson other than his face which was obscured by the digital camera he held up to one eye.

"Hold still while looking straight at the camera."

She didn't know why she did as she was told but knew she could not have done otherwise.

"Stick your ass out as far as you can. Lift your chin higher so your shoulder doesn't block that sexy gag."

She did it. She didn't know why.

"Good girl."

Against all odds the patronizing moniker gave Jackie a pulse of pleasure. In that moment she was startlingly proud not just of her perfect pose and perfect compliance but also of the livid striped she accurately envisioned on her rear. All of her reasons for pride were like symptoms of a disease. The actual disease was that she was happy she pleased and was continuing to please Little Johnson. Oddly, his pleasure seemed worth the price of severe suffering.

Little Johnson took the photo and she wondered if her thoughts could be seen swirling in the blue pools of her eyes. She felt more naked than ever before. No, not naked. More nude.

He approached and removed the ball gag. She gasped and sputtered, splashes of pent up saliva sliding over her chin, dripping onto her swollen breasts. She wished her hands were free to wipe off the saliva. Somehow, she could still be embarrassed in front of this man. Even as the thought occurred he undid the handcuffs and her sore arms fell to her sides, blood rushed back to her feet whose circulation had suffered constriction.

"Stand up, hands on your hips. Look over your shoulder again and, this time, give the camera a huge sexy grin of happiness."

She did as he instructed. It felt weird to be smiling after all that happened. Weird, but it did not feel like a complete lie. It felt surreal to pose around for Little Johnson wearing only wet panties twisted to one side and the monster dildo inserted in her pussy still sliding around with each movement. It was even weirder to be following Little Johnson's every direction as if it was gospel.

She was doing more than following them. She was actually looking forward to each command with a subversive will to complete them to the best of her ability. It wasn't enough to just do as he commanded. She wanted to excel at it. She was curious, almost eager, to learn what he would have her do next. The logical part of her knew cooperating with Little Johnson could not help her cause, would only mire her deeper in the foul mud. Unfortunately, the logical part of her no longer had a vote.

She grinned and looked straight into the camera as he took several more shots from slightly differing angles. In the last one he told her to pull one ass cheek out to the side while using her other hand to pull up hard on the rear waistband of her panties. In effect, he ordered her to give herself a wedgie and she did it.

Her hand squeezing and pulling her wounded right ass cheek released a new stab of pain as well as a flash of arousal. That and the photo in her mind of what he was having her do to herself and for him. She realized this wasn't all for him, though. She reminded herself that everything done was really at the behest of Wayne Jones. Little Johnson was a servant serving Jones. Chauffeurs drove cars, maids dusted, Little Johnson was a talent scout, a trainer, an obstacle remover.

"Fishy the slut, get those sorry panties off and pull that wacky plastic cock out."

She followed his orders, and then stood there, holding the dripping dildo and awaiting further instruction. She looked forward to it. She felt eager and beyond questioning any directions he gave. She knew he would make her do something she shouldn't want to do and she knew whatever it was, she would want to do it. It was insane.

Slut! Dildo-humper! Pain-craver!"

The verbal abuse seemed to soak right through her skin, becoming part of her, part of how she viewed herself.

"It's time to put the dildo away. You must clean it first. Lick it all clean. You wouldn't want your cunt juice to rust it, would you? Lick it all up."

Jackie went to work with a purpose. She was surprised she didn't try to deny, delay, or protest. She had an order from someone she now somehow recognized had the right to give her orders. The best time to follow an order was immediately.

Her tongue swept up and down the sides of the shaft. It was so big and the batteries made it a heavy burden. She found it hard to believe it was inside her just moments ago. She saw Little Johnson was taking more photos and she did her best to ham it up with sultry eyes and nibbling lips. Even she couldn't buy that she was just trying to lull him into a false sense of security. As she displayed wanton passion she really felt it. Like smiling caused people to feel like smiling.

The taste of her feminine essences was wildly exciting. It was such a nasty and embarrassing act. The shameless act of licking them off conversely filled her with shame and a white hot brand of arousal radiating in the depths of her womanhood. She was such a Bad Girl for doing such a bad thing but she knew she was a Good Girl for doing it so good.

Her logical mind had no vote but still had a voice. It was appalled by everything. Her mind even protested the illogic of Little

Johnson's statement. A plastic cock could not rust! Even the copper strips wrapping around it like red on a candy cane could not rust! If it could rust, replacing the pussy juice with spit wouldn't have done any good.

What was Little Johnson going to do with those photos? Give them to Jones? Post them on the Internet for thousands of perverts and possibly her friends and family members to view?

These logical arguments and reasonable concerns were counterproductive. It turned her on that Little Johnson was treating her like an idiot. It turned her on that, as she pictured herself and imagined their reaction, that Jones, strangers, and even people she knew and respected might see her like this.

Would Little Johnson tell her to shove the dildo back up her pussy when she was done licking it clean? Damn! He wouldn't. That would defeat the purpose of licking it clean in the first place. Maybe she could offer to lick it clean again if he let her use it to come one more time.

No. She knew he didn't want her to speak. Just to follow orders. He'll tell me when he wants me to talk and he'll probably tell me what to say. She kept licking for long minutes trying to recover every molecule of pussy juice.

"You've done a good job on that thing. I think if it was a real cock it would have come by now. Just as well it didn't. Thing is so huge if it was real, had a matching set of balls, and you did make it come you might drown."

The ugly little bastard laughed and Jackie felt hurt. Little Johnson could hurt her both externally and internally apparently at will. He could just joke and giggle while she was covered in whip wounds and was working so hard to do a good job cleaning the dildo. Jackie mentally shook her head while keeping her lips and tongue all over up and down the dildo. Her thought process seemed all wrong but she didn't know how to fix it.

"Tell you what. You'll give me the same kind of blow job you're giving monster there. Just all lips and lip nibbles, tongue flutters, no deep-throating. No tonsil-boxing this time. When I come, pull back a little so it goes all over your face."

As he stepped forward Jackie went to her sore knees. She saw he still had the digital camera now held secure by its strap twisted around his right wrist. She supposed he would end up taking more photos. She was fatalistic. Like an Old West Native American who believed photographs stole souls, at the moment she saw no difference between one embarrassing humiliating possibly career-ruining photo or twenty of them. The first one had already plucked her soul. It was all the same.

Jackie noted that even kneeling she actually had to lean down to get her mouth to work on the standing half-Dwarf's perfectly erect cock. Like the other night it was a strange purple hue. She felt lust in the pit of her stomach, renewed flow in her pussy, and was filled with passionate purpose. Make the cock of the semi-man who'd whipped her so horrifically come all over her face. It wasn't just a goal, it was the goal.

She fluttered her tongue all over it, dappled it with wet-lipped kisses, sucked the sides, and then stroked the flat of her tongue firmly across the wide head. Her left hand gripped the base of the cock tightly and jerked it towards her rhythmically. Blood entered the cock through the central arteries but her insistent grip made it more difficult for the blood to retreat back into Little Johnson's body. Her right hand got her fingers into position to jiggle in and out of her pussy with each of her tongue strokes in either direction on the cock. She continuously raked the side of her index finger against her still hard clitoris.

The nastiness of the situation and the picture it presented in her own mind did as much to turn her on as her own fingers. The continual pain from her back and backside magnified her lust. She wondered why Little Johnson didn't just fuck her. She obviously wouldn't put up any resistance to the idea. She actually wished he would fuck her. She felt like asking him to do it. She thought she may as well try.

Jackie pulled her lips away from his cock, looked up at him and asked politely, "Would you like to fuck me?"

"Get your mouth back on my dick, slut! If I wanted to fuck you, believe me, I would. You'd love it too. No, you won't get a real screw from a real cock until you've earned it. The good news is I'll help you earn it and eventually you'll get all the dick you need and more than you can handle. Right now, focus on the job at hand, the dick in your hand. Suck and lick it and make it come all over your slutty face. Be a Good Girl, Fishy!"

Jackie actually felt hurt by his rejection. She'd offered him all she had to give and the little man turned her down. Jackie felt a renewed swarm of buzzing pleasure in her pussy even as she felt embarrassment and outrage. She tried to understand her feelings as she sucked one side of his cock and her left hand squeezed the base harder. Somehow the fact Little Johnson rejected her most personal offer contradictorily made him all the more worthy to receive all she had to give. She had no place wanting him but he was perfectly manipulating her to want more and more the exact opposite of all things she should want not want.

She yearned to prove herself worthy by giving him all the pleasure she could. She would take joy in his enjoyment. His satisfaction was more important than her satisfaction. Without thought, directed by instinct, her right hand abandoned her self-pleasuring and moved up, slick with her juice, to now cup both his small tight testicles, cupping them through the elephant-hide of his scrotum.

She sensed the more she massaged them, the more pleasure he felt, the more semen he would eventually shoot all over her face, all over her. She wanted to drown in it.

Her fingers and legs trembled and he was shaking a little himself. When she heard a noise her lips and tongue and both hands kept working but she glanced up with her eyes. She saw him fumble with the digital camera. He was rushing like he wasn't going to be able to hold out much longer and wanted to get some shots before he was too distracted during orgasm or too tired after. She did nothing to escape as he took a triplet of photos. None of them would change her overall circumstance or impact her plan anyway but Jackie wasn't thinking about that. She was only thinking about how hot those photos must be and how important it was to provide Little Johnson with a fantastic orgasm.

Little Johnson groaned heavily and he nearly dropped the camera as she felt his cock expand slightly in the moment before orgasm. She was so hot she was having difficulty thinking but she pulled her face back until she thought it made a nice target about a foot from his cockhead. She made sure to keep her fingers locked tight around the base of it. A girl at college once commented to her that constriction on the cock made the man's come shoot out faster and further. At the time, she'd thought it a disgusting factoid. Now Jackie wanted to see if it was true.

Little Johnson's groan deepened and a pulse of sperm struck her forehead just above her left eyebrow, sperm drops fanning and disappearing into her blonde hairline. She flinched as she thought that he might shoot into her open eyes. She stayed in position like a slut trooper. The next pulse of sperm struck her upper lip and ran down on either side of her mouth giving her a momentary Fu Manchu.

"Take it come-hungry bitch! I bet you wish you were swallowing it!"

Jackie found she was wishing that as four more major pulses of sperm splattered on various targets of opportunity across her face, the last one hitting her left ear. The constriction trick seemed to be a true story though she couldn't be sure without knowing his normal performance level. She wanted to open her mouth to catch a sperm stream but knew that was not part of the instructions. She must follow instructions. Mostly because it just felt so right for her. Disobeying Little Johnson now seemed almost unthinkable.

"Let go of my cock and balls. You've been a Good Girl, Fishy. Now, let's help you out. Lay on your back on the carpet, legs spread, keep your hands on the carpet at all times, and grind your ass into the carpet until you come."

Jackie was confused, "I'll do anything you want but... my ass is so sore and I won't be able to orgasm like that."

"Do it, slut! I know what's best for you, not you. It's simple, now and always. All you have to do is follow orders. You have it easy."

Jackie didn't feel like she had it easy as she moved her flaming ass into contact with the rough carpet fibre. She was in a crab-walk position with her tenderized rear scraping in little circles on the tough carpet. She wished she had vacuumed that week.

The acid pain from the whip strikes had receded to a volcanic throbbing but the fresh friction brought all the pain back as if the whip strikes had just happened. The pain was unbearable but it reminded her pussy of all the orgasms. Despite the insufferable pain her pussy valiantly released more juices in readying for another orgasm.

Jackie twisted her ass repeatedly into the carpet, harder and harder without any encouragement from Little Johnson other than his dark watchful eyes. Her clit felt hard as a pebble and she desperately wanted to come both for her own pleasure and as a completion of her obedience to Little Johnson. Through teary eyes she saw him studying her, enjoying. A drop of sperm fell from his still hard cock and plunged into the carpet between her spread knees.

Jackie didn't think she could come like this. No clitoral contact, not enough pain. Now she ground and bounced her ass shamelessly into the beige carpet increasing the pain but not enough. Her eyes misted from the pain but even more from frustration.

"Would Fishy like some help from her friend Little Johnson?"

Jackie sobbed and nodded her head desperately. She couldn't speak, overwhelmed with need. Little Johnson slipped away while she continued to grind her ass viciously and with no consideration to carpet burns, sanitation, or the pain that would stretch out over the coming days.

Little Johnson returned. She saw he held the whip. She showed no reaction. He raised the whip. She made no move other than her continued grinding and did not plead for or against. She saw him grin evilly. She was patient and just kept mashing her little agonized ass into the hostile carpet. He brought the whip down, welting her from her taut stomach near her navel down into her dark blonde patch of pubic hair.

Amazingly, that was what she needed. She yelled and came digging her heels in the floor and pushing her body several feet across the carpet giving herself new friction burns on her shoulder blades as her arms collapsed under her. Jackie writhed for a long minute before winding down.

She didn't pass out but she fell asleep moments after Little Johnson shoved a pillow under her head and she felt a tossed blanket settle over her body. She wanted to stay awake for some reason. It had something to do with a plan. Sleep just seemed more important.

CHAPTER 12

Jackie woke up at 3:25 AM. She was on the floor and her body throbbed with pain. Just pushing the blanket aside increased the pain and sitting up increased it outrageously. She smelled something and realized it was dried come on her face and crusting her hairline. She had to get that scrubbed off. She needed a shower and she needed to pop some pills for the pain.

Jackie felt the weight of her slim body driving her tender buttocks into contact with the carpet. Even gravity seemed to be working against her. She felt a curious lack of emotion. All she felt were sets of sensations, most of them painful.

Movement was compounding the pain from the whip slashes and carpet burns. Oddly, she could not even categorize the pain as bad sensation. The pain carried with it the association of all the orgasmic joy she'd released. Then she realized she wasn't lacking emotion it was just that a single emotion blanketed and suffocated all others. It was satisfaction, a deep and profound satisfaction.

How could she feel so satisfied after all that pain and mistreatment and after all that bondage and humiliation? Little Johnson had done more than just disregard her feelings. He actively went out of his way to make everything worse for her every step of the way. Only, it had somehow made it better.

Jackie shook her head in dismayed disbelief because, out of all the bad things Little Johnson did to her, somehow the worst was when he rejected her after she offered him the opportunity to have intercourse. He turned her down! It was so frustrating. She was deeply satisfied but something was still missing. Instinctively, she felt incomplete without a man's cock releasing its load deep in her womb. She marveled that she'd gone from hating the disgusting Little Johnson to yearning for his sperm deep in the cradle of her womanhood in just a couple 'interludes' with him. She smiled reluctantly. Good God, a few more like this and she would be in love with the evil pervert! The idea was funny but scary because it did not seem as far-fetched as it should.

For just a second she pictured a church full of her friends and family, all dressed up, with her and Little Johnson exchanging vows in front of everyone. In front of Wayne Jones dressed as a priest!

Revolting! Most single women fantasized about marriage and

the day of their wedding but that was no day-dream, it was a day nightmare!

Jackie was amazed her subconscious could even experimentally match her with Little Johnson. She knew that never under any other circumstances could she picture herself with him. If Little Johnson was rich, polite, respectful, had a great sense of humour, was loving and kind he never would have gotten anywhere with her. His size, his age, his homeliness, and his probable lack of education all would have precluded him from getting even a single kiss from her of a romantic nature. Instead, he invaded her privacy, intruded in her home, and abused her verbally, physically, and he emotionally and, in return for his efforts, got everything Jackie had to give and far more than she knew she could give.

It was all wrong. Still, she felt immensely satisfied. No, she thought, I must just be drained....

Jackie slowly stood up trying to minimize the pains but only drawing them out. She felt dehydrated, almost mummified. Not too surprising considering all the body fluids that flowed out of her under Little Johnson's ministrations. She drank several glasses of water at the kitchen sink.

She remembered the plan. The Plan! Not everything went according to plan with The Plan but she might have some useful video. She had tried to get Little Johnson to talk about threats or blackmail so he would be on record but the lucky little bastard had acted as if he knew every detail of The Plan. In conversation right before he defiled Jackie he had deftly avoided implicating himself. Still, she had issued her statement that this was against her will. She thought she had. She had also clearly stated she was not willing to have sex with him or to let him hurt her. Of course, she had then gone on to cooperate, become obviously aroused, and come about a zillion times.

Jackie's face flamed higher than her sore ass at the thought of the scene captured on the hidden camcorder. It was so embarrassing but it would have her words recorded and images of Little Johnson whipping her around the living room.

Jackie fumbled at the potted plant she kept on a built-in shelf above the television stand. The camcorder was small and well-concealed but it had a commanding view of the majority of the living room. She had hit the record button right before answering the door and there was space on the disc for two hours. There it was!

Her plan hadn't gone perfectly but she may have enough to counter their evil plot. She had to get out from under their thumb. Little Johnson may agree to swap videos especially if she gave him the ultimatum that otherwise she would bring in the police. It would be a bluff because she didn't think she really would. She couldn't stand the thought of a bunch of law enforcement, prosecutors, judge and jury all watching her performance on video. The concept was mortifying and also a little arousing. That video would be hot! She wondered if seeing it would inspire all the male viewers to purchase whips and the females on the jury to throw themselves at the feet of the first man who looked cruel enough to beat her.

The prospect of watching her performance on video was making her pussy lips slick and her nipples were hardened. The rush of blood to fill her nipples and puff up her labia was making her dizzy. She was still dehydrated.

She could watch the whole video. Just to see how she looked. Just to make sure the picture and sound quality were good. She still had the strange dildo. No reason not to get some value out of it. She wondered if penetrating herself with it would be enough or if temptation would cause her to flick the switch. She'd hated and loved Little Johnson for using it on her and she supposed she could hate and love herself for again inflicting all that unbearable pleasure.

The thought was too tempting to resist. She popped open the side panel of the camcorder that provided the miniature picture screen and pushed the play back button. "No disc" appeared on the screen. That couldn't be! She pressed the eject button. There was no disc in the tray but the tray wasn't empty. There was a folded piece of paper. Her shaky hands pulled it open, nearly ripping it, and she read the rough scrawled block letters – obviously written in a form that would defy handwriting analysis:

DEAREST FISHY, YOU ARE A GOOD GIRL AND A SLUT, SAME THING. THANK YOU FOR AN ENJOYABLE EVENING. YOUR KISSES ON MY DICK WERE SO DEVOTED AND THEY LINGER EVEN NOW. I'M SO HAPPY WE HAVE DISCOVERED ONE ANOTHER. IT WAS SO THOUGHTFUL OF YOU TO MAKE THIS VIDEO CHONICLING OUR PASSION. NO DOUBT YOU INTENDED IT TO BE A GIFT FOR

A FUTURE ANNVERSARY. LIFE IS SHORT SO I INTEND TO ENJOY IT IMMEDIATELY. HOWEVER, I DO THINK A COPY BELONGS IN A TIME CAPSULE TO SHOW THE FUTURE OUR MATING HABITS. I'LL ENJOY IT ALWAYS AND I'LL MAKE SURE MANY OTHERS WILL AS WELL. I WILL KEEP IT SAFE. I WAS ALSO THINKING ABOUT YOU AND LEFT A GIFT UNDER THE KEYBOARD OF YOUR COMPUTER. I THOUGHT YOU WOULD ALSO WANT TO REMEMBER OUR NIGHT OF PASSION IN DETAIL. IT WAS SO ROMANTIC!

I WILL MEET YOU HERE IN TWO NIGHTS. I KNOW YOU WANT TO SEE ME EVERY NIGHT AND THE WAIT WILL HARD FOR YOU. THE WAIT IS NECESSARY. I NEED TO RESTOCK MY RESERVOIR OF SPERM.

WHEN YOU GREET ME AT THE DOOR IN TWO NIGHTS WEAR SOMETHING SEXY. IT MUST BE SOMETHING NEW. PICK UP SOME NAUGHTY LINGERIE. DO THIS AND YOU WILL BE REWARDED. I WILL HELP YOU COMPLETE THE QUESTS OUR MUTUAL FRIEND ASSIGNED YOU.

Jackie noted bitterly that he signed it HERE TO HELP.

How had he known? He must have taken the disc after she fell asleep on the floor. Now he had even more video of her to enjoy. The whole situation was like quicksand. Every time she struggled to escape she just sunk in deeper.

She set the camcorder down and went to her desk. Her computer was on one side at an angle. Scattered across the desk were the various props and items from the Wayne Jones file. Far more than props she now knew. She saw Little Johnson had picked up the strange dildo because it was back at her desk now. She noted he hadn't bothered to clean it. Her dried female essences made it glossy.

She pulled the keyboard slide out and lifted up the keyboard. Little Johnson must have connected his digital camera to her computer and printed up a few of his latest and greatest. Her latest and greatest...

There were four glossy photos. The little monster must have had printable photo paper with him, must have gone out to his car to retrieve it after she fell asleep. She still didn't even know what he drove. He might take a taxi for all she knew. Hell, she didn't even know his first name. She felt like a slut and the photos confirmed and notarized her sluttiness.

The photos were the same size and quality as the ones in the Jones collection on her desk-top. Had Little Johnson taken those photos as well?

The first photo showed her standing, legs spread, whipped back towards the camera. She was looking over her shoulder and actually grinning at the camera. How could she have grinned? She blamed herself instead of Little Johnson's wickedness.

The next photo showed her in almost the same position but this time pulling her wet panties harshly up into her own ass crack – a self-inflicted wedgie – while her other hand pulled one ass cheek out to leave her as vulnerable as possible to the wedgie. Awful.

The next photo showed her saliva slick lips sucking with all their power at the side of Little Johnson's cock. Jackie saw she was quite recognizable despite the difficult angle. Her eyes were slightly hooded in passionate concentration. What an image.

The last photo was an action shot. It caught an image of a thick stream of semen, about half a foot long, in mid flight towards her wide open waiting face just inches from impact. More come could be seen on one side of her forehead. She thought the Jackie in the photo had a sort of blonde Mona Lisa expression. Jackie was humiliated and angry. Even so, one part of her analyzed each of the photos as incredibly erotic. All of them would make fine additions to the existing Jones photo collection. She almost felt pride at that thought. She also felt a grudging respect for Little Johnson for successfully taking that last photo in the midst of his own orgasm. The little bastard was apparently expert at both controlling women and controlling his own lusts. That demented little multi-tasker!

Now what? Jackie went to her bedroom feeling fresh juices enabling the folds of her pussy lips to slip and slide as she walked.

In the bedroom, as she anticipated, she saw her underwear drawer was pulled out, the personal articles in disarray. Nothing was missing but obviously Little Johnson had done his homework, reviewing her entire collection of personal items so he would know if she followed his instructions when he visited in two nights.

Now what? Time to go shopping she guessed.

Jackie looked down and saw she was holding the massive vibrating dildo. She didn't remember having plucked it off the desk.

She lay down on her bed, contact with the sheets causing pain in her sore ass, and put the dildo to work. As she got the last inches all the way up her pussy her juice-slicked thumb hovered over the switch. She recalled she'd thought it was a mistake resisting masturbation the last couple days because it kept her primed for Little Johnson. Well, she wasn't going to make that mistake again! Her wet thumb pushed the flat switch one notch and her body stiffened and flexed as the harsh vibrations multiplied her arousal tenfold. In moments she was climaxing, her damaged rear bouncing on the soft sheets. It was only the first orgasm.

CHAPTER 13

Becca had a new roommate and it was none other than Wendy Carter. Becca still had Lilly Hopkins as a roommate as well so all three of them were sharing the cell /suite. The space was cramped. Becca really hadn't thought the sexual activity level could increase but, with Wendy around needing satisfaction, it had.

Jones and his followers liked to team women in pairs in the cell / suites. There were so many women and so many followers doubling up helped with space considerations. Becca wasn't sure if they were assembled together as a trio due purely to space considerations, or because of Wendy Carter's former importance, or because Becca was still fighting hard to resist their alluring opportunities to submit.

Becca, Wendy, and Lilly were tasked to provide each other nearly non-stop sex. Becca supposed this was done in order to keep them in a sexual thought mode. It was highly effective. They were assigned little tasks to complete. For instance, "Make your little roommate come three times before lunch" or "Make your sexy friend beg for it" or "Find a spot on your bedmate's body free of harm and hurt it". It was hard to think clearly when you gave and received so many orgasms per day.

Becca wondered who was even running the day to day operations at Goethner-Varner especially now that Wendy was incarcerated 24 / 7. It didn't really matter since whoever it was must be a Jones disciple. It was probably Mistress Anni.

It was strange for Becca to be locked up with her idol, Wendy Carter, and doing all those crazy sexual things with the older woman. The more she did the more she appreciated the woman's beauty. Those square shoulders built to support the heavy breasts, the womanly hips, and the thick aromatic patch of pubic hair…. You could get lost in that jungle and Becca frequently did sometimes for up to an hour.

One thing Becca didn't like about the added roommate was that the room was meant for only two patients so Becca and Wendy always had to share one narrow bed. They usually fell asleep exhausted, entwined together in a bundle of sweaty naked limbs. She didn't like not having her own space, not even her own bed. There was nowhere for her to retreat for even a moment. On the other hand, there was something about slick warm skin and falling asleep with the scent of female arousal still radiating from their bodies....

Becca lay imprisoned in Wendy's bare warm embrace. She'd woken up ten minutes ago but pretended to still be sleeping in order to avoid beginning another day of use and abuse. She wasn't sure which was worse; what was done to her, what she was forced to do, or her welcoming reactions to so many of the alien acts, thoughts, and feelings. Wendy was on top of her, her body feminine but heavy compared to Becca's slight form. Somehow, she always seemed to end up on top of Becca, like Becca's body was an extra mattress.

Becca tried to lie still but the hot weight and Wendy's humid sleep breath made her feel claustrophobic. She needed escape. She turned her head to look over at Lilly's bed to see what she was up to. Lilly always got a bed all to herself while Wendy and Becca shared. Becca was actually jealous of that.

Lilly was looking at her, "Rise and shine, Pretty Toy. It's time for another day on the assembly line."

There was no use pretending to be asleep any more. That damn Lilly was always watching. There was nowhere to hide from those black button doll eyes. Now Becca felt Wendy shifting and waking. This was it, the day was starting. It was like a roller coaster going downhill. Once it started it was going to plummet and rocket all the way.

Lilly was rolling and stretching in the comparative luxuriance of space her bed provided, "I just love stretching, feeling all those bumps and welts pulling and twisting, and rolling all over my big bed. I just love it here!"

It was pretty obvious to Becca that Lilly knew she didn't like sharing the bed with Wendy. Lilly liked to taunt her with comments on her bed and space. It was another form of sadism.

"How long am I supposed to be on this "assembly line"?"

"Until Pretty Toy is finished, silly!" Lilly's face glowed at the imagined prospect.

Now Wendy took a side, "If you really want off the assembly line you need to let them finish you. You resist the pain and the pleasure you are given. You don't accept who you are. If you don't give in you'll be stuck in manufacturing forever."

Becca wrestled out from under Wendy and jumped out of bed.

Her outrage was refreshing and invigorating, a welcome change from the sexual morass she'd sunk into in the past several days.

"Wendy, I can't believe what you've let them make you into and I won't be joining you. You used to be so strong, so independent. I looked up to you! Now, you just lay on top of me squashing me while I sleep!"

"Strength and independence did not make me happy, did not satisfy my needs. They were an illusion. They made me lonely. I want you to be as happy as me and Doll."

"Forget you two!"

While Becca paced Lilly hopped out of bed and retrieved the slip of folded paper on the floor near the door. Someone slid them under the door, or through the food slot, every night. Another set of tasks to complete. The Dominants didn't have time to abuse all the submissives that needed abusing so they tasked them to abuse each other.

Jones needed all of their help. Oddly, despite enlisting the guards, Jones had far more submissives to keep occupied than Dominants to keep them in hand. Becca would have thought just the opposite but, apparently, more people wanted to submit than dominate. It sort of made sense from an evolutionary perspective though. Dominants were basically leaders and it would be bad to have a bunch of leaders with few followers. Just like on a chess board each side having a single King and a multitude of pawns.

Becca had no idea if the guards, Jones followers on the outside, or Wayne Jones himself came up with the sexual tasks. They were creative and Becca was often impressed and quite aroused by them. Aroused at the thought of them, turned on by putting them in action, and usually orgasmic by their completion.

Becca's anger drained away replaced by a sexual expectation as Lilly opened the note and read it to the room, "Pretty Toy, alternately pussy lick Doll and Dummy back and forth no more than ten seconds at a time until both have come and you have sucked up their juices. Carefully taste and savor their sex fluids. Pronounce a "Tastiest Pussy" winner. For the rest of the day you will tongue fuck the asshole of the winner and the loser will watch and diddle her pussy while licking her fingers clean of her poor quality pussy juice at least once per minute. Pretty Toy may give herself an orgasm once each time she produces an orgasm in a roommate."

And so it was until about lunchtime.

When the door buzzed open and the three of them heard high heels click across the linoleum Wendy was on one bed fingering her pussy with one hand while she licked the other clean. Becca was on all fours on the end of the other bed with her face in Lilly's crack, her weary tongue stuck up the Doll woman's loose wet asshole.

"Bitches! Pay attention and proper respect to your superior!"

Becca pulled her tongue out just in time as Doll stood up, her asshole tightening and closing with the position change. Wendy pulled her fingers out of her pussy and mouth. They all stared stupidly at the young woman before them. She had coppery brown hair of an amazing length down past her ass. She was nude except for high heels and black panties. She had quite a few tattoos including red and gold oriental symbols on her neck. She was younger than everyone else in the room, much younger then Lilly and Wendy and maybe a year or two younger then Becca.

Nevertheless, based on her demeanor the other three knew how to treat her.

They responded in unplanned unison, "Yes, Mistress. Sorry Mistress."

"My name is Kira but you are to call me Mistress Flamepussy."

Curiosity bloomed and Wendy spoke, "Mistress, I apologize for being so stupid but, will you educate us why you are known as Mistress Flamepussy?"

The young mistress grinned and pulled her black panties down, stepping out of them and proudly arching her pubic mound forward. Becca gasped when she saw. Mistress Flamepussy had a nice thick but trimmed coppery bush. There was a tattoo of leaping flames rising and curling from the top and left side of the pubic hair. The tattoo made it look as if her pussy was on fire!

"How do you little girls like my burning bush? Maybe later, if you're good, I'll let you try to put out my fire with your wet tongues."

Becca felt her cheeks burn with outrage that this girl younger than her was calling her a "little girl". It was embarrassing and wrong.

She had to admit the tattooed pussy was intriguing and the prospect of getting up close and personal with the new pussy was making the fire leap to her own pussy.

Mistress Flamepussy issued orders while retrieving items stored in the closet. The closet wasn't needed for clothes since they weren't allowed any so the space was used for various SM toys and instruments. The "little girls" were quick to obey the orders so in the few seconds it took Mistress Flamepussy to collect the needed items and bring them to the bed the "little girls" were able to assemble as instructed.

Becca and Wendy knelt on tender knees on hard linoleum on either side of the bed. They held each other's hands across the bed. Mistress Flamepussy moved in with two sets of handcuffs. Becca looked at her fearfully and then watched motionless as her right wrist was handcuffed to Dummy's left and vice versa. They were helpless, their rears particularly defenseless. They were able to see each other's breasts and facial expressions. More importantly, they were able to watch and vicariously experience the abuses and pleasures heaped on each other.

Becca saw Lilly catch a tossed strap-on dildo and put it on and heard Mistress Flamepussy putting another on behind her. Then Becca watched as Lilly's fingers groped around from behind Dummy and across Dummy's full breasts to seek out and callously tug both nipples. As she saw this Becca felt Mistress Flamepussy's harsher fingers squeeze and twist her own small breasts though they left her tiny nipples alone. While this went on the vibrating plastic cockheads teased dripping labia.

After a few moments of casual breast abuse Mistress Flamepussy told Doll to do as she did. They moved back and used bare hands to spank bare rears. This went on for long minutes, the overlapping pain building. The pain wasn't alone. There was growing passion. Becca was no longer surprised that her pussy was running with juices. She knew pain really did the trick for her. That's what being a masochist was about she guessed. Sometimes she wanted the pain to stop, sometimes she wanted it to become much more severe, and sometimes she wanted it to go on forever.

"Oh, Mistress. Ohhh!"

Mistress Flamepussy giggled as both she and Becca realized Becca wasn't actually protesting and was not asking her to stop.

However, someone else did.

"Step back, ladies, I'll indulge from here." No one had heard the entry buzz of the door due to the harsh loudness of the spanks. Jones' voice was a shock.

"Mr. Jones, of course, as you wish." Mistress Flamepussy was clearly awed by Wayne Jones appearing in the flesh.

Doll backed away from Dummy and right into a wall.

Becca felt tremendous excitement and Dummy's eyes lit up. Dummy was speechless and Becca was expectant. Becca had often thought of things she'd like to say to Jones. How she would tell him off, tell him to drop dead, tell him to go to Hell. At last he was here before her. Well, he was here behind her bare ass and wet pussy. Her anger had waited quite a few days for expression. She figured it could wait a little longer. She wanted to experience what Jones might offer. She could always tell him off afterward.

"I believe in quality testing my products. Proper maintenance is important. For instance, keeping the delicate working parts well oiled."

Becca felt a shockingly cool wetness plop on her anus and spread, trickling down her crack and moving out on her swollen inner and outer pussy lips. She saw Dummy's eyes rapt on the sight and she looked behind her to see Jones, nude, trickling massage oil from a bottle down onto her body. He capped the bottle and Becca couldn't help herself from looking downwards to see his cock erect and ready for action. She knew that should worry her but she was ready for some action also.

He brought his cock up to her exposed 'working parts' and centred the head against her rear entry. She'd hoped he had simply missed slightly when he dripped the oil down onto her. Not so. She knew now it had landed exactly as he'd aimed. She was resigned. She remembered she'd even wondered a couple days ago if and when they would get around to buggering her. She'd never done it before but she was curious. She wasn't sure if she was anticipating the pleasurable possibilities or the discomfort more.

Jones exerted confident pressure and his cockhead easily popped past her clinging ring and coasted inward, its passage well facilitated by the smooth oil. She gasped and gasped again as he shot a couple more inches in. Once he got it in all the way to the base and his testicles jostled her double oily pussy lips she gave a long defeated groan of confused passion.

Jones drove in and out with good speed, his hard flesh

pummelling her tenderness. He was driving all sorts of feelings into her, pleasure, lust, loss of self-respect. Becca knew good girls didn't do this sort of thing. She was cuffed to Dummy across the bed, hadn't asked for this, or even been asked permission but she felt completely to blame because she didn't protest and because she enjoyed it so much. As usual, her sexual pleasures were inversely proportional to her level of self-esteem.

"Your rear orifice feature is working and up to standard. Is Pretty Toy fully aware?"

"Uh, uh, uh." Each tamping thrust pressed gasps from Becca. She was trying to think through the pleasure and the not unwelcome pain. Jones wanted her to talk and she was fairly sure she knew what he wanted to hear. She wouldn't tell him what he wanted but she didn't mind trying to please him with other words that were true.

"You're fucking my ass and I like it. I'm a horny slut!"

Jones laughed but the non-stop shafting never hesitated, "Pretty Toy, this isn't your ass. It's the ass that belongs to us to do with as we will. You're horny but you are far less than a slut. Don't you recognize it? Don't you want to admit it? Don't you want to tell your sweet suite friends?"

Becca managed to look across at Dummy's fervent jealous eyes and then up at Doll's lustful shiny button eyes. She realized they really were well-named. Doll really was a doll and Dummy really was a dummy. If Becca admitted her own true status it might almost be freeing. If she gave up mental resistance along with the physical resistance she'd already lost there would be no more fighting. It would all become an endless series of doing and having done as she was instructed to do. She knew it would be a fall with no bottom, a horrible fate, but it had become so darkly tempting.

"I'm just an asshole to be fucked and I'm happy to take cock up my ass. Fuck me! I'm going to come!"

Jones laughed and pulled his cock out. Becca yelled in outrage, desperate to have it back.

"No, Pretty Toy, you are not going to come. Not yet. You are not performing up to specifications. Admit you are Pretty Toy, no more and no less. All I ask of you is the truth."

Becca clamped her mouth shut. God help her, those words wanted to come out of her mouth. Were they true? They might be or they might not. But saying them would be the final step and would make them true. She couldn't let herself speak those words!

Jones walked to the other side of the bed and sat next to Dummy, his back to Becca. Immediately Dummy was staring down at his steaming cock.

"Dummy, do you want to please this cock?"

The words poured out of her mouth, urgent, almost hysterical, "I do Master Jones. I'm a Dummy and I beg to be allowed to please you!"

Jones looked back at Becca and crinkled the lines around his intense eyes. It was like he was saying to her "Do you see how easy that was?" Then he spoke again.

"Dummy, are you willing to earn the privilege of pleasing my cock?"

"Yes, Master. Please Master. Anything!"

Becca saw Mistress Flamepussy had a small black leather doctor's bag that she opened and sorted through at the end of the bed. Becca wondered what the monsters were planning and how she could get the cock to return.

"Dummy, you need a mark, just in case you are ever lost. Doubtless you're too dumb to find your way back on your own. A Dummy like you probably can't even read road signs let alone remember and dial a phone number. Flamepussy has a specialty. She wants to tattoo you. Agree to it and you will be allowed to please this cock."

Dummy looked appalled as she contemplated what was being asked of her. Her mouth hanging open in dismay and her teary eyes did make her look like she lacked intelligence.

"A tattoo.... Yes, do it."

Jones nodded his approval to Doll who began fucking Dummy with exquisite slowness. Then Jones nodded at Dummy who lowered her hungry mouth onto his hard cock, still warm from its visit to Becca's anal passage. She showed no hesitancy over its previous use, just bobbed up and down trying to take it deep in her throat, her tongue wrapping and twirling all over it like she was trying to clean every millimetre.

Becca was amazed at how low Dummy had sunk and how high her own lust soared at the sight and the awesome knowledge Dummy was about to be tattooed. She felt so frustrated and needy.

She wondered what she might agree to now if she was asked... or told.

From her position, since Jones was sitting to one side and Dummy was now standing at the bed side leaning down on her elbows while she gave Jones oral, Becca was able to clearly see the rising half-circles of Dummy's lovely rear. She watched as Mistress Flamepussy went to work. Dummy was really being tattooed! It was horrible!

Poor Dummy agreeing to a permanent tattoo to satisfy their momentary whims. And she was doing it in order to earn the privilege of giving Wayne Jones oral sex! Becca felt bad for Dummy but also felt angry at her stupidity. How could any self-respecting human being agree to that proposition? It was horrendous and ridiculous at the same time!

Becca felt lustful and felt bad that despite watching the terrible tattooing of poor Dummy her lust only rose. She even felt a little rejected that she wasn't getting any attention now. Of course, she realized Jones had known better than to try to get Becca tattooed. Obviously he knew her limits and his own as well. She would have told him to pack a picnic basket and go to Hell.

The tattooing and pleasuring took a good length of time and Doll's slow thrusts kept Dummy's passion on a boil. She was intent on pleasing Jones but sometimes had to pull her mouth off him in order to gasp or groan in frustration or pain from the needle work on the top of one ass cheek.

Another thought occurred to the fascinated Becca. Whatever the tattoo turned out to be, any tattoo on the older woman would look out of place. It was not getting inked in a publicly visible location but if she ever emotionally escaped the clutches of Jones and his followers how could she explain it to future dates? Letting them tattoo her was really closing down her options, lengthening the terms of her servitude to forever more.

Mistress Flamepussy saw Becca watching the work in open-mouthed wonder. She paused.

"Pretty Toy, how would you like your very own tattoo? Say the word, ask nice, and admit what you are. All this can be yours." She pointed at the half-finished tattoo on Dummy's ass cheek but she was also pointing out Dummy's passionate total capitulation to the will of others.

Becca was fearful at the prospect, "No way, you bitch. Fuck off."

Mistress Flamepussy and Jones shared a chuckle and the tattooing went on. When it was done, Jones gently pushed Dummy's face away from his cock. Though the veins throbbed and it looked like it was about to explode, somehow he hadn't come yet. Dummy was clearly disappointed she wasn't going to get a swallow of Jones' essence.

They had Dummy stand higher and arch her ass. Her ass rose like a ski slope from her face pressed into the bed so Becca could see the tattoo as best she could in her cuffed kneeling position.

It was of a black box-like cage with wide spaces between the bars. It was tattooed with receding sides in such a way that it looked three dimensional. Inside the cage, in bright letters were words, permanent words: MY NAME IS DUMMY. PROPERTY OF WAYNE JONES. IF FOUND, CALL #555-264-9814. NO REWARD.

Becca gasped. She didn't know what she'd expected but could not have anticipated anything so humiliating. She knew Wendy was theirs forever now and would always be Dummy, never again Wendy Carter. Dummy looked up at her questioningly when she heard Becca's gasp. Becca was mentally revolted to realize Dummy herself had no idea what the tattoo was of so she was trying to surmise it from Becca's reaction.

Becca had no idea what to say, "It's... sort of a three-dimensional looking tattoo... with writing...." Becca just couldn't go on. Luckily Doll thrust more vigorously into Dummy and Dummy let her face sink to the bed sheets focusing on the fucking and gave up any concern over the tattoo. Her concerns and her humanity both melted away. Becca and Dummy both realized it was too late to do anything about it anyway no matter what it was.

While Doll screwed Dummy and Dummy's cuffed hands spasmodically jerked at Becca's arms, Jones turned around on the bed and casually wag-slapped his saliva-glistening cock against Becca's right cheek.

"Pretty Toy, would you like to suck this cock or have it fuck your ass again?"

Becca debated the options. Her mouth salivated for no good reason at the thought of sucking him off. She could swallow the load Dummy was denied despite having worked hard to earn it.

That was oddly tempting. The previous ass-fucking had been a tremendous new sensation though and Jones had left her on the edge. Sucking him could not possibly fully satisfy her but anal sex might.

"Fuck my ass." A moment after she said it Becca realized she had not considered saying no, only which of the two options given she would choose. She was playing within whatever rules he made.

"Is that a request or some kind of misplaced demand?"

"I'm sorry, Mr. Jones. Please fuck my ass if that's what you want." Becca hated the words and submissive tone, felt butterflies in her tummy, felt her asshole clench in anticipation.

"Are you a Pretty Toy and nothing else?"

She said nothing.

"I don't want to waste oil on a potentially faulty product."

Becca felt him get in position, felt the cock head bounce gently on her anus, and then experienced the long, steady, continuous penetration. There was still oil from before up her rear channel so the cock slid in smoothly. The main thing was she actually felt bad for disappointing him. She felt like she ought to tell him she was a Pretty Toy, just to please him. It would be despicable but rewarding to do that. It was fortunate the cock was already all the way in so she wouldn't have to say it.

"Pretty Toy, I shouldn't have to do work. That's why I like to automate."

Jones wasn't thrusting. The cock and the feeling of a dilated ass were good and overwhelming but Jones wasn't moving. She wanted friction. She finally interpreted his words and realized friction was up to her, the automated toy. While Jones stood motionless behind her other than the throbbing veins in his cock, she struggled to arch and thrust her little butt. She thrust out from the bed, the cock sinking all the way down her ass channel and then pulled back to the side of the bed until the mushroom head of his cock was gripped by her flexing sphincter, then back again. She did this again and again, picking up speed, confidence, urgency, and passion. She felt more than saw Mistress Flamepussy, Doll, and Dummy watching her performance. The knowledge was embarrassing and arousing.

She could feel it! She was going to come this way! It was going to be a tremendous orgasm, both from the foreign nature of it and the orgasm delay.

He pulled away from her, his cock popping free.

"No!"

How could he do this to her? Was she ever going to get to come? Was he ever going to come? How could he stand this? She knew she couldn't. She was going crazy.

"I don't want to waste my semen on an inferior product. Is Pretty Toy willing to earn it?"

She was. She had to. She knew she would do anything and knew he knew it also. She had nothing to hide, nothing to give he didn't already own.

"Anything."

"Would Pretty Toy be proud to have her very own tattoo?"

God no! Not that! She had marvelled in horror at Dummy's fate. The last thing she wanted was to share it, "Yes. Tattoo me. Go ahead. Please."

Everyone but Becca was pleased by the collapse of her resistance. Jones knew she was settling in to becoming an owned sexual object even if she did not. Not fully, not quite yet. A few more nudges to push her all the way off the cliff...

She was un-cuffed and repositioned. Doll kept up her doggie style fucking of Dummy while Becca robotically followed Jones directions and lay on her back on the bed. She saw Mistress Flamepussy preparing the needle gun and the black ink well. It was all coming true. She was really about to be tattooed and she had no prospect of resistance or rescue.

Jones stepped up onto the bed and placed his feet on either side of her head, his heels against her shoulders, squatting down to bring his cock to a hover above her face, inches from her mouth.

Even if she hadn't known where his cock had just visited she would have known from the smell. She had a task to perform and she knew what it was. She felt Mistress Flamepussy massage her right breast, her nipple already hardened and aching from denied passion. Moments later she felt a sharp pinprick on her breast very near the nipple.

Becca hoped to delay the inevitable, "Please tell me, what is going to be tattooed?"

Jones was stern, "None of your concern."

The pinpricks and pain continued as Becca stared at Jones cock. No one said anything to her but each pinprick was like a little reminder, a little demand for her to do it. Please Jones. Earn an orgasm.

Step 1; suck that cock clean while having a permanent tattoo placed on product.

She craned her neck and gave the cock wide laving licks up and down its length. Masochistic pain and subservient pleasure joined forces to become a force greater than the sum of their parts.

She lost all sense of time and all sense of self.

Eventually it was done and Jones still hadn't come though she thought he was very close and thought she had done a good job cleaning and pleasing Master Jones' cock. She hoped she had.

Jones stood up off her and jumped off the bed. She sat up and blinked. It was four sets of eyes looking from her chest to her own eyes that reminded her. She looked down.

On her right breast in thick black letters wrapped in a circle just outside her aureole were the words MADE IN AMERICA.

Her mind just blanked, wiped clean of emotion. She looked at them.

"Who are you?" Jones asked evenly, casually.

She could see it in their eyes. They all thought she was pretty. They all treated her like a sexual toy. In their eyes, she could see exactly who she was.

"I'm Pretty Toy."

"Does Pretty Toy want to please her Master?" Mistress Flamepussy asked.

"Oh, yes, please, Mistress Flamepussy. What can I do?"

"Dummy has only one tattoo. I'm sure generous Master Jones would be impressed enough to grant you an orgasm and his seed if you agreed to a second tattoo."

"Yes. I agree to another tattoo. If it makes Master Jones happy it will make

Pretty Toy happy." Pretty Toy had no qualms about a second tattoo and was utterly sincere in her desire to do whatever it took to please Master Wayne Jones.

Jones lay on his back on the bed and, following Mistress Flamepussy's instructions, Pretty Toy mounted him and impaled her small pussy onto his painfully hard orgasm-delayed cock. Following further instructions, Pretty Toy held still, only seeking to massage Jones' cock with the slick warmth of her pussy walls.

Pretty Toy held still a long time, through many painful inky pinpricks to her left round butt cheek. When the tattoo was complete at last, Mistress Flamepussy took a step back, and delivered a ringing spank to the other ass cheek.

"Pretty Toy, fuck the cock, soak up Master Jones' sperm."

At last! Pretty Toy launched into action, vigorously working her pussy up and down the shaft. Jones closed his eyes in enjoyment. He pictured the tattoo he knew Flamepussy had placed, as per his instructions.

Jones climaxed profoundly and Pretty Toy felt the warm living sperm filling her vaginal cavity. She screamed her own tortured orgasm to the world.

Flamepussy looked from the semen leaking out of Pretty Toy's loosened pussy up and to the left a few inches to the fresh tattoo centred on Pretty Toy's tight ass globe. Flamepussy was very proud of the tattoo Pretty Toy herself was ignorant of.

There were five words written in large fancy gold letters surrounded by blazing red fire.

CERTIFIED HIGH QUALITY
INSPECTOR FLAMEPUSSY